The author, Cliff Dix, has worked in the entertainment industry for over fifty years. His autobiographical reminiscences are published in
'Up The Fire Escape And Through The Kitchens'

Fiction books by the same author:
The theatre trilogy
'Theatre Wagon'
'In Which Case'
'And Burnt The Topless Towers'

and the backstage murder mystery
'All Invited To A Murder'

All the characters in this book are fictitious and any resemblance to any person living or dead is purely co-incidental

To Ann, with thanks for her patient reading once again.

PLAYWRIGHT

Chapter 1
Arriving

Gemma stood in the kitchen of their new house, looking out of the window. The sink that separated her from the window-ledge had that utterly dry look of dusty uncared for stainless, steel. The white ceramic tiles on the window ledge showed several rings where containers of cleaning products had stood. Green rings, pink rings, and a stray smear of a bluish powder. Two dead flies lay upside down on the draining board, dessicated by the hot summer sun coming through the window.

The removal men were coming and going between the back of the van and the open front door. There were worrying bumps and bangs, occasional muttered instructions between them;

"Well lift your end up then!"

and once in a while one of them would ask her,

"Where do you want this, love?"

Duncan, her husband, was upstairs somewhere. He was supposed to be guiding furniture into the right rooms, but she had not heard him for a long while now and she was certain that he had sat himself down on a random seat and was fiddling with some trivial item, oblivious to the comings and goings around him.

It was his habit of shutting out the world by appearing to concentrate on some single unimportant detail that had rendered him so unsuitable for his job as a secondary school teacher. He had never admitted it, but the legend was that he had once sat at the front of a class of fifteen year olds, while they were supposedly reading a set text, concentrating his attention on something else to such an extent that when the bells sounded at the end of the lesson he had looked up to discover every single pupil had gone, leaving him supervising an empty classroom.

She smiled fondly. She didn't mind being the chief breadwinner. Her senior position within a nationwide company providing transport, 'logistics' they called it, mainly for firms supplying metal components, supported them both very well. The downside was the fairly frequent re-location from one part of the country to another. This was by no means the first house move that they had made. She counted mentally. Six, no, seven different houses in the last thirty odd years, and all the while Duncan had maintained his distant existence in his own world, emerging occasionally to sit at his keyboard and write some freelance piece for an obscure magazine.

In many ways the keyboard was a curse, providing him with a cast iron reason to sit, motionless, staring into space, just thinking.

'Damn it!' she thought, 'Now I'm doing it.' and she turned the tap on viciously to sluice the surfaces clear of dust and spillages and wipe them with the cloth she was holding.

The tap shot water out in a series of great spurts accompanied by strange banging noises from the plumbing before, recovering from its disuse, it delivered a fiercely satisfying stream which splashed up from the bottom of the sink, spraying Gemma's front.

She didn't mind, it was another hot day after all, but the drops ran down her and gathered like a miniature moat in the roll of material where she had tied the tails of her blouse together. It had been a fashion when she was very young, and today, with the move and the heat, she had copied it. She knew, approaching her sixtieth birthday that the knottted blouse and resulting bare midriff had really been a teenager's style, but it had suited her mood and the expected work when she had got up that morning. She had been looking forward to moving in. They had felt very lucky to have found this house, with its four bedrooms and the large established garden she was looking at from the kitchen. 'Established' was a euphamism for 'unkempt' of course, she realised, but she liked doing things in a garden, so it had been with some delight she had eaten the bed and breakfast's morning offering as she readied herself for the day.

Now she was feeling hot, bothered and fatigued, and the van was only half unloaded. The sheer amount of surface cleaning that needed to be done was daunting, for the house had stood empty for nearly a year before they had bought it. Every item that came off the lorry was providing another obstacle. Even as she thought this one of the men came into the room and dumped a box, neatly labelled 'kitchen', on the work surface she had intended to start cleaning.

She ground her teeth, wiping now as fast as she could, and wondering hopelessly if Duncan was doing anything constructive. Knowing he was not.

Upstairs Duncan was sitting on the first bed that had been delivered. There were no sheets, just the bare matress on the bed base. He had his mobile phone in his hand and had been experimenting with the Wifi. They had arranged for the connection to be up and running a day or two before they were due to move in, mainly because Gemma's work sometimes required her to make arrangements outside office hours. She was really on twenty-four hour call, though she had taken leave for this move, and normally it was rare for her to be called outside office hours.

The removal men struggled up the stairs with chests of drawers and wardrobes while Duncan sat looking at his screen. Downstairs Gemma sweated over cleaning their new home.

Curtains twitched in houses on the opposite side of the road and in one of the neighbouring properties. Curious eyes attempted to assess the sort of people that were moving into Greendale Road.

At number 46, a rather shabby house immediately opposite, John and Jenny were watching. They were young by the standards of the road, and hardly the type of people that fitted in. Neither had 'proper' jobs, and local speculation had failed to establish exactly how they made a living. To watch the arrival Jenny had come through to the front room of their house from her workroom. The workroom had been fashioned out of a string of bare brick outbuildings that extended from the back of the house and had once been the coal-cellar, the washroom and the privvy.

Jenny now used the space for her craft and painting activities. She sold some items occasionally via the town's scattering of arts outlets. She stood beside John in paint splattered denim dungarees and flip-flop shoes. It was fairly obvious, if anyone had looked through the window at her, that she was wearing nothing else. The bib of the dungarees was struggling inadequately to cover her decently, but she had the excuse of the hot weather. John was slouching by the window in old jeans and a tee shirt. He scraped a piecemeal living by a succession of cash in hand odd jobs. The overall impression was of a small hippy commune, though neither of them were old enough to remember the true hippy era. Middle class parents walking their children to and from school tended to use the opposite side of the road.

"A couple of oldies," John said to Jenny.

"Might be worth trying to sell them a few arty bits while they are sorting out their décor," she said, "We need to keep an eye on them and call round when they are re-decorating."

He nodded. It was always better to sell stuff direct as a cash deal than through a shop which took commission and declared the transaction on its books.

Edward Cruikshank and his wife had set themselves up in a front bedroom with cups of coffee to watch the arrivals. They were better able to see than their immediate neighbours as they were one door along from the new residents and on the opposite side of the road. Because of this their view of number 47 was not blocked by the removal lorry, in fact they could observe every item of furniture as it came from the back of the van and was carried in through the front door. Emily commented, not always favourably, on each piece. They were both in their late seventies and had few friends. Their days were normally spent reading the paper and watching daytime television. The newcomers were a very welcome distraction, even if any change in the status-quo did make them nervous about what sort of people would now be living close to them.

"There's a lot of shelves and bookcases," Emily said to Edward, taking another sip of the coffee. It was only instant. Emily reserved the filter jug for the evenings.

Edward nodded, "Perhaps they're students."

Emily looked at him scornfully, "At their age?" she asked, for they had seen the new residents when they first arrived, even if they had both now vanished from view indoors, "they're more likely to be teachers."

"I hope they're all right then," said Edward, "because if they are teachers they'll be here all the time. Back from work by mid afternoon, and more holidays than working weeks."

"You're just jealous. A whole working lifetime of nine to five and just a couple of weeks holiday a year, you envy them."

"And the commuting time both ways." her husband reminded her.

"I wonder where their car is."

"Probably got one each. They'll have parked further along the road so the removal van can get outside."

Councillor Andrews knew exactly where the cars were. He wasn't yet sure who they belonged to, they were unfamiliar to him, and his regular checking of street parking outside 'The Limes' meant he knew most of the vehicles that used Greendale Road to park in during the daytimes. Greendale was unlucky in being the nearest street to the railway station not to have parking restrictions. Brian Andrews was partly responsible for that. Despite 'The Limes' having a generous driveway which curved round so there were gates both ends he had vigorously defended his right to park in the street whenever yellow lines were suggested. His many years as a councillor, coupled with unpleasant agression, had given him both enough seniority for his opinions to hold some sway on matters that others were indifferent about, and experience at manipulating the process to his way. He had argued for residents' parking permits, but in that he had failed, simply because the means of operating such a scheme didn't exist in the area. Now he ran a one man campaign against any vehicle he considered to be badly parked. Official looking notices had been printed on his computer that harranged offenders and promised penalty action if they repeated the 'offence'. He had signed the document Cllr. B. Andrews, which gave it some apparent authoity and pretentiousness, and distributed copies liberally under windscreen wipers.

Sometimes, like today, he added handwritten annotations in case the culprit failed to understand their misdemeanour.

Gemma and Duncan had parked near 'The Limes'. There was no reason any more for the house to have that name, because both of the old lime trees had fallen in Michael Fish's hurricane, and Brian Andrews had replaced them with shrubs. Conscious of the shortage of room the newcomers had squeezed their vehicles tightly together in a space adjacent to one of the gateways till thier bumpers almost touched. Even so the back end of Gemma's Mazda overhung the edge of 'The Limes' left hand gateway by a foot. She had stood in the road and looked at this, had decided that it didn't prevent anyone coming or going via the gateway, and could see that the Mini Clubman in the drive was facing toward the other gate anyway. She locked up and walked back to 47.

When the removal van eventually pulled away she would be torn between annoyance and a sad disappointment at such a curt greeting as a welcome when she found the parking note on her windscreen on coming to transfer her car into their own drive.

"I hope we haven't moved into a street full of petty grumblers," she said to Duncan, showing him the piece of paper. Duncan was getting into his car to go the few hundred yards to the town centre to buy them a Chinese take-away, He shrugged.

"He could have got out if he'd wanted to,"

The Mini stood exactly where it had been that morning when they had pulled up.

Gemma wasn't certain of it, but she sensed that there was movement behind the upstairs curtains of the house. She was tired and felt dirty from the day's activity. She was just in the mood to stand her ground if anyone should come out to complain to them. No one did. She backed her car away from Duncan's to allow him to go and fetch the food and then accelerated away from the gates a bit more viciously than she would normally do.

Back at the new house, and parked, she was surprised to find a figure emerging from the porch.

"Oh, I'm so glad I met you," said Miss Peston. She spoke quietly, but with an impeccable elocuted voice. Gemma immediately thought of Miss Marple. The woman was even wearing a coat and hat on this hot summer evening. Gemma looked to make sure she was not sporting gloves as well, but there was just the shiny black handbag dangling from an elbow. "I've left you a little house warming present on the step, nothing much, but I had the oven on and I wanted to welcome you to the street. You can drop the tin back any time, I'm at number 44, the other side, over there." and she pointed to an exceptionally neatly kept house toward the town centre and two doors along.

"That's very kind of you," Gemma told her, suppressing her simmering annoyance at the parking note. Reluctantly she added, "Would you like a cup of tea?" thinking, 'Please say 'no', my take-away will be here in a minute'.

Miss Peston barely hesitated, "if it's not too much trouble. It would be so nice to get to know you."

Gemma led the way indoors. She filled the kettle and turned it on. As an afterthought she took plates from the cupboard and slid them into the oven, which she turned on to warm them. Miss Peston watched, clutching her cake tin which she had picked up from the porch step as they entered.

"I'm imposing on your dinner," she apologised with more perception than Gemma had given her credit for, "I should go."

She found herself saying, "No, no. It's quite all right. Not a problem. Do have a seat."

The neighbour put the tin down on the table, and perched on the edge of one of the dining chairs. She didn't take her coat off, and looked as though she was ready to jump up and leave at a moment's notice.

The front door opened and slammed. They had not heard Duncan's car. He was speaking while still coming through the hall.

"I got a selection. We don't know what this one will be like, but there are two in the main street, so we can try the other one next time.... Oh! Sorry. I didn't know we had visitors," he said as he entered, holding a bulging carrier bag of aluminium food trays.

"This is Miss Peston, she lives just across the road. She brought us some cakes."

"Adele. Call me Adele. But I'm in the way of your dinner..."

"Nonsense, I'm sure there's plenty. Do stay and have some with us," Gemma found herself saying. There was something about the woman that made you accept her. It wasn't just that her apparent age caused you to be polite; she emanated a persona you could trust. Gemma could imagine her being a doctor's receptonist or an agony aunt.

Duncan nodded, opening the oven and stacking foil containers onto the plates already in there. He waved a couple of bags around saying, "They all seem to give you prawn crackers even if you don't ask for them."

Gemma was making the promised tea in mugs with tea bags . She looked over he shoulder toward their guest and asked, "Sugar?" Adele Peston shook her head.

Duncan asked his wife, "Where have you put the table mats?"

"In that cupboard... Well perhaps the one to the left then."

After a few rather hectic moments, during which the unfamiliarity of the new house resulted in Duncan, particularly, having to search for things, the three of them were sat around the kitchen table sharing out a take-away, drinking tea and learning more about each other. The neighbours who had curtain twitched through the day might have been jealous of Miss Peston had they known, for she, by an accident of timing of her delivery of welcoming cakes, became the first to discover who the newcomers were.

Gemma and Duncan found out about Miss Peston.

If he had been asked to guess Duncan would, unlike his wife, have put her down as an office worker, now retired. Actually she was, she told them once she had taken her coat off and sat down at their table, perching on the very edge of her chair, the town's former librarian. She had spent her whole career in the same building, seeing it grow from a limited collection of tired novels arrayed on old Victorian bookshelves in a one room space, to expand to several rooms, growing by taking over the adjacent building and breaking through a dividing wall, fitted with the light coloured wood shelves and clear perspex frontages of the seventies. Before she had retired the authorities had culled the expanded book collection to make room for a row of computer screens and a fenced play area full of brightly coloured plastic childrens toys. It was not, she told them, a change of style that she welcomed.

One of the changes in those later days of her career had been the conversion of the original library building into a small local museum. As this was run by volunteers it was a natural progression for her, on retiring, to be come part of that operation, and she was now the secretary of the Elveston Museum, meaning that several days a week she returned to work in the very building she had originally started in.

She crunched a prawn cracker and asked, "What do you both do then?"

"It's very boring," Gemma told her, "I organise transport for big lumps of metal up and down the country."

"Logistics?" Adele queried incisively.

"That's one word for it."

"In an office?"

"Mostly. My company has just moved into this area, that's why we bought this place. But I do work from home sometimes. It's all computer stuff these days."

"And what about you?"

Duncan had been rather quiet through the meal, not sure whether his wife wanted him to be friendly to the neighbour, or help her to discourage the woman. They had had no chance to talk privately, and he never found it easy to interpret looks. Pushed by a direct enquiry he said, "I'm a writer."

"You've been keeping me in a job then, as a librarian. Or at least you did."

"I'm mostly freelance, so magazine articles and things like that."

"But like all writers you think you have a book in you?"

"Maybe, maybe not. It's not easy getting published, The world of books is just as ruled by fashions as, as, I don't know, music, or TV programmes. Something that might sell one month could be a big flop the next if the public's interest has changed."

"Perhaps you‑ should write about history then. That doesn't change."

"What people think about things changes. There are things that you could say, or write, just a few years ago that will have people complaining about you today."

"And things that you couldn't write a generation ago that are accepted now."

"Are you going to wave 'Lady Chatterley' at me?" he asked daringly, thinking that the old lady would be put off the subject of what he should write about by such a suggestion.

"Not specifically, but that is one example."

"I've never thought of writing books like that."

"Have you read it?"

"No. Have you?"

Adele nodded. "Oh yes. But I think it's just Mills and Boom with attitude. There's only a few pages that caused the censors to make a fuss.. just a few naughty words, the odd description."

Gemma was surprised. In fact she discovered she was slightly embarrassed, and covered this by getting up and clearing the plates to a pile beside the sink. She hadn't read 'Lady Chatterly, only knowing about it by repute, and feeling she didn't want to discuss it, especially with a near stranger. Miss Peston's frankness was a surprise. It seemed to be at odds with her age, voice and garb. She came back to the table and prised the lid off Miss Peston's tin, revealing an expertly made chocolate cake.

"Miss Peston, this is wonderful, it's so kind of you."

"Adele, I've told you. It seems a small offering now you've shared your dinner with me," their guest said, adding, with an unexpected shrewdness, "We don't have to talk about D H Lawrence if you find him a bit near the knuckle."

"Perhaps we've had sheltered upbringings," Duncan suggested.

"Perhaps I spent too much time in my library reading. There were a lot of rather, how shall I put it, dubious books," she said, watching Gemma slicing the cake into sections and handing out tea plates with a slice on each. "I became desensitised. I think the horror section used to bother me a bit, but then I read the history books and realised that the real world was harsher and crueller than almost anything the writers could dream up."

She watched her hosts taking a first bite of the cake. "I hope you like the cake," she said, and for a moment Gemma wondered if there was something sinister about the neighbour. She relaxed once she had had a mouthful of the cake. The woman might have an unusual attitude to books, and a strange liberality in discussing them, but there was no doubt she was a good cook.

Chapter 2
Meetings

"She's a funny woman," Duncan said as they were going to bed.

There had been some delay in getting ready to retire. Lots of things seemed to have been mislaid in the process of the move, and it was really only the contents of the overnight bag that they had had with them at the bed and breakfast that had saved them from tedious hunting through still not unpacked boxes for nightclothes and toiletries.

"Adele you mean?" It had been some hours since the neighbour had left and they hadn't discussed her until now, being involved in washing up and then sorting some of the cardboard boxes that had been off loaded by the removal men.

"Yes. I mean obviously she's read a lot because, well you would if you'd spent your whole life in a library, but she seems unshockable. I wouldn't have thought a woman of her age would have been so.. liberal."

"She's probably pulling your leg. I think she might have a sense of humour and was seeing how outragious she could be before you reacted."

"Even if you are right it doesn't seem proper for a retired spinster lady."

"You were very quick dismissing writing books with sex in. Maybe you should consider it. They might sell."

Duncan snorted. His aspirations were more highbrow and he wanted to write books that would inform, preferably books that would be literary entertainment. He aspired to worthy and, as he saw it, posh literature.

Gemma's unpacking carried on into the next day. She sent Duncan out into the front garden armed with some shears with instructions to cut back the encroaching shrubs so that they could park their cars in positions that would allow either of them to be able to drive out without having to move the other vehicle no matter who had arrived home first.

The day was even hotter than their moving in day, and dark clouds were forming, threatening a possible thunderstorm. Occasional pedestrians passed in each direction. One or two stopped and made some bland comment about his trimming of the overgrown vegetation, or the weather. Very rarely one would introduce themselves and say 'welcome to the neighbourhood'. Duncan enjoyed the break that these fleeting exchanges gave him. He was not a keen gardener, nor was he used to manual labour.

By lunchtime he considered he had done enough. The front garden now also boasted a high pile of cuttings. He was about to go back inside when he noticed the door of the house immediately opposite opening. A young woman came out. Today Jenny was wearing very brief shorts and a skimpy top. She was barefoot. Her long hair was tied either side with mismatched coloured rags. She was carrying a clearly handmade pot, about the size of a jam-jar, with two different shades of brown glaze erratically applied to its sides. She came across the road.

She was clearly heading straight toward him so he had to look up and watch her approach. He became very aware of her. As she crossed the road she had a sensuous gait which drew attention to her bare legs, arms and midriff. Duncan couldn't decide whether his gaze was held by this overt display, or whether he was like a rabbit frozen by the approach of a deadly snake. He felt there was something frighteningly predatory about the woman. She reached his driveway and took a few paces along it so she was near him before saying, "Hello, I'm Jenny, from opposite. John and I thought you might like a little house-warming present," and she held out the pot to him.

He had no choice but to step closer to her to take the gift. Somehow she pulled the hand holding the pot back in towards her as he got nearer to her so in order to take it he was drawn closer than he felt comfortable with. For a long moment they stood, both holding the rather crude pot, almost touching each other. She was shorter then him and she was looking straight up into his eyes. He could see her breasts moving up and down under the skimpy top as she breathed. He began to draw back, holding the pottery, the exchange having taken place.. it was the moment to step apart. She didn't let go of the present.

Duncan had a second of panic in which he became convinced that the woman was waiting for him to kiss her.. perhaps it was expected as thanks. He was hesitating, dreading being drawn into more than a brief 'thank you' peck when behind him Gemma opened the front door saying, "Hello, who's this?"

It broke the frightening impasse, and Duncan turned away, holding the pot the woman had now released and showed it to his wife gabbling, "This is Jenny, she lives opposite, she brought us a present, isn't that nice of her?"

"Isn't it. Thank you so much," Gemma said. But Duncan knew that her woman's intuition had detected that something more than handing over a gift had occurred.

Gemma took control, made the introductions and repeated the thanks, before saying "Come on Duncan, lunch is ready," so they could escape.

Inside Duncan told her, "Thank goodness you came out when you did. I don't know what was going on. It was like an attack, I think I know what a mouse feels like when an owl swoops down on it!"

"Nonsense," Gemma laughed, "you are just out of practice meeting pretty young girls."

"Do you think she's pretty?"

"Don't you? You looked as though you did!"

"I think she's terrifying," he told her, and poured himself a whisky, "What's for lunch??"

"Oh I don't know, I'll get something ready in a moment," she said.

"But you said... Ah..You came out to rescue me didn't you?"

"Not exactly, but I was a bit worried what you might do next."

It was a fairly silent meal.

For several days the couple continued sorting their new home. Even Duncan was unable to avoid some manual labour as this happened, finding himself moving several items of furniture to different places around the house as Gemma experimented with the layout. At one point she interrupted him as he was staring into space, his mind miles away from what was going on.

"Earth calling Newbons Removals," she said to him jokingly.

He jerked back to the real world.

"Mrs Newbon would like Mr Newbon to move this table to the other side of the room for her."

"Is that where it's going then?" he queried.

"That's where I want to try it."

Duncan knew what that probably meant.

The end of Gemma's leave came near, and she pressed him into joining her on a shopping trip to the nearest of the town's supermarkets. They selected the largest sized trolley and set off up and down the aisles of the store. Half way round they came across John and Jenny heading in the opposite direction and were obliged to stop and chat when Jenny greeted them and introduced John. The weather had still not broken and the couple were both in loose casual clothes. Jenny was managing to display an indiscreet amount of bare flesh, and Duncan was conscious that other customers were looking their way as they stood and talked, women disapprovingly, men in frank appraisal. Duncan, who was pushing the trolley, managed to arrange for it to be between him and Jenny.

The talk was inconsequential till John asked if they had found anywhere for the pot. They both felt guilty, for it was so far from their taste that it had been banished to the as yet unused garden room, a high sounding name that had been given by the estate agents to a small space with a door and window facing from the back of the house that the previous owners had clearly used as a potting shed. Here it had been stood on a high shelf out of the way and destined to be forgotten.

"Well we're still sorting ourselves out," Gemma said, "but we think it will be going on display in the garden room."

Duncan could see her fingers crossed behind her back as she said this, and stayed silent. He was loath to enter into too much conversation anyway as Jenny was once again looking straight into his eyes and he could only interpret the expression as rather predatory.

"Come to the pub tonight and meet a few more of the locals," John was saying, and they found themselves agreeing.

The local pub was only a few hundred yards from number 47 and Duncan and Gemma walked there in the early evening. It was a fairly modern brick building, set back from the road with a large tarmac space in front for car parking. The sign outside announced it as the Dog and Dray and displayed a picture of a small dog looking up at a wagon full or barrels above the word 'free house'.

"Nipper's lost his phonograph and found some beer," Gemma

remarked as they approached.

"It does look rather like it," Duncan agreed, pulling open the dark red door by the worn handle to allow them into a rather gloomy bar with a traditional looking counter bedecked with horse brasses and tankards, incongruous in such a recently constructed inn.

There were a few people at the tables and chairs but plenty of space and they soon spotted the group that included John and Jenny in an window alcove. They waved.

"I suppose I'd better get a round," Duncan muttered to his wife, and the next few minutes were spent on introductions and ordering and passing the drinks from the counter into waiting hands. The group were drinkers of pints, and the newcomers were a bit conspicuous as they sat down with glasses of wine. With their neighbours were another couple, Edward and Tamsin, who, they learnt, lived some distance along the street at 94, and a man on his own called Nick, who lived a couple of streets away. Duncan was relieved to find that Nick was sat next to Jenny, and that John was on the other side of her. He had not anticipated that although this meant he was safely separated from his new neighbour he was now facing her across the table.

His concern that Jenny might continue to flaunt herself at him as at their first meeting proved unfounded as she was blatantly chatting up Nick, a situation that Nick seemed to be both enjoying and encouraging, despite John's presence. John had been deep in conversation with Edward and Tamsin when the Newbons arrived, but they all turned their attentions to the newcomers as the pair sat down.

Edward and Tamsin were said to run a material shop, though the explanations failed to explain whether this was a haberdashers, or dealt with dress making material, or curtains, or all three. Nick was introduced to them as a bank clerk. As the evening wore on it seemed that in fact he might actually be unemployed and in reality had once been a bank clerk.

"You see," he told them at one point, "Now all the banks are doing everything on-line the branches are all closing. I don't expect you can remember the last time you went into your local branch can you?"

"Well actually, because of buying the house, we've been..." Duncan began.

"So we're all being given the elbow from our jobs in the branches," Nick explained, "Of course they tell us we can transfer to some main head office in Aberdeen or Exeter, but that's no good unless you want to move house, and who'd do that for a job?"

"We just did," Gemma admitted, "That's why we're here now, because of my job."

"Nick doesn't want to move away, do you?" Jenny was stroking Nick's arm as she said this.

He turned his head to look at her and said, "Of course not," in a way that the Newbons read quite a lot into.

The sky darkened quickly and behind the bar the barman flicked rows of switches on to illuminate the room. The feel changed from a summer evening to a winter one and Gemma found herself studying the log effect fake fire in the fireplace half wishing that it could be turned on too.

Nick started to explain that he belonged to several clubs in the area, and these dissuaded him from moving away. Duncan assumed that the clubs would be things like golf, so was surprised to learn that the man belonged to the local amateur theatre company and a book club. He wanted to ask about the book club but the conversation was suddenly interrupted by a brilliant flash of lightning visible through the window and a crash of thunder only a moment later.

"Wow, that must have been pretty close," Edward commented, and put his arm round Tamsin saying more softly, "Are you all right dear?" She nodded. Edward obviously felt he should explain, and told the rest of them, "Tamsin doesn't like thunderstorms."

"We've probably been due for one for a couple of days," said Nick, "It will clear the air a bit."

Somewhere more distantly they heard a long low rumbling thunderclap, and as if that was the cue it began to rain. Not soft summer rain gently starting and building, but a torrential downpour whose huge drops bounced whole feet back up when they hit the pub car park tarmac which became an inch or two deep in water within a few seconds.

"Oh no! I left the bathroom window open," said Gemma.

"At least it was the bathroom," Duncan said, "Anyway we're not going back through this. We'll wait it out. I doubt it will last long."

"Another drink everyone?" Edward offered, and they all accepted.

The storm continued much longer than they had expected. It became darker as the sun set, although the black clouds and falling rain made it impossible to tell when this was.

"My mother used to describe this sort of rain as being like stair-rods," Edward remarked.

"What are 'stair-rods'?" asked Jenny.

Nick said, "The youth of today!," and began to explain how staircarpets used to be held in place with a rod between two brackets at the back of each tread.

Jenny looked puzzled, then she said, "But the carpet couldn't go to the edges then, because the brackets would be in the way."

"Sweet," said Edward, "this infant actually doesn't remember. Carpets didn't cover the whole floor, they always stopped short of the walls.. and the edges of the stairs."

There was nothing, Duncan decided, of the 'infant' about Jenny.

There was another flash close by and the loud crack of thunder drowned out Jenny's reply to Edward's taunt, but Gemma was fairly sure it was something uncomplimentary about the older generation.

"You know its a good point," Nick became serious, "there is a lot of 'common knowledge' that is gradually diasappearing. We ought to be trying to preserve it."

"You want to preserve stair-rods?"

"Not that specifically, but there's all sorts of things. I bet the people who lived round here a hundred, maybe two hundred, years ago assumed that their decendants would remember... Oh I don't know, what the town was like before the railway got built."

"We know what it was like," said Duncan cynically, "If you wanted to go anywhere you got on a horse, instead of like now when you go to the station to make sure the train is cancelled and get on a rail replacement bus."

There was some laughter, but Nick said, "No, really, we ought to do something to preserve the old knowledge, the stories, well some of them, you know."

Edward, a comforting arm still round Tamsin, said "Oh damn, he's gone into teacher mode now."

"Isn't that sort of thing the job of museums and libraries?, Duncan wondered, "By the way we met a woman who was something to do with the library, your neighbour," he looked at John, "Miss Peston."

"Adele," said Nick, "Yes, she'd be the sort of person to pull some project together. Elveston's walking answer to the Doomsday Book she is. She knows the history, in fact she was part of the history." He left that comment hanging unexplained in the air.

There was the sound of a bell being rung, and the barman's shout of "Time please!"

"He can't turn us out into this can he?" Tamsin said plaintively, just as the barman arrived at their table collecting empty glasses.

"Sorry Miss, rules is rules. Anyway it's easing off now."

They all looked at the window which was black from the night with the impression of frosted glass from the countless rivulets of water streaming down the panes glinting as they reflected the lights of the bar. The pattern of flowing water appeared to jiggle briefly as another lightning flash preceded the latest thunderclap.

"So I see," said John sarcastically.

The group huddled under the pub's brick porch, jostled by some other customers and watching people running to their cars, dodging back when a car turned past the doorway to leave, sending a solid wall of water out as a bow wave as it crawled slowly away from them. By mutual agreement they accepted there was no choice but to make for home through the rain. None of them had coats and by the time they reached the road itself they were soaked. They formed a sad, plodding procession along Greendale Road. Gemma and Duncan and John and Jenny's houses were the first, they went to their respective doors amid 'goodnights' as Edward, Tamsin and Nick carried on along the road.

Fumbling in wet pockets for the key Duncan looked across the road at their neighbours in time to see their hall light come on silhouetting them in their doorway. Duncan said to Gemma, "She wears few enough clothes as it is, but she really shouldn't stand in a lit door when what she has got on is soaking wet."

"I think you are much too interested in what she is doing." said his wife.

Chapter 3
The Grand Idea

Gemma returned to work after the weekend, leaving Duncan alone in the house. He shouldn't have been idle, as there were numerous lists of jobs to do scattered around the house, but his innate nature led him to an inertia about undertaking these jobs, and he spent a long while during the morning sitting staring into space.

After a snack lunch he drove to the town centre. The original market place still seemed to be some sort of hub for what activity the place could boast. Duncan saw that this was not really very much. Streets leading off the square boasted a selection of stores belonging to familiar chains, with the occasional independent shop among them. Closer study revealed that outlets were mostly fast food stores or charity shops. Some hairdressers wedged between these, and there were at least two closed and boarded up banks, their formerly pretentious stonework showing incongruously amidst the now dusty plate glass and the perspex signage.

Yellow lines had been painted on the road to discourage shoppers, and the area was dead and nearly deserted. A small group of teenagers was hanging around the steps of an empty shop and a single cyclist, with his base-ball hat on backwards, rode along the crown of the road with his front wheel off the ground balancing on just the rear one as if on a unicycle. Duncan found a parking space in a car-park hidden in a side street. The cars mostly seemed to be displaying season tickets, and he guessed that they belonged to the staff of businesses in the town centre rather than to customers. Walking back to the square he was in time to witness the arrival, and shortly after, the departure, of an empty looking bus that no-one boarded or alighted from.

The heatwave was over, broken by the storm the night they had been caught in the rain returning from the pub, and it was cooler and the sky was grey as he walked along the main street. After some distance he came to a pair of ostentatious Georgian houses set slightly back from the pavement. Plain signs announced one as the library, and, in the case of the other, a newer sign with a different lettering style declared it to be the museum. He went into the library, climbing the steps, or at least the half of the original steps that remained, the other half having been covered by a concrete ramp that extended out almost to the pavement.

He expected wood panelling and moulded plaster cornices inside, maybe a small chandelier, a reception desk of carved wood and rows of shelves of books.

The door opened into a plain plasterboard box-like room with lino tiled floor and fluorescent tube lighting. Glass fronted poster frames on the walls displayed the minutes of recent council meetings alongside plain and unattractive announcements of lectures on a variety of topics ranging from recycling to litter picking, at least three of which had happened weeks earlier he noticed. The entrance was guarded by a plywood and formica counter bristling with video screens behind which sat an unwelcoming and bored looking young woman. She was tapping at a computer keyboard and even the novelty of someone entering the building failed to make her look up and stop. He wondered whether she had even noticed his arrival.

He wondered whether to speak to her, but her demeanour did not encourage this so he ventured further into the building.

Rooms off what must have at one time been an imposing panelled hallway, but was now painted over in pastel shades with a brutal commercial stairlift defacing the staircase, were labelled with formica signs engraved so the contrast colour backing showed through the cut away lettering. In each case the legend announced 'The Cllr Jones Room', or something similar, although the names of these long gone worthy councillors were never 'Jones', being more usually long, obscure, or double-barrelled.

These labels gave him no indication of what might be inside each room so he opened the door to one at random.

In the bare room that was revealed a group of perhaps eight or ten middle aged women in tracksuits were rolling on the floor in the middle of what he assumed to be a yoga class. The instructor looked fiercely at him, and he mumbled "Sorry, wrong room," as he backed out.

From the next room's closed door came the sounds of children squealing as they played, and he deduced without looking that the Hewson-Smith Room must be being used as a creche. It wasn't until he went upstairs that he found any books, and the room these were in displayed a somewhat pathetic array of wheeled double-sided metal shelf units bearing what were mostly large format, glossy, colour printed, coffee table books, each with a coloured Dewey system label sellotaped to the bottom of their spine and all rather tired and dog-eared.

On the furthest wall some static shelves displayed a selection of novels, but the whole of one side of this room was occupied by a row of computers and their keyboards and monitors. Two people were sat at these, well apart and with their heads leaning toward the displays. They both turned to watch Duncan as he came in, and, not recognising him they returned to studying their screens.

He went to a vacant screen and tried to use the computer. A succession of welcome screens flashed up, followed by an instruction to swipe his library card. He made a mental note to request one, though the library's system was clearly fairly antiquated and he probably had a better search engine on his phone.

He wandered around the room, idly turning the pages of a few books, before making his way downstairs again. The receptionist was still tapping her keyboard and pointedly ignored him as he stood at her counter until he said, "Excuse me. How do I get a library ticket?"

She paused, and sighed as she handed him a paper form.

"Fill this in," she told him, bluntly.

The form asked him for name and address, which he supplied, along with his date of birth. It then stumped him by demanding he supply proof of his address in the form of a utility bill.

"I can't show you a utility bill," he explained, "because we've only moved in a few days ago."

Again the sigh. "You'll need to bring in some proof of your address," she told him.

Frustrated he folded the form and put it in his pocket, promising to call in again the next day. He felt this comment was probably wasted, as the woman was already back at her keyboard ignoring him. As he was leaving he discovered an unmarked door which led through to the adjacent building. This was the museum.

He had been disappointed by the library, both by its contents and by the disinterested attitude of the only member of staff he had seen. The museum was to be a very different experience. The moment he stepped through the doorway he was surrounded by an astounding, almost confusing, array of shelves and cabinets packed with items on display. A figure was bending over a glass topped display, just closing the lid.

Adele Peston straightened and looked back at him as he came in, holding a paint brush and a yellow duster in one hand as she shut the hinged top of the cabinet with the other. Her face lit up with delight as she saw him and she said, "Mr Newbon, how nice of you to come and see the museum."

"Hello Miss Peston," Duncan said.

"Adele, please. After all we have shared a meal, so we are past formality I would imagine."

Somehow her description of having 'shared a meal' managed to sound more as though they had shared a bed. It came back to Duncan how extrordinarily frank and modern the woman's attitudes seemed to be.

"Did you come in looking for anything specific, or were you just curious about our litle exhibition?" she asked him.

"Just curious. Well actually I came to look at the library originally, but it's a bit disappointing, and the girl on the desk said I couldn't have a library card until I could produce some proof of where I lived.. and that's not easy when you've only just moved in."

"She's a silly, lazy fool," Adele told him, "all she has to do is get you to sign a declaration form. You always have to do that with new residents till they get a utility bill. Do you want me to come through and sort her out?"

"No, no," Duncan didn't want to stir things up, and he could imagine that a former employee blustering in and telling the sullen girl how to do her job would be a certain way to make a permanent enemy, "Show me your museum. I didn't think there was enough history in Elveston to make an exhibition out of."

Adele was delighted to show him around, and lurched immediately into full lecturing mode, explaining that the town stood on the site of several earlier skirmishes, if not battles, and was the former home or birthplace of a number of notables.

"The Iceni chased the Romans across Britain at one point, and the Romans tried to make a stand here, but got driven back still further. The fighting then totally destroyed the little hamlet that was here originally, so there's nothing left from those days, but every so often someone will dig up a scrap of Roman stuff. Look, over here in this cabinet. These are all bits from the Roman occupation."

She led him to displays of a large quantity of what to Duncan was rusty or dirty scrap. She assured him that these little pieces of brownish junk were valuable artifacts, and he nodded sagely, hoping that she didn't detect his lack of enthusiasm for the finds.

"I didn't know anything had happened here over the centuries," he said.

"Elvestone's had lots of things happen in it," she told him, "You want to talk to Nick, he's keen on local history."

"Oh yes, I think I've met him."

"I think he's frustrated by the way people just ignore what has happened here in the past. New people move into the town, begging you pardon of course, and they never find out anything about the place they are living in."

"But you're doing your best with this place," Duncan said.

"If we don't record things now we'll lose them."

""Surely the records are better now than ever before, with computers and the internet and photography...."

"You need to persuade people to listen. A museum isn't much good if no-one comes in." she shook her head sadly, "I've had whole days during which no-one has come in here."

Duncan felt the conversation was becoming a bit depressing. He looked around for something to distract from the subject. In a far corner he saw shelves displaying some swords and helmets. She saw where he was looking.

"The civil war," she told him, "The parlimentarians were chasing Charles and they passed near here. They thought he and the Royalists must be in the town so they burnt it to the ground, all except the chuch, and they didn't do that much good."

"I had no idea."

"It doesn't count as any sort of battle, it was just another bit of destruction that Comwell's men did. Apart from the church there isn't a single building that pre-dates the Civil War in the town. And that's why.

"The locals all ran away and hid in Greendale Wood, that's what our road is named after you know, until the military had gone. They lived in tents and hovels while the town was rebuilt."

"What was the town for? I mean was there an industry, like milling or was it the market for the area?"

"Not then. It wasn't until much later that they had the wool trade."

"Wool?"

"The big Victorian building at the bottom of the High Street near the bridge," she told him.

"So there must have been sheep farming round here then?"

"Elveston market was the biggest livestock market in this part of the country for over two hundred years," she told him, "It made the locals very rich, that's why there's the hall up the road and all those public buildings scattered around the place."

"Like this one?"

"Among others. The Library.. this was it originally," and she gestured around the spacious room they were in, "was built by one of the mayors in the Victorian era. All the local notables built something. Schools, hospitals, workhouses, assembly halls, we've got them all. They seem to have been trying to get rid of as much of their wealth as they could."

"Do you think it was for tax purposes?"

Adele fixed him with a stern look.

"No I don't. I think it was philanthropy."

She led him through more rooms of the museum, drawing his attention to displays of period costumes, domestic furniture and utensils, a series of town maps through the ages, showing the spread of the buildings and, ultimately, a diorama of the market place with some sort of fête in progress.

"What was this?" he asked her.

"The annual Dragon Fair," she told him.

"Dragon?"

"The church is St George's, so for over a hundred, or a hundred and fifty, years the town had a fair at the end of April. They used to have a big carnival dragon, and someone dressed up as St George to fight it."

She seemed to hesitate before continuing, "It was a bit raunchy I suppose. They used to have all the girls draw lots and the winner, or maybe you could say, the loser, got carried off by the dragon. We think that the girl had always had to spend the night with the dragon ever since the tradition began. That was why St George then had to try to rescue her the next day and fight the dragon. When he had won the girl was given to him for the next night as a prize. There's records of girls who didn't want to be in the lottery, but they were mostly compelled. They started being entered in the draw at very young ages back in the early eighteen hundreds. The whole thing died out in the nineteen sixties, really because it had become unacceptable for a town to run an annual event that was sort of legalised rape, or at best prostitution."

Duncan mulled that over. Once again he was slightly surprised at Adele's frankness, just as he had been the evening he first met her.

She waited while he thought about it, then she said, "I wasn't the last one, but nearly, there were only two more years of it after the year I was chosen."

"You were one of the victims?"

"I wouldn't really use the word victim. Brian who was the dragon that year wasn't very nice, but my St George was really sweet and kind."

"That's.. It's awful, disgusting. It must have been illegal even then!"

"I suppose so. I don't think so. Maybe. But the entrants were all above the age of consent by then. When things have gone on for generations it's.. Well it's tradition. Anyway we were a very select club, those of us who had been the maidens. Just like a town's carnival queens. We were special. Our peers were secretly jealous, even if some of them despised us. We'd sold ourselves, so that made us whores, but the prize money made them envy us."

"Prize money?"

"Yes. A lot of prize money. I put the deposit on my house with mine. The council and the church put up the money."

"Could I write it up as an article? I mean could I interview you, and any of the other girls, and perhaps the Dragons and Georges. It would be a really great story to publish."

"I don't think that would be a very good idea," Adele told him firmly, "It's not impossible, even now, that someone might try to bring charges, Anyway it's probably not the sort of publicity the town would want these days."

Duncan was disappointed. He remained pensive through the rest of the guided tour Adele led him round as she showed off her empire. Somewhere in his mind he was wondering about reviving the fair, or maybe getting a television documentary out of the story. He was impressed that Elveston had kept this salacious annual event from its history so secret. He had known little about the town before Gemma's work brought them here, but he was certain that rumour of, what had she called it? The Dragon Fair, would have reached him, especially once he told people where they were moving to. He could imagine aquaintances saying 'Oh! That's the place where...' but no-one had. Somehow, despite still having been happening within living memory, the event had been hushed up.

Chapter 4
Revelations

He told Gemma about his visit to the library, and museum when she came back from work that evening, but she was more interested in describing the frustrations of her new job, and clearly wasn't paying much attention to what he said. His mention of meeting Adele produced an off-hand 'oh yes' and that part of the conversation more or less co-incided with her discovery that he had failed to do most of the small tasks that she had wanted him to do.

They were eating a rather scratch evening meal of bacon and egg, which Duncan excused as he prepared it, saying disingenuously, that he hadn't known what time she would be home, when there was a knock at the door.

"Damn," said Duncan, shoving a last piece of fried bread into his mouth and going to the front of the house to answer the knock. He was still chewing the mouthful as he opened the door to find Nick standing on the step.

"Have I caught you eating?" Nick asked.

"Just finishing, come in."

Gemma and Duncan installed Nick in a living room chair and she produced cups of tea for them all, learning that Nick was a milk-no-sugar man.

"I felt I had to come round and see you when I heard you'd been talking to Adele," Nick said.

"Yes I went into the library, well the museum really, this afternoon. It's not much of a library is it?"

Nick ignored the assessment of the library.

"I don't really know how to say this, so I'll just come out with it."

Duncan and Gemma were intrigued, They wondered what had happened that could possibly have caused such a hesitation. They realised that Nick had made a special visit to them and now wanted to get something off his chest. As newcomers to the town they were surprised that he was visiting them with such an aim. They were acquaitances due to having a drink in the pub, but hardly saw themselves as likely to be on Nick's list of confidants.

Gemma said, "What have you done now, Duncan?"

"It's nothing you have done, well at least not yet," Nick assured them. "I'd better start at the beginning."

"Look," he began, "I think that Adele is going to try to persuade you to help us organise a show. We've talked about it for ages, years even, and there are several people like us who think it would be good for the town. Marketed properly it could bring some money and trade in... heaven knows we need it, the town needs it I mean, and it would bring people together, give them a cause."

"What sort of show?" Duncan wanted to know.

"Something to do with the town's history. That's why Adele is so keen. But it's also why there's a problem."

"Not enough history?" Duncan hazarded. Adele's evident enthusiasm at the museum had hardly disguised the fact that there had been only a few historical happenings locallly.

"Rather the reverse actually. You see there are things that used to happen here that might be, let's say 'controversial' in this day and age."

"You mean the fair don't you?"

"I mean the fair. I see you've heard."

"I haven't," said Gemma innocently.

"It all stopped a long time ago. You must remember that," Nick told her, "But there are still people about who were part of it. So even if nothing actually illegal happened in living memory, well people would say it's not exactly politically correct."

Duncan grunted. Political correctness in all its forms rather annoyed him, He often found his writing confined by what he knew his clients would think was accepable nowadays. It was sometimes difficult to write articles that completely avoided offending the more censurious members of pressure groups. Occasionally he felt he had spent more time skirting round contentious issues than actually writing the piece he had been asked to produce.

"Don't start, dear," his wife told him, trying to waylay a possible outburst of annoyance, especially until she had got the measure of where Nick stood on the subject and what he was talking about. She remembered he might well be at odds with Duncan.

"If we're talking about history surely it would be right to report it, show it, whatever you're going to do, as it happened, not some sanitised version. You don't hide the fact that the Romans conquered Britain, you just report it." Duncan was determined.

"I think it's a question of not wanting to stir a hornet's nest."

"What hornet's nest," Gemma still wanted to know, her curiousity now piqued.

"When it was still going on, in the early sixties, lots of people were worried that they'd get up one morning and find a TV crew in the street with someone like Fyffe Robertson holding a microphone and letting the world into our little secret. They decided it was safer to stop the thing, and they put so much pressure on that it was eventually abandoned."

"What was? What secret?" Gemma was frustrated.

"Sorry, I naturally assumed, since I guessed Adele had told Duncan all about it, and he seemed to know, that he would have rushed home and told you."

"He hasn't told me anything."

Nick told her about the fair, and the Saint George and the Dragon. Particularly he explained about the town drawing lots for which girl would be the 'maiden' and end up spending a night with the Dragon and then with Saint George.

"But if the girls agreed..." Gemma refused to be shocked by the revelations of something that happened so far back in the past.

"They did, and their parents, if they were young, signed their consents. There are still people who don't want all the tabloid coverage that's likely if it became common knowledge."

"There can't be anyone left who was involved," Gemma said.

Nick shook his head slowly. "I'm afraid there are, "Duncan's just spoken to one, Adele. She was nearly the last, there were only two more years after that till it ended, and those two girls moved out of the area, but some of the men are still here."

""You mean Adele, the Adele who lives over the road, Miss Peston, she was a 'maiden'?"

Nick nodded.

"She was raffled off as part of a village fête?"

"It's about fifty years ago. She was a grown woman even then. Well at least she was legally speaking an adult. She's almost seventy now you know."

"That's not the point!"

Duncan said to his wife, "She seemed rather proud of it when she told me about it this afternoon. She just didn't seem to want it to be published. I asked if I could do a magazine article or something and she said 'no'. I think Nick is saying the same."

"I'm saying I, and others, would like you as a professional writer to join in with us and work on some sort of show about the town's history. But, and it's a definite 'but', it mustn't include details about the dragon fair..." he held up his hand to stop an interruption, "I know, I know, it's probably the most exciting thing that happened since the Roundheads, but it's off limits."

"To hear you talk you'd be forgiven for thinking you had something to hide too," Duncan joked.

Nick looked from one to the other of them very solemnly, and then said, "It's off limits, OK."

Chapter 5
Persuasion

Duncan and Gemma talked with Nick for a long time that evening. He used all his persuasion, not in order to keep them from enquiring more deeply into the fair, though they were both naturally curious about it and he fended off any questions, but to try to convince Duncan that some sort of performance could be devised to celebrate the town's history.

"It's all very worthy, I'm sure," Duncan said, "But why? And why now."

"Next year will be the town's quincentenary."

"Its what?"

"Quincentenary.. five hundred years since it was incorporated as a borough."

"And you think there should be an 'event' to mark it?" Gemma said.

"Certainly. It's a big deal, lots of people think so too, but we never had a famous writer to script it for us until now."

"Duncan is definitely not a 'famous' writer, he's just a backroom boy and would want to stay that way," Gemma said, protectively. "Anyway who's the 'lots of people' involved?"

"Well, they're not involved yet, but they will be."

"Will be because you've asked and they've said 'yes', or will be when you eventually ask and persuade them?" Duncan wanted to know.

"Look, it's a big occasion. Every club in the town will want to join in. Musicians, youth clubs, schools.. you name it. The council will want it to happen because it promotes the town, the press will have a field day and the public will get a free show."

"Oh it's free is it?"

"Well I don't know yet. I think Adele and I would like it to be, but it depends."

"Depends on how many people you can get to do things for free, starting with Duncan here," said Gemma flippantly.

Duncan scratched his head. Part of him was curious, envisaging a cross between the Edinburgh Tattoo and some Medieval Miracle Cycle play. He looked across over Nick's shoulder to where the calendar hung on the kitchen wall. An implausibly perfect, air-brushed view of this town's market place sat above the white squares counting off the days of the current month. Though they'd only just arrived, and the calendar had been a jocular present from a friend in the town they had left, so had only just been pressed into use, it was already covered in notes and appointments in a variety of different inks. Even allowing for some of these being notes of dustbin collection days and when milk payments were due the planner showed a busy schedule in the household. Gemma's work commitments predominated, naturally, but Duncan had added very, very occasional copy deadlines for himself. Could he really sandwich in writing a script for a big event? Did he know how? He had never written a script, apart from a short speech for a managing director to open a new office block once. Did he actually want to?

Probably he did, he decided. After all he mused, think how infuriating, how galling, it would be if he refused and Nick went off and found someone else to do it. They would almost certainly be obliged to watch the show, cringing at a possibly banal script and wishing he'd agreed. Duncan always believed he could write better than anyone else. He was not even dissuaded from this belief by the relatively sparce orders in his diary.

What would Gemma say if he agreed, he wondered. Or would she be more annoyed if he refused. He hated trying to second guess a decision like this. If Nick had made casual mention of the project one day and then levelled the question at him after he'd chatted with Gemma he would have known which way the wind was blowing on the subject. Her comment about his writing for free had not really enlightened him as to her feelings about the project. He wished they had discussed this side of the thing more before he was asked to make a decision.

"What do you think, dear?" he asked.

"It's up to you," she replied, unhelpfully.

This was one of those moments when Duncan knew he couldn't win. Say 'yes' and there was a chance Gemma would ask why on earth he had done so, say 'no' and he might be lectured about how they should be supporting their new community. He steeled himself for a potential future domestic disagreement and said,

"All right. But certain conditions. You've got to give me a list of what you want covered and who to get the facts about it from.."

"I think you know 'who' already. Adele will give you everything you need."

"..and I need to know where it's going to be performed."

Nick looked uncertain. "I'll come back to you on that. There will be pressure from some groups, some interested parties let's say, for it to be in particular places. Personally I'd like to think in terms of a a rolling moving pageant, a performing procession through the town. You talk to Adele and get some ideas going and we'll see." and with that vague information and opinion he rose to leave. "Thank you so much for agreeing. We're so lucky you've moved here."

When he came back from letting Nick out of the front door he found Gemma washing up the cups and glasses with that hard sort of handling that stops just short of breakage but relays a message and knew at once he had made the wrong decision.

"You're an idiot!" she said to him, over her shoulder.

"You don't think I should have agreed?"

"Of course you shouldn't have agreed. It's a poisoned chalice. They're going to dictate what you can write the show about, they're going to tell you who's going to be in it, and where it's going to be staged. And when their parocial ideas don't work it will be you who gets the blame... and in any case, what do you know about writing scripts?"

"I asked you whether I should do it and you said it was up to me."

"I couldn't tell you 'no' in front of him could I? How would that have looked? I can hear them now, 'He's right under her thumb, she wouldn't let him write our show...' "

"So how was I supposed to know?"

"If you had given it any thought you would have known exactly what my view was."

"I'm not a mind reader. Anyway I think it might be quite interesting."

"Darling, you're an idiot, but you're my idiot," she said, and turned and hugged him with wet washing-up soaked hands, "I just hope it all works out all right for you."

Chapter 6
Learning

He seemed to be spending a lot of time with Adele. Her voluntary manning of the museum meant that they often discussed the show while she was there, and this allowed her to sometimes show him exhibits that she said related to the historical incidents she was listing for him. He was frequently unsure about the link, feeling that tables full of pewter tankards, or a display of a Victorian hip bath, were neither dramatic, nor could he deduce a proven connection with an incident in the town's seemingly largely bland history.

After these meetings he often returned home and sat apparently vacantly staring at nothing as he puzzled over what he could make of all this.

Gemma was unusually unhelpful when he explained his quandry as they talked when she came home from work.

"There really isn't enough 'history' to make anything of," he grumbled.

"I did warn you. You've made a rod for your own back with this."

"Well what would you suggest?," he asked, hoping she would come up with some idea, even just a tiny titbit to make a start from.

"I told you, say 'no'. I can't help you with this. Best thing you could do is back out of it, better now than later."

He prodded the food on his plate. He had cooked, again, and as usual it was not an outstanding success. Meals were always better if Gemma cooked them. Today his attempt was marred by underdone potatoes, so the mash he had tried for was lumpy, 'just like my old school's dinners', he thought, and chops that had distinct signs of charring at the edges. Gemma didn't complain, but he knew she was frustrated by his attempts at catering. Nearly as much as she was by the town event and his having become embroiled in it.

One day, when the weather was bright and sunny, Adele asked Duncan, "Have you got your car here?"

He said "Yes, why?"

"There's plenty of volunteers here today, Let's go and see the site of the battles."

Following her directions he drove out of the town a little way until they came to a piece of open country where the land sloped up from the minor road to a ridge on the left.

"Pull off anywhere here," she instructed him, and he ran the car onto the grass beside the road.

Adele climbed out and stood beside the car straightening her coat and hooking her handbag firmly over her arm. He locked the vehicle. They were on a largish patch of grass bounded in the distance by trees and shrubs. The grass was short, cropped by rabbits, he decided, spotting the droppings all over the place. Looking further away he could see a few of the animals nibbling at the grass in the sunlight. Away from the road the land formed a ridge about a hundred yards away.

"Come on," Adele commanded, setting off up the slope with energetic strides that belied her age. He followed, trailing a bit and making heavy weather of the unaccustomed exercise. They reached the crest of the rise and he found that there was a small cairn of slabs and stones with a metal plate attached.

He bent to the plaque and read,

> *'On this site in AD 60 the Iceni under Boudicea met the*

Roman IX legion in a skirmish that drove the Romans down this hillside. In 1648 The Parlimentarian Army camped here while pursuing King Charles I, before raising the town of Elveston to the ground.'

The plaque was small and the engraving weather-beaten. There was a crest at the top, which he recognised as the council emblem incorporating a dragon like creature winding itself around a spade with a crown above it.

He squinted at the text, confused at first by the combination of two historical incidents on the same plate. The pile of stones that it was attached to seemed rather wobbbly and unsteady and bore a striking graffiti of a heart with initials K and L rendered onto the flat part of one of the stones in red spray paint.

"Your work?" he asked her, for she had rather pointedly indicated the memorial. "The plaque I mean, not the graffiti," he added.

"Hooligans," she commented, "I know they probably came up here to consumate their affair, but surely they didn't have to bring a spray can all this way to record the incident." She rubbed her hand on the graffiti as if she thought the paint might brush off. Finding that it didn't she turned to the direction they had come from, facing the town, which could be seen behind the belt of trees that marked the edge of the grass space.

"That's Greendale Wood," she told him, "Where the townsfolk hid when Cromwell's men destroyed their homes. Most of the artifacts in the museum came from this field. We organised some metal detection work and a dig about, let me see, probably twenty-five years ago now."

"You must have known this was the site before you started digging about though."

"Yes and no. Local rumour had always said that Boudicea fought the Romans in this field. Poor woman, she didn't best them very often even with the powerful motive of revenge to help her, but this was one place she got the better of them. Anyway we started digging and turned up the Civil War camp quite unexpectedly. It was very confusing really, because the Parlimentarian army had stopped the night right on top of the earlier battle. We spent weeks sifting the finds, just to separate the eras."

"And it all ended up in the museum," he stated the obvious fact.

"Mostly. There were a few really exciting items which got sent to London and never came back to us. I think the big experts thought that our little museum wasn't good enough to display the important things."

"Such as?"

"There was a almost perfect Roman sword, and quite a lot of coinage, I suppose the star item was the chest with the full suit of Parlimentarian armour in it... well the chest wasn't in very good condition, but the armour was immaculate, in fact a lot of people thought it was a modern reproduction."

Duncan mused, "I wonder if we could use the quincentenary and the show as an excuse to get those things back here where they belong for you."

Adele gripped his wrist excitedly, "I hadn't thought of that. Could you try?"

"I don't think I'd be much use, but surely the museum could try."

"Believe me, we did. But a special occasion might be an excuse to try again."

They began walking down the hill again. Half way Duncan stopped.

"I strikes me that old history is just a long account of wicked men, well people, and nasty things they did."

"A lot of modern history isn't much different," she told him sadly.

"How would it be if we did the show here?"

"You mean on this hill?"

"Yes. If we staged it somehow so the public could sit on the slope and picnic, and watch it, and it would be like a sort of amphitheatre the way this hill curves around."

Adele now became increasingly excited by this idea, and by the time he had driven back to the museum she seemed to have decided that the show should be an open air event on that site.

Using the nearest local newspaper and radio they advertised a public meeting to discuss the project. Nick had become an unelected spokesman for the scheme, and the radio station, always welcoming any minor local item that could put forward someone for interview, put him on air in the middle of a hot drowsy late summer afternoon. Whether anyone was listening or not was debatable, and Duncan always felt afterward that it was probably some of the others' tireless door to door leafet dropping through letter boxes that really swelled the numbers at the meeting.

They had managed to get the loan of the Village Hall, though they had had to hire it and in the absence of any funds Nick had paid the hire fee from his own pocket, and that still sunlit evening a little group of them, feeling like conspiritors, laid out the chairs and then clustered on the platform of the hall.

There were seven of them on the platform. Adele and Nick put themselves in the centre of the arc of chairs they arranged. John and Jenny were to one side of them, and Edward and Tamsin the other. Duncan sat next to Tamsin, on the extreme end, and tried to be as inconspicuous as he could. A trickle of curious people began to come into the hall.

The self appointed organisers whispered among themselves nervously. Their biggest concern was that it would turn out that they had laid out a hundred chairs, but only a handful of people turned up. It got nearer to the publicised start time, and they stared out over what seemed a wide expanse of empty green coloured plastic seats. The pale cream walls, with cheap hardboard panels, bulging outward slightly and edged around with pale green painted timber strips to hide the joins, only exaggerated the bleakness of the near empty space.

"This could be a bit embarassing," Nick whispered to Jenny, next to him.

Jenny shrugged, which caused the shoulder strap of the short lurid flowery dress she was wearing to slip down, leaving a revealing expanse of bare flesh. By her standards of costume she had dressed very smartly, Duncan thought, but still managed to expose herself to the limit of decency. Duncan was sure that the dress was brief enough to be displaying her underwear to the, as yet empty, front rows.

"Our friends will turn up, don't worry," she promised Nick.

He looked at his watch. They should be starting now. He had just made up his mind and was raising an eyebrow at Adele for her approval when there was a flurry of arrivals. 'Good,' he thought, 'that doesn't look quite so bad.'

The new arrivals seated themselves, mostly right at the back, so he would still be talking to them across a sea of bright green. Adele nodded to him. He got to his feet, and as he did so another group came in. He waited while they chose places and took a breath before starting to speak. More arrived, and in this fashion, over a good ten minutes, during which he stood, feeling unsure whether to greet everyone, gangs of late arrivals filled the seats until some were standing in the gangways.

At last, feeling he could wait no longer, he said, "Welcome everyone. It's good to see so many people here.." and they were under way.

Adele watched with fond pride as Nick explained the coming centenary and their idea for a performance of some sort to provide a focal point for the town's celebrations. He introduced Duncan, who blushingly discovered that he was both a newcomer to the town but also a noted writer, and that he had agreed to script the show. There was a mild ripple of applause. Nick introduced the others on the platform; Edward and Tamsin smiling politely at "who you'll all know from the material shop", and John and Jenny waving at the crowd when they were mentioned.

"We need volunteers. we need performers, we need fund raisers, in pracical terms we need somewhere to perform," Nick told the audience.

A voice from the back shouted, "You need a licence."

"Thank you Councillor Andrews. You are quite right, there will be many official things that need to be arranged, Tonight we just want to see if there is support and what style the event might adopt." Nick knew Brian Andrews of old. He wanted to get through tonight without crossing swords with the man.

"You can't expect the public to support something that isn't officially sanctioned," the councillor replied.

"As I said, just a meeting to see what support there is, Councillor. And I'm pleased to say that from the turn-out it looks as though there are lots of people who are interested."

There was a murmur of agreement. It was the first reaction the audience had given, and was probably, Duncan thought, more from being against the councillor's officiousness than from supporting the scheme.

"We're looking at trying to do the show at the end of April the year after next, so that gives us over eighteen months to script the show, involve local groups, rehearse and deal with costumes, scenery and props, and, of course, the legalities that Councillor Andrews has been kind enough to remind us about," Nick looked over his shoulder at the others on the platform for support. Adele was sitting very upright and appeared to be glowering in the direction of the councillor, Edward and Tamsin avoided his eye, and John and Jenny were both exchanging some sort of meaningful looks with a group in the audience who were clearly together and seemed to know the pair. Duncan was shyly shrinking into his chair. Nick decided it was best to try to change the subject.

"On to other matters," he began. As he did so the setting sun reached a point where it shone directly through the side windows of the hall onto the people on the stage, dazzling them all. From the audience, none of whom they could now see, a voice asked,

"Where are you going to do this show?"

"That's not been decided yet..."

"If you want to do it in here you must remember we get booked up very early. As it's only a show I assume you wouldn't need the hall till about seven on the night, but we do have the bridge club in on a Tuesday, and the footballers use the changing room at the back on Wednesdays, Fridays and Saturdays," annonced the voice, anonymous in the glare.

"Thank you, but I think we probably need somewhere rather bigger," he started to say, but was interrupted by the voice.

"Why did you hold the meeting here then?"

Diplomatically Nick said, "We wanted to have this first meeting somewhere that was fairly central and everyone knew where it was."

Another voice chimed in, "What about the Community Centre?"

The meeting disolved into a succession of suggestions, ranging from the school hall to the Market Place.

Nick turned back and made a mute appeal to Adele for assistance.

She spoke for the first time since they had started the meeting. She didn't shout over the crowd, in fact her voice was rather quiet, but authorititive. Crisply and with perfect enunciation she said, "We will be considering all the options. I'm sure those of you who represent particular venues may want to talk to us privately about what facilities you are able to offer."

The crowd simmered down again.

Nick found it was much the same when he tempted fate by enquiring if there were any groups or organisations that might wish to help. From the floor he was informed that people were 'sure' that the Scouts would probably put up posters, that the 'Men's Shed' would be able to build scenery, that the WI would be able to undertake refreshments, but no representatives of these, or other clubs suggested, seemed to actually be present.

Eventually he came to realise that he was handling the meeting all wrong. This rag bag of disparate interests included no-one with the power to offer more than individual help, aside, perhaps, from Councillor Andrews, who was being less than encouraging, having at one point added the problem of parking for the audience to his objections.

The sun had set far enough to no lomger dazzle those on stage before Nick told the audience that there were sheets to fill in on the tables at the back of the hall for anyone who would like to volunteer and wrapped up the evening.

The gathering left slowly, some stopping to fill in name and contact details on the forms they had printed off for the purpose.

They'd left half a dozen pens on the tables with the forms, but despite that they had to go hunting for pens and pencils in the end as the original supply had all been taken by the audience. This further annoyed some of the attendees, and Nick heard grumbles about a lack of pens right up until the last person left, their "..not at all well organised," hanging in the air behind them as the automatic closer on the doors swung them shut with a rattle of panic bars.

"Perhaps we won't try that again," he said to his small gang of volunteers on the platform.

Edward said, "Tamsin and I found that a bit scary. It wasn't what we'd expected, I mean you'd said it was all about doing something for the town, about its history and so on, to entertain people. But it seems to be a lot of arguing."

"The history of the town has always consisted of a lot of arguing.. There wouldn't really be much to show people if it hadn't," Nick tried to make light of the evening.

"Anyway, I don't think we want to be on any organising committee, I'm afraid. We'll help all we can, but don't want to be in charge of anything."

"You don't have to confront the public if you don't want to, just lend your names to the organising committee so it looks as though we've got solid support."

"No, I'm sorry.. we're sorry. People would be coming in our shop and telling us what they thought. It's too much worry for Tamsin," and without any more discussion the couple left, Tamsin looking back and mouthing 'sorry' as they reached the door.

Once again the exit door swung shut and the panic bars rattled.

"Oh dear," said Adele, "I didn't think people would start to drop out before we've even started."

Nick shook his head sadly. For an instant Duncan thought he was going to put his arms around Adele, but he straightened as if throwing off a weight, went down the short flight of stairs to the level of the hall floor, and began stacking chairs into piles along one wall.

"The next meeting had better be much smaller and in private, he announced above the metallic scrape and clatter of his task.

Chapter 7
Approaches

The knock at the door surprised Duncan. He had been in one of his daydreams, or as he preferred 'deep thinking'. He had promised himself that today he would arrange his work space, but piles of unsorted papers and files still mingled with parts of his computer and associated cables. Gemma had sorted her 'desk' much quicker, and she really didn't need it as she had an office at work.

He went to the door. A small grey haired man in a black suit stood there. Despite the summer heat he had a scarf wrapped around his neck, so it was a few moments before Duncan noticed the dog collar.

"Hello. Sorry about my voice, sore throat you know," the vicar started by saying by way of explanation.

"What can I do for you?" Duncan asked.

"Well firstly I came to welcome you to the town, because I understand that you and your wife," he craned his head about as if trying to see past Duncan into the house, possibly expecting to catch sight of Gemma, "are new to the area. Are you churchgoers?"

Duncan shook his head.

"A shame. Never mind. You'd always be very welcome to join us you know, even if it's only special occasions. Lot's of people only come to church at Christmas, and perhaps Easter."

Duncan wished he hadn't opened the door. He had a long practiced, firm, 'no thank you' that he adopted for door to door salesmen and Jehovas' Witnesses, but he felt guilty about being that abrupt with a vicar. He had been brought up and schooled in

60

a system in which the church was accepted as a part of life, at least as being part of your life at the 'hatched, matched and dispatched' points, and like most of his generation he had been through a school regimen that included a daily service. Like so many he had lapsed from this on leaving school, but he had no real anitpathy toward the system.

"Thank you," he told the vicar, "We'll remember that."

He was gripping the edge of the door preparing to say 'goodbye' when his visitor said,

"There was one other thing, if you have a moment."

Afterwards he could not decide whether the vicar had accidentally caught him at a moment when his resistance was at a low ebb, or whether the man was exceptionally skilled and slick at getting people to listen. However it was he found himself inviting him in, and, a few moments later, boiling the kettle and making coffee for them both.

"Sugar Vicar?" he enquired.

"Yes please, two please, and do call me Luke, Luke Grainger. I try to avoid the 'vicar' title except when I am, so to speak, at work. Not that this is entirely a social call.. Thank you," and he took the mug from Duncan, balancing it delicately on a coaster on the table. "You see I heard about this show, and the script you are writing. Have you decided on a venue yet?"

"Not yet. It isn't really my decision, I'm only the words man. You probably need to talk to Nick."

"Nick Canforth? Used to be in the bank here until they closed it?"

"Yes. That's him. He's really the driving force behind all this."

"I'll talk to him, of course, but if you are writing the play surely you have to have some idea from the outset of where it will be performed?"

"It would be helpful," Duncan conceded, "We're not very far advanced yet though."

"I came to offer the church. Saint George's."

"Is it big enough?" Duncan wanted to know.

"It's pretty average for a small town parish church. Decorated period, very nice, and despite the parlimentarian army's destuction of Elveston it survived. We've got a splendid stained glass window showing St. George fighting the Dragon."

Duncan was reminded of all the questions that had been in the back of his mind ever since he had been told not to include the Dragon Fair incidents in his script. He still nursed some idea of a magazine article as a commercial piece of writing.

"Perhaps I should drop in and have a look," he hinted, thinking he might be able to do some investigation while he was there.

Ten minutes later he and Luke were leaving the house to walk to the town centre church. Jenny was in her front garden, revealingly dressed as usual, bending down and apparently collecting small stones from the gravel patch around the base of the bay window. Duncan hoped she would not see him and call over to him but some sixth sense made her look round and see them as they reached the pavement and she was across the road like a shot, clutching Duncan's arm and saying, "You must drop in for a drink sometime," as she ran her forefinger down his cheek, still gripping the pebbles with the rest of her fingers. She pressed against him as she did this and he couldn't decide whether it was a blatant come-on or something conspiratorial, as she opened her hand to show him the pebbles and whispered, "I'm using them for texture on a batch of pots."

"Interesting," was all he could think of to say, sidling away from her, conscious as always of her scanty clothing, "Must go."

They walked away down the Greendale Road, and the vicar commented, "I see you've made friends in the area already."

Duncan didn't want to discuss his neighbours. He didn't know whether the vicar knew Jenny, whether he had inferred some improper relationship, whether he disapproved. He felt it best to try to ignore the incident and they walked to the church in silence. Luke lifted the latch and opened the gate to the churchyard. They followed the path, which curved slightly to bring them, through a sea of venerable gravestones to the West door. His guide turned the worn rusty brown and black ring shaped doorknob and the heavy wooden door swung open. Inside the church was exactly as Duncan had expected. Two rows of pillars straddled a central aisle and dark wood pews were sandwiched in serried ranks facing the pulpit, lectern and steps to the chancel. To one side some rather modern glass doors were set into light wood panelling and led to an enclosed area on the north side of the church which had once been one arm of the building's cruciform layout, but now housed a tea urn and childrens' play equipment.

The opposite arm of the layout had escaped modification and there the pews were arrayed facing North across the main seating of the nave.

"What do you think?" asked Luke almost at once.

Duncan was taking in more details now. At the East end an impressive stained glass window showed a traditional crucifixion scene, but prominiently, below the cross, an armour clad saint mingled with the usual depictions of Mary and the apostles dragging a dead dragon by a chain around its neck.

"That's unusual," he commented.

"Very," said Luke, "We probably make, or made, much more of

Saint George than most churches do for whoever they are dedicated to." He pointed to the window he had described, where an armoured knight was locked in an endless stained glass battle with a fierce dragon.

"In fact.." and he stopped, before saying weakly, "Perhaps you've heard?"

"I've heard some things."

"I assume you won't be including that in the play."

"I've been warned off it. But I'm interested. I'd quite like to do an article about it in my freelance capacity. I just don't really know how to get any information."

The vicar said, "I can't let you have anything about recent years, I mean nothing in living memory, obviously. But we have some interesting circumstantial records in the tower."

"The tower?" Instinctively Duncan looked toward the West end of the building.

"Yes, all the old records are stored up there, if you don't mind a climb."

The stone spiral staircase wound inside the thick walls of the tower which supported the spire. They emerged in a dusty room, separate from the bell-ringers' domain, and guarded by a locked door that Luke produced an oversized key for. Rows of shelves housed bound volumes.

Luke said, "I got interested in this after I came here about ten years ago. I met the same secretiveness that you seem to have done whenever I asked anything so I did my own investigating. No-one ever looks at these parish records, so I marked the relevant pages with post-it notes, like this," and he pulled one particular volume from a shelf. A series of half a dozen luridly coloured scraps of paper peeked from the top of the closed book. He opened the volume at the first marker.

"This is the first hint I could find," he explained. He ran his finger down the lines of calligraphy, saying, "These are basically the parish accounts. Ah, here we are."

"What does it say?" Duncan asked , peering at the writing. It was gloomy in the tower room.

"It says, 'To expenses for the Dragonne Fayre £10/5/6½.' That's in 1810. So you see there was an enormous amount being spent right from the very start. We can't establish when it first happened, but it was obviously earlier than that because there's no explanation for the phrase 'Dragonne Fayre', so everyone must have been familiar with it."

He turned to other marked pages. Repeatedly the parish was shown as spending huge sums on the event, increasing each year. In the mid 1850s the description changed from 'expenses' to 'prize money'.

"If the women were potentially winning that much, surely it would skew the local economy. I mean if a common worker came by those sorts of sums they could give up work, employ a servant, whatever?"

"Probably, but that's where the politically incorrect bit come into play. If we're right that it started right at the beginning of the nineteenth century, or even earlier the girls in the lottery could perfectly legally have been as young as ten. The winner would probably have had the money taken away from them by a father. So it might not have been that good a deal from the girls' point of view."

The vicar sighed.

"It's so difficult to discuss these days, and since there are still

people alive who actually took part..."
"We keep assuming that the girls were young. Was there an upper age limit?"

"Not so far as I can see. But they did have to be 'maidens', so that probably limited the number of more mature women in the draw."

Duncan came to realise that not only had his new acquaintance researched his potential article already but that he was also much happier to talk about the town's little secret than anyone he had yet chatted to.

"And given the salacious activity that seems to have gone on, wouldn't there have been a risk of, well you know..."

"I'm ahead of you there. It was one of the first possible consequences I thought of. I found three that I can reasonably be sure of." He took a different book from the shelves. "This is a record of baptisms," he said, turning to coloured page markers.

"This says, baptism, blah, blah, blah... 'Illegitimate. Mother Daphne Southall, spinster of this parish. Father: George Dragon!' and another. Similar wording...different mother of course, 'Father: George and Dragon', and the other one, ' Father: George Dragon.' The church was accepting these babies as a consequence of the fair. And all these baptisms are around the end of January in different years."

"Well if there had ever been any doubt there isn't now."

"More shocking than that, really is what else I found."

"Go on."

"I went back through the baptisms to find each of the mothers. It took ages, because I hadn't got any sort of date to aim for. Assuming that they were baptised as infants, and that would be normal, these three mothers the church's fair created were about fifteen, sixteen and twelve when their babies were born."

"Now you are going to tell me you know who the babies grew up to be."

"These cases are too far back to be interesting. They're born about the same time as your grandparents or great-grand parents. I do know something about one of the much more recent offspring, but don't press me. I'm not telling."

"People have told me that the girls, the 'maidens' were chosen by a lottery. What about the Dragon and St George?" Duncan deliberately avoided pushing the question about who the vicar was talking about. The man was keen on his subject and quite garrolous, and Duncan felt sure that the information about a 'more recent' child would be spilt sooner or later.

"Lottery again. But by all accounts there were almost pitched battles to be selected. They couldn't affect the outcome of a draw, but I get the impression that there were attempts to get more than one entry in with your name on it if you were keen. Has Adele shown you the picture of the Dragon Fair in the museum yet? If you look carefully you can see what we think is the drum they drew the entries out of."

The church clock had been chiming out the quarter hours as a background to their discussion. Now the heavier tolling of the hour of midday attracted Duncan's attention.

"It's been fascinating," he said, "but I really must go."

"You never told me if you would want to stage your play in the church.

"No. I'm sorry. It's up to Nick, of course, but I doubt it would be suitable," he said guiltily. And he left.

Chapter 8
Beseiged

Gemma was clearly disinterested in the account of his day. She had told him about her day at work and been only too aware that he was barely half listening. As he told her about the vicar, and the records in the tower she had some slight sympathy for him. They were involved in completely different things now, and the house itself was the only over-lap. As she didn't really trust Duncan to make domestic choices that she would wholeheartedly agree with she couldn't tell him to arrange things in cupboards or on shelves, and certainly not to make a start on the bits of redecoration she wanted done.

Duncan was secretly pleased not to be left instructions to do any decoration, a task he was not fond of. Gemma's daily absence left him free to explore the town, though he soon found that these outings were almost always under the control of an existing resident. The word had got out about the show, and one by one the leaders of the committees that ran the town's small selection of venues came to his door, just as the vicar had done, and dragged him off to admire their hall.

Over a fortnight he was shown two churches of different denominations, a parish hall, not unlike the hall they had held the meeting in, and a Georgian coaching Inn's yard.

He became adept at warding off decisions by pointing out that he was merely a writer and that Nick was responsible for the staging. Despite that the small town mentality meant that at least one member of the committee controlling each of these inappropriate venues felt that, if the event was to be a major landmark occasion, their hall should have the cudos, and more importantly the income, from being the chosen location. Many saw the possible income as worth fighting for, especially where they had some form of catering outlet, usually behind a shutter in the body of the hall, which they controlled.

The Georgian courtyard attracted him most, being part of a hotel, that was still open, and served lunches, though its passing trade now consisted almost entirely of drinks sales in its bar on weekends, alongside accomodation for the occasional travelling salesman. In the back of his mind Duncan vaguely remembered reading somewhere about an old tradition of performances in pub yards. He began to research historic staging styles.

He had managed to get a library card, following Adele's advice about the required form, rather, he felt, to the annoyance of the sullen girl on reception. The credit card sized piece of plastic now nestled in his top pocket as he began to scour the thinly populated book-shelves.

Theatre and performance was very badly represented in the reference sections, what books there were mostly being large format coloured picture books about a few famous pop musicians, some film stars and directors and, obscurely, a single slim volume on the history of the Noel Coward Theatre in London.

After a frustrating morning he emerged with two books. One, a dull, wordy, closely typed text book about Medieval Miracle plays, and the other a child's picture book called 'At the Theatre' which featured brightly coloured drawings of backstage in a conventional, Victorian looking, theatre apparently staging a pantomime.

The girl scanned his ticket and the books with no comment or greeting at all, and checking the volumes out would have been a silent operation had it not been for the soft bleeps of the scanner.

Back home he began reading.

Nick called on him one morning later in the week, saying he had made a list of the significant events in the town's bland history that he thought might offer some posibility of dramatic content for the show. He had conceived the possibility of introducing the history bits by having some characters, 'possibly a child asking its mother or father' he suggested, explaining events which were then enacted by the cast as if the child were visualising what it was being told.

Duncan said, "Maybe," as he studied Nick's untidy writing on the list of events and Nick chatted away eagerly.

When Nick ran out of steam Duncan told him how he was being asked to visit possible venues.

"I wanted to talk to you about that," said Nick, "All these places are likely to want to charge us a lot to use them, and we haven't got any finances yet. There's somewhere I'd like you to come and see if you can, which we could get to use free, or at least very cheaply, I think."

Duncan followed Nick's directions as he drove them across the town.

"What are you going to do about money?" he asked.

"We can put in for a grant from the council for a one-off project that 'involves the community'. Adele is getting the forms for that. But we could do with some commercial sponsorship. I think it will all be much easier once we have some firm idea of the show and a venue. Turn right here."

They arrived eventually at the gateway of a private house. The high stone boundary walls curved inward from the road to a pair of square pillars which flanked the driveway. There had been a white painted timber gate to fit the gap at one time, but it now stood wide open with the gate hanging limply from its great hinges, sagging to the ground beside the gravel drive.

Instructed by Nick he turned in.

The drive curved through the trees, so the house, when they reached it, was a surprise which came in view. The drive approached the house from one side, so a visitor didn't see the Georgian double frontage until they were actually at the foot of the low steps that led to the front door. In front of the building a vast lawn led away to a heavily reeded pond or lake that might just possibly have been part of a small stream.

"Whose is this then?" Duncan asked, more than a little jealously.

Nick got out, saying "Basil Carnthorpe's. He was the manager of the bank I worked in before they closed it down. His family had owned this place for years. I remember he wasn't too delighted when he inherited it because of the cost of the up keep, but he got a big hand-out when they shut the bank. I think that saved him."

A figure came around the corner of the house. Basil was a tall, rather skinny figure, whose old fashioned clothes hung from him as if there wasn't enough of him to fill them up. He was balding with grey hair, and he peered at the visitors myopically as he approached them.

"Hello Basil," Nick said.

"Er, it's Nick isn't it?"

"Yes, I said I'd bring Duncan along to see your house, or rather the garden."

"So you did," Basil said, giving the impression he had no recollection of Nick having said anything of the sort,"Something about a show, wasn't it?"

Duncan held out his hand, "Duncan Newbon," he said. He gripped Basil's bony hand and the older man murmered a 'How do you do'.

Nick took charge. He walked out to the middle of the lawn with the other two trailing behind. Duncan realised the lush green tended grass was an illusion, for once you stood on it you were aware that it was well overdue for a cut and the green was at least in part due to a variety of weeds that were flourishing among the proper grass, which was yellowing from the long hot summer.

Nick stopped, turned to face the house spread his arms wide with a gesture, almost of pride, as if he were selling the property, and said, "There!"

Duncan saw that the house provided an impressive backdrop. The central door at the top of the brief flight of steps was flanked and surmounted by sash windows, and a later extension of the original building each side made for a wide facade. Shrubs and trees nestled close to the brickwork alongside. He thought that Basil must have had to duck under the lower branches where he had appeared from. He turned round. Nick clearly had in mind placing an audience where they were standing. The space was large enough to accommodate several hundred spectators.

Nick was in intense discussion with Basil. 'Could we do... How would you feel about... Any chance of...' Duncan could hear Basil being pressured into agreeing to a whole string of hypothetical requests.

By the time they left the whole thing seemed to have been agreed in principle. This then was the space he would have to write for. Nick had got agreement for various marquees to be erected around the area, to the installation of mobile toilets, to using the house's electrical supply and much more.

They drove back to Greendale Road. Duncan was quiet, mentally trying to sort out how something, as yet unclear, could be made to work now he had seen the space Nick had decided on. Nick prattled beside him in the passenger seat, saying how he had known that Basil would agree, how lucky they were to have such a site for the event with such and amenable owner, and how now they could start planning properly. Duncan thought that the retired bank manager had been bamboozled, but he held his tongue. It was almost eighteen months yet until the quincentenary. Time enough to smooth any ruffled feathers, he felt.

The planning process gathered pace after that visit to Basil Carnthorpe's home, which he discovered was called 'Elveston Lodge'. Adele seemed to become embroiled in a flurry of form filling and paperwork, which she reported back on to Duncan whenever she saw him, apparently revelling in the minutiae of the bureaucracy involved. Applications for licences, for alcohol, for performance, for admitting the public, a simple written agreement with Basil for the use of his house and gardens, which in itself would eventually neccessitate the formation of a properly consitituted committee to run the event, a bank account, with a nominal pound deposited in it, and some press releases, all kept the woman busy.

For his part Duncan was beginning to develop some ideas. His reading, and some searching of the internet, led him to discover an old medieval staging format that he felt might suit. He found pictures, artists impressions mostly, for contemporary information was clearly very sparce, suggesting a series of what were mysteriously called 'mansions' scattered along a wide space to represent different locations. He discovered that each of these, and they were usually religious in connotation, reperesented somewhere like heaven or hell, and were made of a platform on legs with a canopy roof over.

He was starting to learn about modern lighting too, and realised that he could arrange, or ask Nick to arrange, for different locations to be lit to draw attention to action on a specific stage while actors readied themselves on another one. The more he thought about the possible format the more excited he became.

He realised that he could possibly use big groups of volunteer performers, schools, youth clubs and so on, to be whole armies, keeping a small handful of leading characters on a little platform to deliver dialogue or explanations.

All he really needed now were the final lists of historic incidents

and the agreement of sufficient organisations to become involved.
He was talking this over with Nick one day when Nick said, "If
you had singers and dancers and things like that the group in
question could go off and rehearse their bit quite independently
and we could just fit them in when we were near the performance
dates."

"If we had groups of singers and dancers and musicians they
would all bring their friends and relations, and it would swell the
audiences."

"I doubt we've got a problem with audience," Nick assured him,
"Haven't you talked to people in the town? We're over a year
away from the event and it's the talk of the wash-house."

"That's good. What are they saying?"

"Well.." Nick seemed hesitant, "some of them are saying it will
be a flop, and some of them seem to think it will stir up old
memories, you know, the controversial stuff." He paused, "You
aren't including any of that are you?" Duncan shook his head.
"Good. The trades-people all want it to happen obviously. The
council is broadly in favour, though I probably don't need to tell
you who is against it."

"The bloke who was heckling the meeting? The man with the
private parking tickets?"

"Yes. Councillor Andrews. But Brian has a huge chip on his
shoulder. Always has had. I think we can get him out-voted."

Duncan asked, "Why is he so against everything?"

Nick brushed the question aside, "Don't worry about him," adding
"I think we're at the point where we should have a go at getting
some groups involved. Can you jot down what sort of
organisations you need and we'll sound some out and get them
together."

So Duncan found himself writing lists of participants at the same time as drafting an outline script.

When you came down to it, he thought, there were more people necessary than he could ever have imagined.

His list started with a set designer, and then carpenters and painters, and that put him in mind of posters, and poster designers and printers, and perhaps programmes, and tickets and someone to run a box office, even if they did have free admission, and would they need front of house staff and catering?

Did they need musicians and sound for sound effects? What about lighting, if it got dark during the show, and did they have to have exit signs?

If Nick was the director, did they need a choreographer too? And if they used local school children to appear for crowd scenes would they need chaperones? There would have to be auditions for the cast, and he was now envisaging a large cast, and that meant lots of costumes, so they would need a wardrobe mistress and a team of people to make and sew costumes, and transport too, so many things to be moved onto the grounds of Elveston Lodge.

His phone rang. It was Gemma. It had to be. All around him people had mobile phones in their hands day and night it seemed, but he had only just got his first mobile, at Gemma's insistance. She had been given a new one for her work the moment she started the new job, and he had noticed that she now carried it like a badge of office. It was her, reminding him to take something out of the freezer. He assured her he would, and fumbled with the tiny buttons, never quite being sure if he had actually hung up. That brought another thought to his mind, how would they communicate across the Lodge's gardens to synchronise starting the show?

He carefully added this query to his list, and immediately forgot about the freezer contents, a mistake that would result in sighs of exasperation from Gemma, and lengthy defrosting in the microwave before she could start to prepare their evening meal.

Chapter 9
Formation

Duncan's apprehension continued to grow as the days went by and he realised the enormity of the task he had been given. He was more careful now to make sure that he noted Gemma's daily instructions, and resisted the regular attempts to drag him away to discuss the project. Nick was most often spurned by him and began to wonder if the newcomer was less interested than he should be. Nick's batchelor existence left him free to concentrate on the proposed show day and night, and he became frustrated, even angry, when people did not exhibit the same obsessive enthusiasm that he felt. His single mindedness was leading him to forget other people had work, and families.

He and Adele had prepared a submission to put in front of the town council. They had orginally thought that this would only need to be a simple 'we want to do this, we hope you will give it your blessing' type statement, but after much deliberation they compiled a document that incorporated every currently fashonable concept they could come up with.

The result was a moderately thick planning submission which, after explaining the broad outline of the event, laid on the benefits to the town, culturally, financially, and in bringing the community together, involving both adult residents and children, with a trowel.

The pair typed this up on Adele's computer, printed multiple copies, and delivered one to each councillor's home address a few days before the next scheduled council meeting.

Nick drew the short straw for delivering the brown envelope containing a copy to Brian Andrews at 'The Limes'. He parked a hundred yards away and walked to the house to avoid a confrontation with the councillor. Starting up the curved driveway he was relieved to see that the man's Mini was not there. Quickly he scuttled up the steps to the door and fumbled with the letter box. It was one of those where the outer flap had to be lifted to put the letter in, but an additonal flap was fitted to the inside of the door. Making the process more awkward were the black bristles fixed in a narrow strip inside and the fact that the slot itself was set into the bottom of the door.

Nick found himself kneeling to get down low enough to make the attempt to feed the bulky letter into the man's hallway. As he was doing this the door was jerked open, and Brian stood there challengingly.

Nick caught a brief glimpse of the hallway beyond the man's legs; patterned carpet, and dark wood hall stands with an array of shooting sticks and umbrellas, guarding the way to a staircase with a mahogany bannister that swept down to a horizontal swirl at the bottom. There were framed pictures along the walls, but Nick could not see what they showed. The overall impression was of a small reproduction of some baronial hall.

Brian said, "What do you want?" and, recognising Nick, "Oh, it's you. What are you doing?"

"I'm just delivering this to all the councillors so you have got it and can study it before the next meeting." Nick immediately felt like some sort of inferior supplicant grovelling at the feet of a ruler.

"Is this the performance thing? I saw that in the agenda. I suppose I should have guessed you'd be involved. I don't think it's something we would want happening here."

Nick struggled to his feet, still holding the envelope, and held it out to Brian.

"Have a read of this before you condemn it out of hand," he suggested.

The envelope was snatched from him, and Brian turned back into his house without another word, slamming the door in Nick's face.

He told Adele later.

"We rather expected that from Brian," she said mildly, "though I don't know about you, but I had hoped he might have mellowed over the years."

"It doesn't seem so. If anything I think he's got worse."

Adele laid a reassuring hand on Nick's arm, saying, "Don't worry, I'm sure he will be out-voted if it comes to it."

When the council meeting convened the few rows of chairs for the public were, as always, sparsely occupied. The meeting was held in the Victorian Gothic town hall's Council Chanber, where portraits of long past former mayors clad in their robes stared unhappily and scowlingly down on the ornately carved table that the councillors sat around. More recent mayors were represented by a relatively small framed colour photograph, and the quantity of these now occupied nearly a whole wall.

The councillors roughly divided themselves so that the conservatives were one side of the table, and the labour, liberal and green members were on the other. There was no rule about this arrangement, but some force of traditional habit led them to sit this way. The business of the meeting was boring in the extreme, ranging through rubber stamping the accounts to agreeing a handful of planning applications that would be passed to the county level for decisions. The event came up under any other business, by which time the local press reporter was tucking his pencil back in the top pocket of his jacket and closing his notebook and the married couple who had come to make sure their planning application got passed to higher authority without comment were wondering if it would be frowned on if they left before the end of the meeting. Several of the other attendees in the public seats were closing handbags, and picking up coats and clearly preparing to depart.

Duncan sat with Adele and Nick. He wasn't sure why they had insisted on his coming. He had no experience with local government, and was slightly worried that he might find himself having to put forward arguments in favour of the proposd event. He worried that, were that to be the case, and should the proposal be turned down after he had said anything, Nick and Adele might blame him for the scuppering of their long held plans.

He heard the Town Clerk, Nigel Warren, an oily civil servant in an anonymous grey suit, who was chairing the meeting, announce that there was only one item under any other business, and give a brief description which he had clearly culled directly from the paperwork Adele and Nick had put in.

Duncan tried to read the faces of the councillors, but with one exception he did not know them, and didn't know what their normal expressions were. They all looked rather serious and sour to him.

He was surprised when, following the Clerk's rambling preliminary introduction, one the ladies seated around the table said that she welcomed the idea, and that it was high time that Elveston had a major public event. She went on to say that she hoped that the Council would support the scheme that these members of the public had put forward and that the show should be encouraged to bring the 'community' together.

Another councillor said much the same, adding his hopes that the event would draw in people from the surrounding areas to be entertained.

Duncan felt quite encouraged. And then Brian Andrews spoke.

He told the assembled councillors they should be wary, that there was every reason to suppose that this scheme was a sly attempt to re-introduce the old dragon event by stealth, and that if so it would bring unwanted attention, even scandal, to the town.

There was a muttering around the table. Duncan strained, but could only catch occasional words as the councillors spoke in low mumurs to their neighbours. He heard 'dragon' and 'scandal' and 'public disgrace', and saw a few of the council members looking severely at Adele and Nick.

One middle aged lady, in a tweed outfit, which made him think of hunting, said that she was very opposed to anything that might develop into wild behaviour and loud music, or bring undesirable people into the town. He saw Adele put a restraining hand on Nick's arm.

A scrawny man wearing thick glasses, who Duncan recognised as one of the town's independent shop keepers, said that he was in favour of anything that might increase trade, and a few 'here here's encouraged the show proposers.

He was supported by a slim, studious looking woman who manged to announce, in case anyone didn't know, that she was a school teacher, and that she hoped the producers would make sure that all the children in the town had the chance to be involved, and how pleased she was that a community event was being arranged, and these little speeches were contradicted by the tweed wearing lady, who said that the town had no facilities for this sort of thing, and that nobody wanted the council to permit a return to the 'riotous shenannigins' that used to go on.

The Town Clerk had no gavel, but banged on the table with the base of an empty glass from the tray near the water jug.

"Quiet please!" Warren ordered, "No time for long discussions on any other business. Just a quick vote. Those in favour of the propsed event," hands were raised, "And those against?" two councillors, Brian and the tweed lady, put their hands up.

"Carried. I declare the meeting closed."

And with that it was over.

People rose and drifted away. The slim teacher, passed them, smiled, and said "Break a leg". Nick said, "Thank you for supporting us, I don't suppose you'd like to get involved would you? We could do with someone to supervise the bits of the show that include kids."

The woman hesitated.

"Do join in, Susan," Adele encouraged her.

Nick agreed, "Please, it would be so useful to have someone who could help us organising the youngsters who get involved."

Susan nodded thoughtfully. Then shrugged, saying, "All right, I'll join in, but I can't spare much time. Perhaps you could drag me in nearer the actual date."

They promised they would, hoping that the woman wouldn't come up with some further excuse later, and parted company at the doors of the town hall, under the overhang of the ornate porch with its narrow stone pillars and carved stonework. Duncan had a feeling of being on the set of some horror film as the gathering darkness cast the entrance into gloom.

Nick was ebulliant about the meeting. As they walked towards their houses Adele said, "Now the real work starts."

Chapter 10
Press Ganging

"You must go and visit her during one of the classes, I've told her you're coming," Nick instructed Duncan. So he was outside a small hut like hall, pondering the number of these the town seemed to have, and wondering why it should be, and hearing a tinkling tune being played on a portable music system inside the hall. On the grass verge where he stood a small, amateurishly lettered, 'A' board announced 'Freya Culpitt School of Dance' above small lettering that said 'Classes from 3 years old to adult.'

He hesitated at the wide open double doors going into the green painted hall. Inside he could see a temporary portable arrangement of wooden stands and a rail was providing a ballet barre for a dozen leotard clad little girls who held it with one hand while bending and stretching in a series of exercises directed by a young woman. The girls faced away from the door, holding the barre with their left hands, and the woman was at the far end of the room near the platform facing the door. She instructed in the loud voice of a strict disciplinarian.

Seeing Duncan in the doorway, and without any perceptible break in the lesson, she pointed to the corner of the hall near him that he could not see from where he was. Drawing breath for a second, and as the girls continued bobbing, she announced,

"Miss Culpitt is over there."

immediately shouting "Plié!" and the children, feet turned out like Charlie Chaplin, bent their knees again.

Duncan took another pace and turned right, seeing an elderly woman, huddled in what seemed to be multiple cardigans and a woollen skirt, seated on a stacking chair, intently watching the pupils. She eyed him fiercely. He quailed under her scrutiny, thinking he would have hated to be one of her pupils.

"Yes?" the woman said.

"Miss Culpitt?"

"Obviously. I'm in the middle of a class, what do you want?"

Duncan began to explain the idea of the quincentenary event, making much of how the whole town would be involved and how the show would include all sorts of performance styles.

"We do ballet," Miss Culpitt informed him, "and we're very busy at that time of year with exams. If you want a short ballet piece we have already rehearsed we might be able to oblige for a fee. Is that what you want?"

"We were thinking of your pupils dancing with some ribbons to represent the flames, perhaps." he told her tentatively.

"Certainly not! My girls are being trained to follow the cherography of known classical pieces, not to skip about randomly. If you want 'modern' style stuff you need to talk to Catherine James." The woman tightened the outer cardigan more completely around her shoulders as if shutting him out. He could see the instructor, still ordering her charges through their movements, studying him curiously as the conversation with Miss Culpitt came to an inconclusive end.

He said, "Thank you for your time," a bit insincerely and almost scampered from the hall. When he was outside he walked away, and the tinkly music and shouted instructions followed him till he was out of earshot.

Later he said to Nick, "Who's Catherine James?"

"How did you come across that name?"

"Freya Culpitt said that was who we should talk to about girls for the fire effect ribbons."

"Yes, I suppose it was a bit of a long shot talking to that snobby old battle-axe."

"Why did you send me to try then?" Duncan wanted to know.

"You really don't understand the politics of the small town do you... or of productions for that matter. Freya Culpitt's ballet school has been here for decades. She has a pretty good reputation for getting girls into the London ballet schools. If you asked any average member of the population who the dance expert in the town was hers would be the name they would come up with. That said the audiences for her village hall shows are pathetic, because they only consist of mums and dads.
"Catherine James uses the community centre, and does her shows there. She teaches what they call 'modern' stuff, so her girls come out doing tap and show dances, popular stuff. She has no qualms about her girls doing sexy moves and rauchy routines, a bit like you used to see in 'Top of the Pops' or even 'Kenny Everett', and guess what? Her shows are packed out. Even the Mayor goes."

"So why send me to Miss Culpitt?"

"Because it's vital that we have been seen to try to include the 'correct' organisations. We have enough image problems with the people who think we're resurrecting the Dragon Fair without approaching Catherine first."

"I thought all the opposition because of the old Fair had gone away."

Nick laughed, "You think councillors change their minds?"

"But.."

"Look, some of the population is po-faced and likes classical ballet and Shakespeare, the other half would rather listen to rock music, watch Hot Gossip on the tele and girls disco dancing. We aren't in the market of changing either side, we just want to do a popular show. But if we don't pander to the straight laced ones we'll never hear the last of it."

Duncan considered this statement.

"This show seems to be more about what we might be allowed to do than about what you and Adele want to do," he observed.

"Small town activities always are," Nick told him, "I hope you're not too disappointed. I mean having to write what will be acceptable."

"Most of my freelance work is a case of 'having to write what will be acceptable'," he admitted candidly. "I suppose I had thought that this might have been a bit less restrictive though."

"Don't worry. We show them what they want to see, then we change it to what we want to do nearer the performance. By the time someone leaks the news the show will be on and it will be too late to do anything about it."

"You sound as though there's things you want to put in that I don't know about." Duncan was grumpy.

"You know all about them, but you also know that people have said they're not to feature.. but we want some mention of St George in there somewhere. Decently, of course," he added quickly.

Duncan began puzzling over how to tackle that, as Nick continued, revelling in the near certainty now of his project coming to fruition and the town having a show.

"Shall I take you to meet Catherine?" he asked.

"Now?"

"She'll be holding a class in the Community Centre about now.

86

Come on," Nick said, and they set off.

The Community Centre was bigger than Duncan had imagined it would be. It was not an attractive building. Externally it greeted the passer-by with blank brick walls and even its entrance doors seemed designed to provide an obstacle to getting in, held shut by over fierce spring closers and with the upper, glass, panel of each door blanked out by a black painted plywood panel screwed onto the inside. Duncan assumed that at some time the hall had fallen prey to vandals breaking the glass of the doors, and that a second line of defence had been installed.

Inside a bleak brick and concrete tiled entrance led to more doors which guarded the main hall. Loud music thumped within and Nick pulled open one of the doors to allow Duncan to pass through into the cavernous hall.

He was slightly bewildered by what greeted him. The hall was big enough for three badminton courts, which were, indeed, marked out on the floor. A high pitched roof supported by RSJs made the space a huge echo chamber, at one end of which the whole wall was missing, leading to a low platform stage with luridly pink curtains. These curtains were open at the moment, and some dozen teenagers were performing energetic routines to the pounding sound-track that was playing.

At the opposite end of the hall, seemingly miles away from her pupils, a woman he assumed to be Catherine James was leaping around mirroring the moves of her girls.

Catherine was wearing a lime green tracksuit, though her pupils wore a variety of different coloured leotards. Nick marched unhesitatingly across acres of bare floor to her.

The dance teacher saw him coming, smiled at him and, as the music track finished, shouted "Well done, do the 'Steps' number next. Someone could be seen on stage crouching over the music player and some bursts of random bits of popular numbers indicated that they were searching for the track they had been told to rehearse. Between the brief snatches of music Catherine shouted, "Take over, Simone," and a girl in a vivid blue leotard, half covered by baggy camouflage cargo trousers, waved a cheerful acknowledgement.

"Come outside where it's quieter," Catherine told them, as the music system blared forth again.

"Well Nick, what can I do for you?" she asked once they were outside.

"This is Duncan. He's writing the script for the show that we're doing for the quincentenary. We're trying to see how many people would be willing to be involved. Would you like to have some of your dancers be part of the show?"

"I think it's about the same time of year..."

"Late April."

"Yes, roughly when we normally do our own show here," she gestured to the Community Centre, "but if you could fit in a routine we had already rehearsed we could join in. Is it a case of making up the numbers?" she asked perceptively.

"Not exactly," said Duncan, "but I need to have some idea of how many people I can use in different scenes. I mean, if we try to do something about the Romans fighting Boudicea I might script it one way if we only had, say half a dozen actors, or differently if we had a hundred."

Catherine laughed, and said to Nick, "A hundred? He's a real Cecil B. De Mille isn't he. Anyway I don't think my girls would make very good fighting soldiers," she paused and appeared to consider, "Though there are a few..."

"I wasn't thinking of them for battles," Duncan said quickly, it was just an example.

"Well," said Nick, "It's not a bad notion, done as some sort of stylised marching routine.."

"A tentative yes," said Catherine, But I'll let you know what the routines consist of once we have set them for our show."

The two men thanked her and watched her go back inside.

"She's a helpful sort," Nick declared, "and now we have the ball rolling it will get easier."

Duncan nodded thoughtfully as they walked home, wondering how best to use a group of girl dancers doing a routine not of his choosing in the show.

Chapter 11
First Draft

"It's only a draft outline," Duncan excused himself.

They were all crowded in Nick's house, a small terraced home which was crammed with old furniture, that Nick proudly explained had been his parents', alongside some rather startling modern pieces. A visitor felt uncomfortable, not only because they were probably balancing on a stool or kitchen chair because there were not enough comfy seats to go round, but also because there seemed to be a large number of clearly breakable things, ranging from large vases to delicate little tables. When Duncan handed out the printed copies of his draft he could see the recipients hesitating over whether to try to continue holding the mugs of coffee they had already received, or find somewhere to put these down so they could turn the pages of his opus conveniently. The assembled supporters of the event were split on this decision.

He knew most of the people there. Nick introduced some, but he forgot their names almost immediately. He himself had managed to get an armchair, simply because he had been early arriving, and Gemma, who he had persuaded to come along, had insisted on sitting on a stool beside him, despite his repeatedly offering the chair to her. Actually it was a singularly uncomfortable armchair, certainly from Nick's parents, and parts of the padding and springing under the seat had collapsed, so you were tilted to your right as you sat on it. The covering was worn, and bare patches showed on the arms.

Nick had given them a few introductory words, in which he clearly assumed that he would be the director of the piece, before pushing Duncan forward to explain the outline of the project. Now Duncan found all eyes on him, as he proposed a succession of scenes against simplistic props to establish location. He was suggesting roughly following a chronological sequence, and had found scenes to play that covered the town's historical growth.

He had to admit that the twentieth century had offered no historical developments at all, even the second world war had only offered a single bomb that had presumably been jettisoned as unwanted by a passing German bomber. Certainly it had not hit anything significant, having only succeeded in destroying an unoccupied and disused outbuilding on a nearby farm. He appealed to the guests in Nick's home for any ideas for a dramatic finale for the show, which promised to peter out as it came to the present day.

There were no suggestions that evening, but the assembly read his outline with great concentration. Nick had seen it already, and kept interrupting their reading with comments on how he thought he might stage certain bits, some of which the slow readers had not yet reached, or the fast readers had gone past, so they had to turn back if they were paying attention to what he was saying.

Adele, unsurprisingly, was a fast reader, She said, across the room to Duncan, "I think that should work very well. If you don't mind I'd like to go over some of the historical details with you, but well done."

He felt as though his homework had been marked for him.

John and Jenny were sitting on the floor. As usual her costume, he never thought of them as clothes for her now, was revealing, and having chosen to sit there, either through choice of through lack of chairs, she was displaying a considerable amount of her breasts and the cheese-cloth skirt was split from hem to waist so her thigh was totally exposed on the side facing Duncan. It distracted him. Perhaps it was intended to.

Jenny said, "What sort of things will you be needing us to make for you then. Swords? Spearheads? Crockery? ….

Nick promised, "Duncan will write you a props list."

Gemma leant to her husband's ear and whispered, "You've just been given another job."

Duncan was less bothered by the prospect of compiling a list than by the thought of having to hand it over to Jenny. He was resolving to get it typed up and post it through her door.

Tamsin, seated with Edward on hard dining chairs in the very corner of the room, asked, "When will we know what material is wanted for costumes?"

"Once we have a full list of who's taking part, and what they are doing," Nick told her, "Does the offer of some cheap material from your wholesalers still stand?"

"We'll be delighted to see what we can do to help. We do get roll ends and remnants sometimes, and so do our suppliers, so I'm sure something can be worked out."

"That's great, we'll let you know as soon as we've cast it and someone has done some costume designs." Nick was ebullient.

"Who have got for design?" Tamsin wanted to know.

"We haven't sorted that yet for either scenery or costumes," Nick admitted.

Edward nudged Tamsin, "Go on."

She offered tentatively, "Edward and I would take all that on if you wanted us to."

There were mutters of approval all round.

Gemma whispered in his ear again, "Do they know anything about design, I wonder?"

Adele either had very acute hearing or guessed the content of the whisper, because from her side of the room she told them, "Edward and Tamsin were both commercial designers before they started their fabric shop."

Duncan said "Oh, I see. That's good." Actually he had little idea of how design for theatre worked. Like most members of the general public he gave it scant attention. He guessed that someone designed costumes and scenery, he even assumed there must be people in charge of the look of lighting.. 'Will we need lighting outside in late April?' he wondered. When he and Gemma got home she left him in no doubt about the need for both designers and makers, pulling out an old theatre programme from a drawer where ephemera had been tucked as they moved in, and turning the pages until she found the close typed list of backstage personnel.

"See," she said, pointing.

"But we're not doing a musical," he said, flipping to the programme's cover to see what it was for.

"Oh yes you are. Think about it. There will have to be music for all sorts of scenes. Anyway it doesn't change the number of people you need. Someone has got to get busy rustling them all up, otherwise there's going to be a terrible panic at the last minute."

"Nick and I are getting people together, anyway it's more than a year yet," he protested.

"Too slowly. You need groups, not individuals, and groups plan a long way ahead."

"What groups do you mean?"

"Your girlfriend, Adele, should be able to come up with lists of local organisations, shouldn't she?"

He chose to ignore Adele being described as his 'girlfriend'. He realised he was spending a lot of time with both her and Nick, but Adele. while certainly now a friend, was no longer a 'girl'. Really she had latched on to both of them as soon as they moved in, and it was only Gemma's work dragging her away all day every day that meant that most of the discussions about the show happened in her absence.

He said, "Yes, I suppose she probably could."

Chapter 12
Growing Impetus

"I'm sure we can produce a list of organisations for you, It's what libraries are for, well partly anyway," Adele told him as she led him through to the library part of the building from her museum domain. She went unerringly to shelves of local directories and atlases, running her finger along the shelf edge as she scanned the spines of the rather worn and neglected paperbacked volumes.

So far as he could see almost all of them bore the bold advertisment of some local trade company, with the actual title of the book hidden in small print at the top or bottom, usually with a year date to show when it had been published.

"Ah!" said Adele, "This is a likely one," and she pulled out a small, but thick book entitled 'Elveston Guide', flicking quickly through the pages until she came to a whole section of 'Local Clubs and Organisations'.

"Thank you," he said, "I'd better start copying them down," for he had noticed that the secion they were standing in bore bright red signs at the top of each set of shelves saying 'Reference Only'.

"Don't bother about that, we'll run a copy of the pages," and she went to the desk where the sullen girl had her head buried in a book.

"All right if we copy some pages of this?"

The girl hardly looked up, "Ten pence a copy, you know where it is Miss Peston."

As they copied the pages, laying the directory face down on the glass and closing the cover over it as the green light swept back and forth, before turning the page and repeating the action, time and again, Duncan said to Adele, "Is that girl always like that, or does she just not like me?"

"She's been like it ever since she arrived. Honestly I don't really know what her problem is. It's such a wonderful job. I loved it. Helping people find the things they wanted, whether it was fiction books or for some sort of research they were doing, and keeping the shelves in the right order. Of course it's more a case of dealing with room bookings now I suppose, but even with that you're helping groups of people." She sighed.

"You miss it don't you?"

"Frankly, yes. But I'm not sure that the world is still set up to 'serve' people any more. People like her," she nodded to the counter as she turned another page and laid the book down, pressing the copy button, "don't really want to serve, and half the population is quite happy to get the tin of beans off the supermarket shelf themselves and scan it through the self service till without even seeing a member of staff."

The copying machine stopped for one of those unaccountable pauses that follow pressing the button and precede scanning before the green light swept back and forth again. Another sheet of paper flopped into the tray on the right of the machine.

"Do you think we need to have the lists of nursery schools?" she asked him.

"No, but I'm thinking we ought to circulate everyone so there can't be any complaints about having been left out."

"Yes, you're right, of course. Maybe we could get a body like the Scouts," she held the book to him as they happened to have reached that page, "to distribute the letters for a donation which is less than the postage would be."

"We really need some funds don't we?"

"I don't mind contributing a bit to start us off," she told him, "but

I don't have enough to finance the whole thing."

"Of course not, no-one was suggesting any of us should were they?"

"No. But we may have to bale it out at first to get things up and running. I think there should be a rule. We'll put it to the next meeting, that we mustn't run up more debt than we organisers could afford to underwrite if it all went terribly wrong. No-one's house must be at risk," she laughed, mirthlessly. "That would be a bit ironic in my case I suppose."

The last page crawled out of the copier and flopped down into the tray. They picked up the pile. Adele took the directory back to the shelf, and Duncan went to the desk.

"Thirty-eight I think," he told the girl.

She took the neat pile of sheets from him and began counting. Adele joined them.

"Three pound eighty," the girl said.

Duncan fished loose change from his pocket and gave her the money.

"We really ought to get a receipt," Adele told him as they left, but he shook his head.

"Let's not get bogged down in the petty, petty cash. Certainly not yet."

"Don't spend too much, we're relying on you for a script, not a subscription," she said.

Later they showed Nick the circular letter they had prepared. Using his computer they set it up so a personalised greeting opened each printed piece of text, but essentially all the letters would say the same.

They gave Nick's address and number.

Nick read it through and nodded slowly.

"I think that's fine," he said slowly. If people come forward how will we know if they can actually do what we want them to do? I mean we could audition for actors, and everyone accepts that, but we can't make people audition to be a programme seller or a scene shifter can we?"

"Isn't that always the problem with an amateur production?" Duncan suggested, "Do any am-dram companies vet their front of house staff? Does the one you belong to? Aren't all am-dram stage crews made up of the people who aren't good enough to have got a part?"

"That's a bit unkind," Adele interrupted him, "Some of them might not want to appear in front of an audience. There must be lots of them who want to be involved by doing something practical rather than being thespians."

"All right, but how do we know if someone who, let's say, wants to build scenery has any idea how to go about it?"

Adele said, "Stage scenery building is a specific trade, uses very precise methods and techniques. I read about it somewhere. I doubt we're going to come up with anyone who knows how to do that locally. We just have to work with whatever we get offered."

Duncan went home to type in the organisations' names and addresses and to set his computer to printing the mail-merged letters.

Chapter 13
A Company Forms

He decided there were two types of organisation. You could describe them as large and small, as formal and informal, old and new, but the result of those differences was that they responded to a letter asking them to muck in with a show in just one of two ways.

It was obvious that the announcement of the production had struck a chord with the public at large and there were stirrings of interest through the town. It was also clear that large organisations, old organsations, formal organisations, found it hard to make any sort of commitment. The younger, newer and smaller clubs came back to Nick almost instantly with promises of help. They offered labour, they offered performers, they even offered materials.

He commented on the other clubs when Duncan, Adele, Gemma and he were having a drink in the pub one evening.

"The trouble with them," he said, referring to larger and longer established societies, "is that they all have top heavy committees. So the real active people have to wait for several months to the next committee meeting before they can ask permission to do something. I think we'll see a slow trickle of them signing up to help, but it will take ages, because the committee only meets four times a year of something... worse they might even have to refer to head office if they are part of a national organisation, and we'll have to wait for yet another committee, higher up."

"I told you this," Gemma said, "I said you needed to get on with it or you'd run out of time to organise things."

"It seems so far away yet," her husband said.

Nick nodded, "It does, but the time will fly past once we really get under way. Christmas, New Year and then just the summer to do any outdoor rehearsals ready for the show itself in the spring.”

Duncan said, “When exactly is the Quincentenary really due?”

“It's a bit unclear,” said Adele, “We know the charter was in 1515, and the actual document locked in the town hall just says 'in the year of our lord 1515', but there's a few scraps of paperwork that have dates ranging from mid February to late May. I think that everyone accepts St. George's Day as being as good a date as any.”

Duncan noticed that she avoided catching anyone's eye after she said this. He was still unsure about Adele's attitude to the old St George's event. She had been very straightforwardly open about the things that happened at it, and even her own involvement one year, but had a very reserved approach whenever it came up in conversation among them as a group. And it did come up in conversation, time and again. It was a constant elephant in the room, and in the town, or perhaps, his writer's mind thought, the dragon in the den. Having set the performance date for St. George's day brought the old event to mind repeatedly. He resolved to keep avoiding the subject. It seemed politic.

“Who haven't we heard from then?”

Nick listed, “The Scouts and Guides, two different marching bands, the Lions Club, all the schools, three of the different church denominations, all the shops that are part of national chains, and a few of the local independents..... Rather a lot of people really.”

“Three churches? How many are there?” Gemma wanted to know.

“Four with their own buildings,” Nick told her, “but a couple who are sort of itinerant and use other people's halls. St Georges, the parish church, has sent a note saying they will help however they can."

"I bet they don't want to put up the modern equivalent of the amount of funding they used to finance the fair with," said Adele.

"I met the vicar the other week, Luke something," said Duncan.

"The reverend Grainger," Nick said, "Rather a fanatic about St George. But we're doing this about the quincentenary."

"You're right," Duncan told him. "But he showed me some interesting church records."

"Leave them right out of your script," Nick said, "When will we see a script by the way?"

"Very soon, in draft form. I'm still stymied by not knowing how many actors we have got, but I'll press 'print' on where I have got to in the next couple of days and let you all have a look."

John and Jenny came in noisily. They joined the others. Duncan found himself obliged to go and get a round in from the bar. By the time he had ferried the glasses to their table he found that the only available seat was next to Jenny. Warily he squeezed into the space, hemmed in on one side by the wooden end of the bench seat, and on the other by the thigh that the woman was, as usual, brazenly displaying. Gemma was opposite, and he saw her grinning at his obvious embarassment. Jenny thanked him for the drink, turning to him to do so, flaunting her cleavage almost into his face.

"We've got wonderful news for you," she burst out.

"We weren't going to tell them till it was firmly settled," John said.

"Oh John, don't be such a boring kill joy, I want to tell them," said Jenny, "We've got a sponsor!"

There was a flurry of questions from the show planners following her announcement. Nick came out on top with, "Who, and how much?"

"I buy all my art stuff, clay, dyes, paints, well everything, from a supplier in Anderton, it's just down the road, you know," they all nodded, they knew. It was a larger, busier town. "and I was telling them about the show, and the props and so on, like you do, and the sales manager said that they'd supply all the materials I need, free, for a programme credit.."

"Are we having programmes?" asked Nick. Somehow, though he was pleased at someone succeeding in the drive to get funding he was irritated that it was being presented as a fâit-accompli. Now he felt Jenny was making assumptions about programmes. Mentally he always classified John as a dull, but useable labourer and Jenny as a rather wild and silly young thing. That she frequently pawed at him and partially exposed herself always left him unsure whether it was a genuine come-on. He was constantly confused by seeing her do the same with everyone else.

".....and I said 'is that all?' and he said he'd put up five hundred quid as well if he could have a whole page," she finished triumphantly.

"I guess that's a good deal," Nick conceded, "When might they pay up?".

"I expect they actually want to pay after they've seen the programme, but I'm sure I could charm him into rather sooner," Jenny promised, "What do you reckon, Duncan?" and she touched his leg rather suggestively, looking him in the eyes to see his reaction.

"Yes, err, I'm sure you could," he muttered. He could see Gemma desperately trying not to laugh at his embarrasment.

Jenny saw this and said to Gemma, "You don't mind me

borrowing him sometimes do you?"

Gemma let the laugh out and told her, "Of course not, you borrow him all you want."

"Oh thank you, I'll take you up on that," said Jenny, using the hand on his thigh to squeeze his leg rather higher up than he felt common public decency would normally have implied. Worse, he found she left her hand there as the conversation went on.

He was cross with Gemma when they got back home.

"I don't see what was funny about what that woman was doing," he said as he opened their door, checking that John and Jenny had already gone inside their house and closed the door.

Gemma burst out laughing. "You poor dear! Surely you could see she was toying with you. Everyone else there thought it was funny. She does it with everyone, well all the men, and you're the only one who is embarrassed by it. It's just meaningless flirting."

"It's embarrasing, and I never know where to look."

He wasn't really a prude, but he had no experience of such loose behaviour. He hadn't realised that Gemma had either.

"Well at least she's only making some of the props," he mumbled.

Chapter 14
First Draft

"...Then the narrator says, ' Join us now as we take you back to 61AD as Boudicea leads her Iceni army against the Roman occupying forces, just outside the town here.' "

"And the armies are the other side of the stage?"

"Well they'll have to come on as that's being said, but yes, I suppose, the other side so the audience looks across to them next."

"Like a tennis match, it's going to give them neck ache."

Duncan hadn't expected an analysis of every word and stage direction. They were hardly more than two or three minutes into the script and everyone had interjected at some point already. Anyway, surely it was up to Nick to direct the thing how he saw fit. The trouble was that Nick was putting up most of the objections and raising most of the queries. Duncan was becoming fractiously annoyed with him, with the other members of the loosely formed committee, with the whole concept of the drearly contentless show.

He had struggled with the script for several days on end. No that was untrue, he had stared into space in his habitual way for several days on end. Great gaping periods of nothing interspursed by brief sessions of rapid keyboard pounding. Then, frequently he deleted what he had just written and went back to staring into space.

Sometimes he had walked about, looking out of the windows. He avoided the front windows now with their view of the door of number 46. Twice his idle look out had been disrupted by the sight of Jenny coming out into the little front garden, or returning to the house. When she came out it was to bend down and search the gravel for some particular stone flaunting her cleavage when she faced his way. Decisively he had drawn the curtains of their front bedroom and gone back to his typewriter. Then he wondered whether she would think he was hiding behind the curtains to spy on her.

None of this had made the text flow onto the page.

"Then we have the scene with the armies and the battle," Duncan told the meeting. "Someone says something like, 'Greendale wood is the perfect place to camp for the night' and the Roman soldiers put up a couple of tents and maybe light a fire and settle down, then there are shouts from off-stage, and Boudicea and the Iceni charge on and fight the Romans. We'll have to stage the fight so no-one gets hurt, but the end of it must be the Romans being driven off."

Someone asks, "How many of these soldiers have we got to get?"

"I thought," Duncan explained to them, "That we could get a society, or a couple of societies to make the armies. Maybe scouts, or something."

There was a chorus of suggestions of suitable groups. Or at least, thought Duncan, groups that are probably unsuitable, but people have remembered them. He felt more inclined to rely on the list he and Adele have printed off from the directory, especially as every suggestion was followed by some uncertainty and some occasional disagreement about who the correct person to contact about that group might be.

He ploughed on through the proposed show, describing, and reading snippets of script that depicted the town. Even he admitted to himself that the script was tedious, lack-lustre and possibly boring, as a chronological account of not much happening in an unimportant town.

"We have a couple of semi pastoral scenes, 'tableau vivant' if you like, you'll see the details in your copies, before we get to the Parlimentarians camping on Greendale, before sacking and burning the town.."

"How are you going to burn the town?" asked a voice.

"Let's do it for real!" said some wag.

There was an ironic cheer.

Nick, who seemed to be feeling the reading was a bit unsatisfactory, said, "Oh come on, people." which had a further dampening effect on an already rather dreary and depressing meeting.

Duncan said, "We're hoping to get some help with some special effects lighting, well we're going to need stage lighting anyway, so let's not worry on that score yet."

He could see Nick shrugging.

"The actors being the towns people run about shouting and eventually, when they've failed to put the fires out they set up camp in tents and things on Greendale. I rather thought we could do a sequence at this point with lots of activity, ladders and wheelbarrrows and things, you know, to show the rebuilding of the town." He flipped pages and said, "Starts on page twenty-eight, where 'a worker' says 'Bring that ladder over here'.."

Some of the people turned pages, and there was a bit of rustling as they did. Duncan saw that most of them were not reading his script at all, just passively allowing him to try to describe action he himself was unsure of. He regretted agreeing. Coming round to what Gemma told him he was more and more convinced that he should have encouraged Nick into writing and directing. She had been right, she always was, he knew nothing about writing scripts, there was little or no meat in the story of the town, aside from the 'off-limits' subject, and he was floundering.

"Then we have the evacuees arriving during the war," he said desperately.

"What about the men who died in the First War," came a shout from the back.

"If we have enough people, and uniforms, we could have them marching away to war," he told them hastily. "Anyway, the evacuees give us a chance to involve some children in the cast."

"You'll need chaparones."

"Yes, we know."

Nick said, "Can we stick to the business of the evening please. Just the script for now. Go on Duncan."

"Then there's the scene where one of the evacuees asks questions about the town, so we can cram all sorts of minor things in there that aren't enough to fill a scene on their own. The way the pond always floods, the building of the by-pass.."

"The evacuees had long gone before they started building the by-pass."

Someone was yawning. Another said, "If George is falling asleep just hearing this, I don't think there's much hope for an audience watching it staying awake."

"Remember," said Nick, "there'll be actors and movement and music and, well lots of visual things we haven't got here tonight."

A voice said, "The public only wants to know about the dragon thing."

"No! Absolutely not," said one of the audience.

"Go on, be good sports. It's the worst kept secret in the county and our sole claim to fame, you've got to use it."

There was a burst of argument. Clearly some of the assembled group agreed, some did not.

Duncan looked in mute appeal at Adele. She, he thought, will be the only voice of reason if this debate spirals out of control as it seems to threaten to do. But Adele was sitting impassive as if her mind was miles away.

It was an insoluble dilemma. Some of the townsfolk trying to suppress and ignore the story, some wanting to cash in on the salacious nature of a long discontinued event.

Nick found he was unable to keep real control of what turned into a wide ranging, and at times, heated debate. The meeting broke up before Duncan got to the end of the script he had written. He left embarrassed and annoyed at the poor showing he had made. Days of typing and editing had been revealed as thin and lacklustre when paraded for the scrutiny of people who really should have been considered supporters of the project. What hope was there for it if it was presented to the general public?

Nick hardly said goodbye to him as he left. Clearly he was as unimpressed with Duncan's efforts as the others, as critical of his bland attempt as the nay-sayers. In his heart Duncan knew that a word of encouragement as he left would have been disingenuous, but he still smarted at being slighted if not snubbed.

At home he hurled the ring binder with his copy of the draft script across the room as he went in. Gemma looked up from some work she was doing at the noise as the folder hit the edge of the settee and fell to the floor, its locking rings springing open under the impact and a shower of pages flying out and scattering across the floor.

"Didn't it go well then?" she asked mildly, slightly surprised at such a show of temper from her husband.

"They argued about every sentence, and I don't really blame them. It's a load of rubbish. There's no plot, no characters, no action... frankly no hope."

"Cup of tea then?" she said, getting up and making for the kitchen.

"Maybe something stronger."

"I'll do coffee then and put some whisky in it for you," she promised him.

He muttered 'thanks' and began picking up the scattered script rather ashamed of his outburst. The doorbell rang.

"Damn!" he said, and abandoned the pages to go and answer the door.

"Another coffee please Gemma," he called as he led Adele into the living room.

"Sorry to come round late, and after you had all that stress at that reading," she was saying, before halting at the sight of the pages scattered about. "Oh!"

Duncan dropped back to his knees trying to gather the scattered script, making incoherent apologies for the mess and trying to pretend that the folder had come undone accidentally. When Gemma emerged from the kitchen, clutching three mugs, two in one hand and one in the other, Adele and Duncan were both scrabbling among the mess scooping pages back into the folder. Duncan would have settled for just trapping the escaped papers, but Adele was carefully sorting them back into order and threading each one onto the curved metal prongs of the ring binder, her natural desire for tidy organisation coming to the fore. He kept muttering 'thank you' as she sorted the pages.

Chapter 15
Christmas

'Like two children,' Gemma thought as she put the mugs down on the coffee table near her husband and Adele, crawling about collecting loose sheets.

"Coffee, you two," she said, because they didn't seem to have noticed her arrival.

Duncan got up rather slowly and creakilly. There was a time, not so long ago, he would have managed getting up off his knees perfectly well. He extended a hand down to Adele to help her up, but the sprightly woman got to her feet unaided, cllutching his ring binder with most of the script back in it, and said to Gemma, "Thank you. You must think I'm an awful nuisance coming knocking on your door so late, and after that meeting too."

"Duncan was just telling me," Gemma said, "I don't think he felt it went very well." She ignored the look Duncan was giving her. He wasn't sure he wanted Adele to know that he had doubts about his offering.

"No," Adele agreed, "They were a bit critical weren't they.. Oh, you've put something in this coffee!"

""Just a drop of whisky. I hope that's all right"

"Very much so dear. Very welcome after this evening. I'm sure Duncan wanted some."

"He certainly needed something to put him in a better mood," Gemma said.

"I'm sorry you had a bad time at the meeting, Duncan. It may have been my fault," Adele told him.

"Oh I don't think so," Duncan replied, "I made a botch job of presenting it and haven't managed to make any sort of entertaining show out of what material there is."

"Just what I meant by it being my fault, our fault," Adele corrected herself, including Nick in the statement, "there's two problems.."

"Only two?" he was still grumpy.

"..one is a shortage of material, the other is our telling you to omit the dragon fair."

"It's tricky if we omit anything, there's so little meat to work with."

"So that's why Nick and I have come up with a suggestion. Could you put a bit in that told the story of George and the Dragon with no reference to the town's Dragon Fair. I mean, just as if you were telling a fairy story to kids."

"Would the vicar like the idea of calling George and the Dragon 'just a fairy story'?"

"You don't have to literally say 'this is a fairy story' you just don't say it's history, or even particularly local. It's just on the excuse of what the church is dedicated to."

Duncan downed his coffee.

"I suppose I could try, if you still want me to.."

"Of course we want you to."

Gemma laughed and said, "You don't have to say that. You asked him to do it with no idea whether he could produce a script for you. Now you've found out... Well, you could drop him now you've seen what he's produced."

Duncan knew she was trying to get him off the hook he had become stuck on. However he did feel a little slighted, ashamed that his wife was prepared to admit that his effort was not good enough. Part of him would have been delighted to have found a way to walk away from the project, part of him wanted to have another stab at the show, to see if he could rescue anything from the debris of the first draft. She had told him he was an idiot when he originally agreed to write it, had called it a poisoned chalice. How right she had turned out to be. And yet..

Adele was still talking to Gemma, "He was having a hard time because of the Dragon Fair, or rather not being allowed to mention it, but if he does the traditional St. George story instead that covers all our tails. No come back from the people who want it all hushed up, no grumbles from people like the church who think we're suppressing the local saint because of the old traditions. Everyone's happy."

"Having seen them tonight I can't conceive of any way that 'everyone' could be made to be happy," Duncan grumbled.

"Oh all right. Go on, Duncan. Give it another try," Gemma told him grudgingly.

"I'd better talk to the vicar again; make sure I get the right slant to satisfy the faithful." he said.

Adele looked worried for a second, saying, "Be careful with Luke, he's got a real bee in his bonnet about the Dragon Fair. Go in there with questions about St. George and he will have an excuse to start on his historical research about the fair."

"I seem to have had that conversation with him already."

"Unless it lasted a whole day, you haven't started to hear everything our vicar has to say about the fair," Adele grinned to show she was partly joking.

"I couldn't make my mind up whether he was for it or against it."

"He's in an awkward position. His organisation was very much involved in running something that the modern world thinks infra-dig," Duncan grinned at the use of the old fashioned term, "So he has to be critical," Adele went on, "but his personal interest is all consuming. He is passionate about trying to track down every detail of the thing that he can."

"Voyeurism?" Gemma asked.

"Maybe. Yes very possibly. The great regret for him is that there are virtually no contemporary reports or pictures. Even in the sixties, when you'd have expected people to be out with their Box Brownies or even taking colour slides there's hardly anything. At least," she qualified, "if there are pictures, people are keeping them hidden away.

"Anyway, I shall ask him about the saint, and see if that could give us another scene."

Adele nodded. "Do that." She got up. "Thank you for the coffee. And have a good Christmas, if I don't see you before," she added as she left.

It was getting much closer to Christmas before Duncan managed to talk to Luke Grainger. He seemed very elusive, maybe because of the coming festive period, which saw him, like all vicars attending school carol concerts and playgroup Nativity plays as well as an increased number of church services. Duncan caught up with him in St. George's church late one afternoon. The vicar was balancing on some rather unstable looking wooden steps hanging lights and baubles on a Christmas tree planted in an old metal dustbin by the archway leading to the choir stalls.

"Afternoon vicar," Duncan called.

Luke wobbled unsteadily as he looked to see who was calling.

"Could you just hold this ladder while I put this bauble on please," he begged, "I'm having to reach rather a long way over."

Duncan did as he was asked, getting profuse thanks when the worried man finally reached ground level again.

"Not my favourite occupation, ladders," he explained.

"It looks as though it's seen better days," Duncan commented, giving the steps a gentle wriggle. The elderly joints between the sides and the steps all seemed to have movement in them, so it swayed alarmingly when in use.

"Another thing we probably can't afford to replace," said Luke.

"You'll wish you had if someone comes a cropper," Duncan predicted.

"Please. I don't need a real life Job's comforter." the vicar looked back up at his tree, "I can probably reach the rest from the pulpit," he said optimistically, "What can I do for you? Ready for more information about the Dragon Fairs?"

Duncan saw an eagerness at this possibility. He remembered what Adele had said about the man having an apparent obsession with the old event.

"Actually it was the real St. George I wanted your knowledge of."

"Oh." for a moment Duncan thought the man was disappointed, then the vicar said, "You'd better come in the vestry."

He led Duncan into the cramped, dark cupboard like space. The medieval windows were partly boarded up with venerable old planking. Duncan wondered if it had been put there during the war. Whatever the case it added to the gloom of the winter afternoon. Luke switched on the light and a single naked bulb, hanging from a cable in the middle of the room, made a useless attempt to light the place. He could now see, however, that the dusty room had some storage, locked behind dark wood panelled doors, along one side, and a tatty table against the other with church paperwork on it. There were two bentwood chairs. All the available surfaces were filled with untidy piles of metal containers, obviously intended for flowers, and the vicar's cassock and surplice, incongruously clean, hung on an over-ornate hook.

Luke sat on one of the chairs, waving Duncan to the other. Duncan felt, although he had never been in one, as though he was trapped in a confessional booth.

'Forgive me father, for I have got cajoled into writing this show' he thought.

Luke lent back and appeared to study the light bulb for inspiration.

"What do you want to know about him?" he said at last.

"I don't know. I mean we all know he slayed a dragon and that's about it.

Luke said, "Hmm. Look he's a rather obscure character. The story you're describing, the one our local fair used as a basis for its activities, is that there was a dragon, which the king and his people could only keep at bay by sacrificing their women and girls to it. Eventually the king's daughter got selected by the lottery they were using to pick victims. There's that lottery thing again. Just in time St. George turned up and killed the dragon. The king was so pleased that he gave him huge amounts of money..."

"Not his daughter then?"

"No, not in the widely accepted version of the story, just money. St. George insisted on the money going to the poor and that's why he became a saint."

"You said 'the version of the story I was describing'. Are there others?"

"Historically the dragon is probably just a fable that sprang up around the saint."

"You mean 'which came first, the dragon or the saint?' But that's what everyone knows about St. George."

"True, but really he was a Roman soldier, one of Emperor Diocletian's personal guard, who became a Christian got executed because of that, so he's a martyr. This would have been around the fourth century. People started venerating him about the fifth century, but the dragon story came along much later."

"So why have we got a Roman soldier as our saint?"

"He's the saint for lots of places. It seems likely he was Greek anyway, not Roman, The dragon story didn't turn up until the twelfth century in Europe. It started in Lybia. He's accepted as a prophet by some Muslims. One version has him being ressurected. In the West they latched onto him being some sort of protector, I suppose that relates to the dragon. St. George's day was one of few church festivals that survived the Reformation in this country."

"It all seems very confused."

"Every region developed its own version of the stories. Picures of him usually show him in armour that would have been being worn at the time the picture was painted. There's no real contemporary information."

Duncan asked, "What about the dragon? I mean does it always look the same? What's it meant to represent?"

"It changes appearance from century to century, nation to nation, but it's always representing evil, the devil, sin... whatever you want to call it."

"Could it be shown as like a Chinese dragon?"

"Good heavens no. Why would you want to do that? The Chinese dragon is a symbol of good luck, it's quite different. Is this something to do with the show?"

Duncan nodded, "Just wondering how we could include St. George, and your church, of course, without mentioning the dragon fair thing."

"Have you seen what the dragon looked like at the fair?"

Duncan suddenly realised he hadn't. The most significant thing in the most salatious annual event for the town for decades, and he'd not seen a picture or description.

"Come on. Up the tower again I'm afraid, but all the secret papers are up there." Luke laughed.

Chapter 16
Image

They left the vestry. The church seemed darker than ever. He realised this time, as he climbed, that the spiral stairway was lit by tiny slit windows at intervals, but now it was a winter afternoon precious little light made its way onto the steps. He groped and stumbled his way after Luke. Once the oversized key had been used to unlock the book filled space Luke set about finding the paper he wanted by the inadequate light of another dangling naked light bulb like the vestry one. Duncan waited, somehow feeling that he was trespassing into some secret world.

The yellowing scrap that Luke eventually handed to him was almost a relief in its mundaneness. A few column inches from a local newspaper, headed with a photograph made up the fragile cutting. Duncan laid it carefully on an empty bit of shelf and studied it, wishing there was more light. The photo had been taken from some high vantage point, maybe the upstairs window of one of the shops in the main street. He guessed that you could probably work out where with great accuracy if you tried. Crowds thronged the street and, some distance away, a small platform, populated by what were clearly important figures in the town, one wearing a mayoral chain, included in their number a young looking girl in a white frock. They were all looking toward the wooden double gates of the yard of the coaching inn in the town, which had opened enough for the dragon to emerge.

The 'creature' was a one man costume, with an almost round body, seemingly formed from some sort of wickerwork, covered in cloth scales and a ferocious head with wide toothed mouth on an extended neck. The legs of the man inside were very obvious, in ordinary trousers, but the animal's tail dragged behind it on the ground, some of it still inside the inn yard. The whole image was rather unclear due to the print technique for photographs in newsprint being composed of numerous dots, so no real detail was to be seen. It would be impossible to identify any individual.

Duncan read the newspaper write-up below the picture.

'Dragon Fair in Elveston'

it said;

> *The annual Dragon Fair has been held again in Elveston. Last Saturday's traditional celebrations saw the town packed to capacity. Organisers thanked the public for their support, numbers swelled this year by the early spring sunshine. Highlight of the event, as always, was the selection, by lottery, of St. George, The Dragon, and the maiden to be 'sacrificed'. Mr Edwards and Mr Lambeth were this year's George and Dragon respectively, and sixteen year old Mavis Waddington was chosen as the maiden. Mavis wins a substantial undisclosed cash prize and two nights in the local hotel.'*

The article meandered off into descriptions of the fairground attractions at the annual event. Duncan went back to peering at the picture. He thought he could vaguely discern the draw drum that Luke had previously mentioned.

"What paper did this come from?" he asked, hoping that he could contact them to see if the archives still contained the original picture, without the dots.

"The Argus, but you won't find their archive, if that's what you were thinking. The newspaper offices were gutted by fire in about 1990 and the paper closed down. You may have noticed, we don't have a local newspaper any more, just one of those monthly glossy advertising free sheets."

Duncan nodded, disappointed. "Is there any way I could get a photocopy of this page?" he asked.

"I don't see why not. There's a copier in the rectory. It's not very good, but we'll give it a try for you." and they left the bell tower records to climb back down to ground level. Luke was right. It wasn't a very good copier, but after Duncan had pleaded for another attempt, and Luke had adjusted the density a bit they achieved a reasonable print of the picture. Duncan stowed it carefully in his jacket pocket, enclosing it in one of the early attempts, folded in half, to protect the better copy.

"Would you be happy to see some representation of the St. George story in the event, just to acknowledge the church's saint?" he asked, getting an agreement to this before thanking the vicar and heading home.

He was studying the photcopy of the newspaper cutting on the dining table when Gemma came home. He showed her, and, unusually, because she had adopted a firm disinterest in the proposed show, she read it thoroughly.

"Do we know what date it is?" she asked.

"No. And the newspaper offices were burnt down, so the records are all gone seemingly, but I'm guessing late nineteen-fifties."

"I wondered if any of the named people were still about, Mavis Waddington, or these blokes, Edwards and Lambeth."

"What if they are? I can't write about them. I really got this for the picture. I want to see if someone could reproduce the dragon costume so I could do the St George story as the church's section of the show."

"Oh." Gemma seemed disappointed. The cutting had peaked her interest suddenly, "I thought you might have decided to say, 'so what' to the censorship and research the thing for an article or even, you had said maybe a TV documentary."

"I can't do that. We've made friends with these people now. I'll have to do the show their way whatever happens. Perhaps, once its all over, maybe then I could do something independently. But they'll be very upset. We could fall out with them very badly over that, I think."

Gemma shrugged. "Well I'm going to see what I can find out." she promised. He knew that once she started on a project she wouldn't stop until she had completed it. Sooner or later she would be telling him titbits of information about the fair. She didn't have the advantage of Luke's access to parish records, but he was sure she would turn up some information.

Christmas arrived.

Gemma announced that she had a long holiday from work, due to the way the bank holidays fell, giving her a whole ten days at home. She set about decorating the house for their first Christmas in this new home. Cards began to arrive from old friends in their previous town, from family scattered across the country, and from some of the new acquantances they had made since they arrived. It was these that caused the most decision making over the pile of cards spilling, with their envelopes, from the Christmas box. Gemma had bought new cards for this year, to add to the usual left-overs from previous years. The left-overs mainly consisted of the less appealing ones from selection packs, that had been passed over last year. These were usually an emergency supply for odd neighbours who they had forgotten, or who had unexpectedly sent a card to them.

They sat facing each other across the table. "Your Aunt Hilda," Gemma said, reading from her list. The list had started as a tidy aide-memoire many years ago, and included a series of ticks and crosses which indicated whether the particular person had reciprocated with a card. Some names had been crossed out entirely, many more had been added, and this year a whole swathe of additional names and addresses from Eleveston had been added at the foot of the list. These alterations and additions were in a variety of inks, and the whole list now had a very scrappy appearance.

Duncan grunted, reached out, and picked up a card with a stage-coach in the snow, selecting an envelope that fitted it.

"You can't send her that, she's a relative."

"Well hardly. We haven't spoken since I was about twelve. Anyway she'll probably like to be reminded of stage-coaches."

"Duncan! Here, send her a robin." and Gemma snatched the card he had picked up away, passing him a smaller, smarter one. He helped himself to the address book, once he had written their names in the card, and riffled through the pages. "Is she under 'A' for aunt, or 'H' for Hilda?" he asked.

"'M' for Mattisen," said Gemma, her tone implying 'of course'.

He found the entry. "Don't we have a post-code?"

"For Aunt Hilda? No we never have known it."

Duncan sighed and wrote the address on the envelope. His wife selected another card as he sealed Aunt Hilda's, and passed it to him saying, "Edward and Jean."

"Do we still do them?" he asked her.

"They're your friends. It's up to you. Leave it this year if you like, but they sent us one last year," she told him, consulting the sheet in front of her. He was hesitating when the doorbell rang.

Rising to answer it he found Jenny on the doorstep. As usual, and despite the winter chill, she appeared to be partially dressed. She carried a bulging, second hand carrier bag.

"I've got something for you," she said, It was a phrase open to interpretation. She acknowledged the possibilities by adding, "No, not that, you naughty boy. Well unless..."

Duncan thought he might be safer in Gemma's company, so he invited their neighbour in. Jenny went through to the living room where Gemma still sat, surrounded by the debris of card writing. He saw his wife give a knowing sort of smile as she saw him ushering the visitor in. Gemma regarded Jenny frankly, short skirt, loose top showing too much cleavage, her wild hair blown about by the wind even in the short journey across the road.

"Hello," she said, amused.

"I came to bring you these for Christmas," Jenny said to Gemma.

"That's very kind of you," Gemma told her, taking the bag and peering into it.

"Not at all. Your first Christmas in the street, I had to do something." a pause, "Duncan might not have let me do what I first thought of, so I made you those."

Duncan blushed, wondering if the first thing she had thought of was the same thing he was thinking of, and coming to the conclusion that the local flirt probably did mean that. Gemma began taking things out of the bag.

There were several individual items, each wrapped in a piece of old newspaper. She unwrapped them as she lifted them out. Each was a clearly hand made pottery piece. Together they made a collection that comprised reindeer, a sledge, sacks of presents and a fat santa to sit on the sledge. Each piece had been hand shaped, fired with appropriate coloured glazes and had been executed with great care and more artistry than Gemma and Duncan had thought Jenny would have displayed. She arranged the pieces in an appropriate line one behind the other across the part of the table that was clear of cards and envelopes.

"Thank you so much," said Gemma, "That's really kind of you. I'm afraid we haven't even got round to writing your card yet, we're a bit on the drag with Christmas preparations."

Duncan muttered a blushing 'thanks', trying to keep his eyes away from the tease, also rather embarrassed by the near neighbours having decided to give presents. A new town meant a whole set of new behaviours to learn. He never felt very secure with the correct 'form' with acquaintances at birthdays and other celebrations. Gemma seemed to cope so much better, so he usually left arrangements to her. Now he saw her pick up one of the reindeer and study it.

"You've done this really well," Gemma told Jenny.

"It is my trade, it's what I do." the woman said. And there was an implicit 'why shouldn't it be?' in the phrase.

"Yes, sorry, of course.. I didn't mean.."

"Thank you," Jenny rescued herself. She had clearly made a faux-pas.

Duncan was politely offering a cup of tea, surprised when Jenny accepted. He filled the kettle and got cups out, "I assume you want one?" he checked with Gemma. She nodded, still turning the pottery items this way and that on the table. Drinks made he scattered mats and the mugs joined the Santa and his reindeer on the table. Gemma waved Jenny to sit down. She chose the chair nearest to Duncan's, contriving to make her skirt ride high up her thigh, at least on the side next to him. He leant close in to the table so its surface hid the display from him.

The conversation was inconsequential as they sat and drank, Jenny and Gemma exchanging vague plans for Christmas and agreeing with each other about how the long holiday created extra shopping and how wasteful it all became if you tried to stock enough food for the special days as well as your usual weekly provisions. After a while Duncan felt Jenny pat his leg as she said, "How's the show shaping up now?"

He floundered around trying to answer the enquiry. Gemma

guessed what was happening by the way her husband was blushing and becoming a bit incoherent in his answer to what was a simple enough question. She laughed and told Jenny, "Duncan's still fixated on the dragon thing. He's been talking to the vicar about it, haven't you dear?"

Duncan nodded. Then with sudden decisiveness he pulled his leg away from Jenny and got up to fetch the photocopy he had made at the rectory. He put it in front of her asking, "How easy would it be to make a reproduction of the dragon costume from this?"

Jenny was suddenly serious and professional. She lent forward and studied the grainy image intently. At one point she picked up a ruler that was lying among the litter of stationery Gemma was using. Gemma replaced it with a pencil, because it had been marking how far down a column of Christmas card recipients' names she had got. Jenny made a number of measurements of the dragon and of nearby doorways and people, before saying, "It's not too big to deal with. I reckon it must have had a cane framework under all that.. is it scraps of material making the scales? Cane would make it light enough for the man inside to carry it about. You can't see his hands, so I suppose they must be inside it lifting the thing up. It does look as though the head had some sort of mechanism for the jaw to open and shut... you'd have to operate that somehow so maybe... Oh! Perhaps it hangs on shoulder straps like clown's baggy pants on braces."

"You think it's possible?"

"Someone made it originally. It's obviously possible. Do we know anything about the colours?"

"No, but I imagine a dragon is green."

"Probably. But it must be lots of different shades of green. You can see in this that the material they made the scales out of seems to be different on the back from underneath.. the scales are different sizes too if you look." She pointed to the picture.

Duncan leant over, forgetting, momentarily, his usual wish to keep a safe distance from her, and seeing that she was right.

"Do you know someone who could make one?"

"I can do that. Might be an idea to get Edward and Tamsin involved, if only to get material on the cheap. Are you hoping for a replica, or for a one man dragon that reminds people of this one?"

"Maybe not too close a replica. People seem to be a bit sensitive."

Jenny dropped her hand down to his knee, "Yes they are aren't they," she said cheekily.

During the run up to Christmas Duncan and Gemma were surprised by the number of people who, as Jenny had, called in to see them, bearing small gifts for the newcomers. In truth they themselves no longer felt like 'new' residents of Elveston, but this being their first Christmas the locals clearly felt that they were. There were visits from Edward and Emily, saying the hoped the show was coming along well and full of apologies for not being active in the arrangements; from Edward and Tamsin, who'd somehow heard that they might be required sooner than they had thought for materials; and from Nick himself.

Nick and Adele called together one late afternoon. The curtains were drawn against the darkness outside and Gemma was in the kitchen armed with a cookbook and the pressure cooker attempting to make soup. Duncan answered to door. He invited them in, offering tea. The guests sat in the living room while he boiled the kettle and brewed.

"Gemma will be out in a minute," he promised, handing round the mugs, "she's making soup."

"I'm glad someone still acually makes soup, I think most of the modern generation believe it's impossible to do at home and that it only comes in tins."

"I blame that all on Andy Warhol," Nick said.

A hissing noise started in the kitchen.

"Pressure cooker," observed Adele, "I remember when everyone had one of those. They were really good for dealing with cheap bits of meat... and making soup, of course."

"Something of a Christmas season item," Duncan said, "it comes out for soup, and the ham, and the pudding. But it does sit in the cupboard for most of the rest of the year."

Nick said, "Now, about things that come out once a year." He studied Adele, and she nodded, "We hear that you've asked for a dragon for the show."

"Who told you that," Duncan asked, "Jenny?"

"No, actually it was Edward and Tamsin. They thought they'd better be sure the material asked for was really for the show. Obviously they don't mind it being on tick until funds appear, but when the heard what was being made they quite rightly checked with me."

"Am I being told off?" he wanted to know.

"Not really. But I did think we'd agreed not to go near this dragon thing. It's a sensitive issue. Look how Edward and Tamsin immediately wanted to check."

"I'm not intending anything to do with the fair, I've been talking to the vicar about how we rope the church into the thing, and we figured that some sort of acknowledgement of St George was in order."

"You do realise that Luke is rather obsessed about the Dragon

Fair don't you?" Adele asked him.

"Oh yes, I gathered that. Anyway he came up with the picture we're going to use to base the costume on. Have you seen it?"

"Picture?" Nick asked rather sharply.

Duncan nodded and found the photocopy to show them. They poured over it for a while before Adele said, "At least it's far enough back to be reasonably safe. I would guess it's at least five years before my year. I can't remember any of the names they mention."

"I think I remember Mavis Waddington," Nick murmured, "I reckon she might have been in the year above me at school. At least there certainly was a Mavis."

"Common enough name in those days," said Duncan.

Gemma came in from the kitchen. The background hissing of the pressure cooker reduced slightly as she shut the door. She was holding her tea mug, and sat, joining the gatering.

"Sorry about that," she told them, "Had to make sure the thing was behaving itself. What are you all looking so serious about?"

"Just the show," Nick told her, "but I hope you can keep your husband in line. He keeps wanting to write about the dragon thing. We're trying to keep quiet about that."

"So I understand. I do think it's a bit silly. It's a piece of the town's history, in fact it's the only reasonably recent bit of history, and leaving it out almost draws attention to it. I'd just give it a mention and go on to something else. Not that I can see there's much else to dramatise."

Duncan frowned at his wife, making half concealed 'keep quiet' gestures out of Nick and Adele's sight. Gemma went on, "You're directing it, you're going to see any script first, you could always censor anything that you didn't like. Why not let Duncan have free rein and see what comes out?"

Their guests exchanged glances. "To be honest," Nick said, "we'd rather there wasn't too much investigative research being done. The town has settled down over the past decades and it's all in the past. None of the older generation want it all gone over again."

Duncan and Gemma stood on their step and watched Nick and Adele go. Duncan said, "I don't think they're too happy about my including St George."

"What they're not too happy about is the possibility that you might include the Dragon Fair. For some reason they're worried sick about it coming back into the public's mind. Maybe they think someone will try to ressurect it."

"I think the vicar might if he had the chance. He seems almost smitten with it."

"I don't think it's an obsession. I think he's just fascinated by the whole thing. I bet he knows a lot more than he's let on to you." Gemma said. "Anyway it's probably a bit voyeuristic with him. I can imagine a vicar drooling over prurient details of maidens being deflowered in the local hotel by two different parishoners in forty-eight hours while he sits in the lonely confines of his vicarage."

"You're just speculating, and type casting too. You've no reason at all to suppose Luke's interest is, what was it you said? 'Prurient'. I think he's simply into local history. He's been posted to a town with an oddity in its past, so he's been looking in to it."

Gemma told him, "I've said it before, you can be very naiive sometimes. He's researching something the good people of this borough have decided he should leave alone. Like you have been told to." she paused, "So where else can we go for information?"

"What?"

"Where else can we dredge up information. They don't want us to know, so of course we want to look into it. Whether you use it in the show, or get some mileage out of it if and when we move to another town, is almost irrelevant. We both want to know."

The dull gap between Christmas and New Year saw them both pounding keyboards, Duncan in a furious attempt to produce a more interesting and useable script, and Gemma trawling the internet for any mention of the fair, or similar events around the country. She soon discovered that Elveston's secret was apparently unique in the British Isles, or if not everyone else's version had been utterly obscured. The few mentions that had escaped onto the web were vague, and usually described as a rumour. She turned her attention to what parish records and census information she could dredge up, paying out to use the various sites intended for tracing family trees.

On New Year's Eve she wandered into where Duncan still tapped at his keyboard. She leant over him, reading his screen while massaging his shoulders. He seemed very tense. She told him, "Don't get so serious about it. It's a small town production. There's no chance of it going out on a national tour, whatever you write."

Duncan finished his sentence and leant back. The cursor on the screen winked impatiently where he had stopped typing. "I think I may have sorted out how to present it," he told her, "It's not exactly original, but it should work, and it allows Nick to use lots of volunteers in his cast."

"And local dance groups and schools and musicians?" she checked.

"All of those," he assured her.

"Come and look at what I've found then," she said, almost dragging him to her computer. The screen displayed a rather lurid red border around the website's text. A constantly scrolling title at the top announced "Naughty things your grandparents did." Gemma had parked the text below at the point where it read:

'..and a small number of local traditions where willing or unwilling victims were raffled for sex with other members of their communities. This tradition was usually linked to some religious or pseudo religious festival and probably originated around the time of the Druids. It is unclear how such raffles worked in those times, but it is certain that where the church was involved in the organisation of the event the victims, always female, were selected from the younger inhabitants. The age of consent was as low as ten years old between the sixteenth and nineteenth centuries, only rising to twelve years old in 1861, a year older a quarter of a century later, not being set at sixteen until as late as 1885. The few records that remain all have huge prize money, from church funds, for the victim and imply that being selected was viewed as an honour rather than a disgrace.
Heaton-Bassett's raffle chose a girl to be offered to their 'River snake' and Elveston's dragon received a girl too. These, and a few others of whom there is no record except dubious word of mouth shared a commonality that the girl was handed over to a man playing an animal part, who spent the night with her.   Elveston's girl seems to have been doubly unfortunate in that she was traditionally rescued the next day by St. George, who then spent the night with her in his turn.
Other animals that have been mentioned include a bull, a ram and a lion. It is assumed that all of these were men in costume destined to abuse or possibly rape their young raffle 'winner'.'
These unusual events were distinct and somewhat different from the several hundred conventional pageants which existed alongside them.'

"See!" Gemma said, as he read the screen.

Duncan said, "But it doesn't tell us anything we didn't know does it? I wonder where Heaton-Bassett is."

"About fifty miles away, I looked it up. Do you want to go on a visit?"

"If it's got a museum, and it's open, it would be worth a shot."

Heaton-Bassett nestled beside Heaton-Broadwater, though modern expansion and housing developments had merged the originally separate towns into one sprawling connurbation. It looked particularly drab in the cold rain. They visited on one of those post Christmas days when the decorations are still up, but the festival is finished. In the main street the council had hung moulded plastic shapes and characters in strings from one side to the other every twenty or thirty yards. It was a somewhat sparse display, and the santas and stars, reindeer and holly, looked drab and neglected in the cold afternoon air. At one point a timer had become incorrectly set, and there, between the upper storeys of a burger bar and a charity shop, two reindeer faced each other across a yellow star, lit from within by crude low wattage lamps, which highlighted random and mostly unsuitable parts of the mouldings.

Duncan drove his elderly and boxy Fiat with Gemma in the passenger seat. Gemma rather wished they'd come in her Mazda, which was a decade newer and equipped rather better. They were lucky locating the town's library, hidden in a side street. They had even more luck with parking, finding that the library boasted its own, free, car park, which was virtually empty. The building itself was similar in age to Elveston's, but unlike that one had survived the worst ravages of the seventies plasterboard and formica era, still welcoming its readers with the ornate woodwork and carved decorations that the original design had given it. There was a slight acknowledgement of the season in a number of paper lanterns strung from a piece of fishing line stretched across the entrance hall, but the first impression was of 'business as usual' and a friendly welcome. The woman on reception smiled at them as they came in, saying "Can I help?"

Leaning on the counter they explained their interest, and asked her what information the place held on its history.

"Ah," she said, half jokingly, "Looking for the salatious gossip, are you?"

Duncan protested, "No, no, nothing like that. We're doing some work for Elveston and Heaton-Bassett came up in an internet search as having had a similar event back in the past."

"Yes, the woman said, very similar. Actually you'll find more about Elveston when you start looking into it, because their Fair lasted much later than ours. I think it stopped in the nineteen-sixties sometime. Heaton-Bassett abandoned their River Snake event in the eighteen-nineties. We've got some pictures, contemporary drawings and paintings, obviously not photos, if you want to look."

She led them to a cabinet of wide shallow drawers in an adjoining room from where she pulled out a big folder of loose paper and laid it on the table, saying "Everything we've got is in this folder. Take as long as you like, but we do close at five. I've got to mind the desk, but come and ask me if there's anything you want to know."

Gemma watched her go. "Very helpful isn't she. I reckon she fancies you." but Duncan had already opened the folder and was slowly turning over the loose sheets.

First came a watercolour of a market scene. There was nothing remarkable about it and Duncan turned another sheet. This bore a line drawing in ink of what they deduced was the River Snake. The costume had a serpent's head mounted above the shoulders of the wearer and leading down to a tight covering for the performer's body and arms, some sort of opening to allow the legs out, and a long sinuous tapering snake's tail. The drawing showed scales, though with no indication of whether these were painted on or formed of individual bits of material as the Elveston Dragon's scales seemed to be. The River Snake's scales covered the whole of the costume except the head, which seemed to have been shaped to a bulbous rounded form with staring eyes and a small mouth, from which dangled a forked tongue.

Other drawings and paintings were of the event itself in progress in a street thronged with people with the snake generally some way away in the distance.

At the back of the folder a small document file housed yellowing paperwork in the cursive hand of past times, recording random names and amounts of money. Gemma was rather disappointed. They went back to the desk, asking if there was any chance of getting copies of the drawing of the snake and the few pages of documents. The woman was happy to oblige, and fed the things they requested to her photocopier for them. "You did notice the phallic nature of the Snake of course?" she asked them, "In our case that was the excuse for the girl being handed over to the performer in the costume."

"You think it looks like... you know.."

"All the people who look at this paperwork say so. Don't you think so?" the woman asked Gemma.

"I suppose so. I'm no expert you understand." She laughed, suddenly embarassed. "Do you think that was the intention from the start?"

"They say there had been a long tradition of offerings to our River Snake. But all snakes in legend and imagery have some sort of sexual connotations don't they?"

They came away from Heaton-Bassett feeling that they knew no more, but had, at least, been given a friendly welcome and help. Back home Gemma prepared tea. Duncan examined the copies they had brought. After a while he got a magnifying glass and began trying to decipher the handwritten pages of records.

"Cold turkey again," Gemma said, laying a plate beside him with Christmas left-overs on it.

"Look at these amounts of money," he said, "I think these are church accounts. The sums for what they call 'snake expenditure' are astonomical for the time, but the real eye openers are the ones marked 'prizes and payments'. I mean, a hundred pound prize in the eighteen nineties like they show here would be about sixteen thousand today I think."

"Well how did that much get put up as a prize then?"

"No telling, but it looks as though it did. I suppose like Elveston it was a combination of the church and the council."

"But a snake thing wouldn't have had anything to do with the church would it?"

"Maybe, serpent in the Garden of Eden perhaps? Anyway just like here it looks as though the girl was almost winning the lottery in cash terms."

"Might have made it worth the risk of the snake man being unattractive," Gemma said, "Here, eat your tea."

Duncan got up and went to fetch a jar of pickle. "Sorry, I forgot," said Gemma, prodding her fork into the left-overs on her plate. Duncan returned to his food, and to sifting through the papers they had acquired. After the meal he settled into an armchair and gazed at the ceiling. It seemed possible he had dozed off, but Gemma knew this apparent reverie of old and went quietly about, careful not to disturb him. He had gone into his 'staring into space' mode. Somewhere in Duncan's mind the whole show was gradually forming, alongside a very vague scheme to create a documentary about the salacious things that local communities had done as entertainment down the centuries.

Chapter 18
A script at last

Nick was becoming increasingly irritated. He was irritated by Duncan's continued failure to produce the script he so desperately wanted. The man had supplied him with a long, and very detailed, list of the cast required, but, although assembling those was keeping him occupied, Nick longed to be able to at least have some serious read through, to be able to make some stab at imagining what the final production might look and sound like, and to have some firm idea of what would be required in terms of scenery, costumes, props, even lighting and special effects. He was irritated by the way this absence of a firm, printed thing to hold in his hand and put under people's noses was resulting in those he approached saying that they were willing to help, but telling him to come back when he had something definite he wanted them to do. He was irritated by a phrase he now seemed to encounter every time he mentioned his pet project.

'What you ought to do...' people said to him, following it with their own particular ideas about what the show should be like.

He had heard it so often now that he was no longer considering the views as possible ideas to incorporate into the scheme. Even members of the council advising him on how to approach raising the finances required, or the reporter from the local paper tipping him the wink about the editor's preferences for press releases, or officials in organisations that could be useful to him, all said, 'What you ought to do...' and riled him slightly. He was hearing the phrase now as a criticism of him and the project. Repeatedly he was now being told what to do about some aspect of the thing, with the implication that what he had been doing up to now, up to the point at which the speaker had imparted their superior wisdom, was all wrong.

If he had been less confident, less convinced of the likely success of his brainchild, he might have been made nervous by the phrase. As it was he became irritated.

"What you ought to do," said the man, "is involve lots of local organisations.."

"That is what we will be doing."

"You see if you rope in an organisation with, say, a dozen members, that will be at least that number of seats sold."

"We're hoping to make it free admission.."

But the man wasn't listening. And the ambition was likely to be unfulfilled once the real costs became known. Nick resigned himself to receiving yet another batch of un-asked-for advice and to biting his tongue.

There was still over a year to go, but news of the project had now spread, so most of the town's population were at least vaguely aware of the coming event. Nick was feeling further irritation due to having discovered that the Town Council, ignoring the fact that they knew all about the project, at least in as much detail as Nick did, had spent some time at the last meeting discussing what it should do to mark the quincentenary, adding insult to injury by deciding, according to the minutes pinned to the board outside the offices, that his event, his show, should be recognised as the council's official event.

"They're going to pretend it was all their idea and that they organised it!" he ranted at Adele.

They were in the 'Dog and Dray'. She was sitting rather primly with her coat on and her black handbag hanging from her elbow in front of a small glass. They had been there long enough for the glass to be empty. Nick expected Duncan, and possibly Gemma any moment. He had seen him across the road and asked if he was coming as he and Adele had left her house after he had called for her. He was hoping that the writer would appear soon so that it would be his round. He wasn't naturally mean, but had come to thinking that a few drinks were the least the man owed him after all this delay.

"Penny for them," said Adele.

The barman was moving some beer-mats rather pointlessly on the counter, looking over to the two of them, clearly wondering if they would be ordering another drink. Nick roused himself from his brown study and asked her if she would like another drink. She was saying "Same again please," as Duncan and Gemma arrived. Duncan was carrying a thick ring-binder under his arm.

"Is that...?" Nick began.

"Yes," Duncan said, and handed the file to Nick who flipped a few pages saying, "Drinks all round then," passing the script to Adele to hold as he headed to the bar.

"Champagne I would have thought," she shouted after him. The barman was quick to hear this and was thrusting a bottle into an ice bucket and setting glasses on the counter before Nick had navigated the chairs and tables between where they sat and the bar. Normally he would have resisted such extravagance, but the arrival of a script at last deflected any parsimonious thoughts and he allowed the barman to run his credit card through the machine, returning to the table with the bucket and glasses. He was in the process of pouring when they were joined by John and Jenny, who were delighted to arrive at that moment. Nick fetched two more glasses with good grace.

"What are we celebrating?" John asked.

"Duncan's arrived with the script," Nick told him, adding, "at last," under his breath. Gemma heard him and grinned at him to show she at least didn't take offense.

"Oh! Script!" Jenny said, excitedly, and took the file out of

Adele's reluctant hands, opening it on the table and beginning to thumb through it.

"I know what you're looking for. It's toward the end," Duncan told her. She clutched his wrist, saying, "Bless you. Once I know what it's got to do I can make a proper start."

Nick felt he was being elbowed out of the decisions, but bit back any complaint. He was quite pleased, secretly, that there was enthusiasm being shown. He watched as Duncan pulled his wrist away in embarassment and Jenny continued her search of the pages. He had noticed Duncan's reserve around Jenny before. Personally he revelled in the woman's tactile behaviour, accepting any touch and every revealing choice of outfit as a bonus, a highlight of a day. He guessed that Duncan was withdrawn and seemingly shy because he didn't want Gemma to be angry. It was easier for Duncan to reject and avoid the casual flirting Jenny habitually did with everyone than to be accused of anything by his wife. Yes, Nick thought, that was it, Duncan was attracted to Jenny and didn't want Gemma to know. He concentrated on where Jenny had got to turning the pages. She was near the end of the show now and studying a page intently.

"So it just comes on and dances about a bit?" she queried.

"It's got to roll over and die when it's defeated," Duncan said.

"Oh yes. Got it here on the next page. Right, now we know. Do you want to see designs, or will you trust me?"

"What's this about?" Nick wanted to know, feeling excluded.

"St. George's Dragon," she told him.

Nick grabbed the file and started reading the page. He looked tense, but after a few moments seemed to relax. Adele asked, "Well?" and he reluctantly replied, "Just the Church's Saint George story I think."

141

Adele looked relieved and said, "Thank you, Duncan," before taking a sip of her champagne.

The script was handed around and people dipped into it, mostly without any comment as the evening wore on. Extravagantly Nick ordered another bottle and the six of them had become comfortably merry by the time it was closing. Jenny had taken a blank page from the file at some point and had been drawing for a long while before moves to depart were made. Coats were being donned as she held up the results of her sketching. Duncan and Gemma hadn't previously seen any drawn item from her and were surprised at the skill shown in the idle doodle. It depicted a champagne glass, with the famous 'Babycham' deer standing in it, with the animal's head replaced by an instantly recognisable caricature of Nick's face.

They all laughed. Adele took the paper carefully and studied it closely. "May I?" she asked.

"Of course, I thought you might," said Jenny, and Adele rolled the picture, tucking it delicately into her black handbag.

They said their goodbyes to the barman and went down the steps onto the car park. They walked together along Greendale Road. As they were passing 'The Limes' they all instictively looked up the driveway at the house. There was an impression of movement, and they were all convinced that Councillor Andrews had been watching the street from his window. Nick said, "Nothing better to do I suppose."

Adele held his free arm possessively, he was carrying the script in one hand, saying, "Just leave it."

Nick muttered a reluctant, "OK" and they carried on past the house. There was a parting of the ways with scattered 'Good nights' near Duncan and Gemma's. Once inside she said to him,

"Well, everyone seemed pleased didn't they?"

He went to the kitchen and filled the kettle to make coffee, saying,

"Thank goodness for that," over his shoulder.

Chapter 19
Committee

Catherine James repeated her insistence. "I'll bring you as many girls as you like, but we can only do routines we've already rehearsed for our own show, with the music we're used to, and we've got to do at least three dances to make it worth while."

Wearily Nick asked her to supply him with a list of the music she had routines for, knowing there was almost no chance that any pop based dance would fit seamlessly into the show and the script he was desperately trying to sort into a performance.

"Maybe you should go back to Miss Culpitt," Adele suggested to him.

"Go back?"

"Duncan said you made him go and enquire with her."

"That was just a public relations move. I wouldn't want the old girl's classical ballet girls toddling around on pointe, complaining about the grass being uneven and trying to stage Swan Lake in the middle of my show..."

"Catherine's girls are going to insist on trying to stage their disco numbers in the middle of your show," she reminded him.

"Maybe we can find a way of working some sort of link into what they are doing. I very much doubt we could find an excuse for the 'Nutcracker' to make a guest appearance, but popular stuff is easier."

Adele wondered if that would prove to be true.

Other areas seemed to be going more smoothly. Somehow word had got round, and members of local amateur theatre companies, from the town and the surrounding villages, were clamouring to take part. Volunteers for backstage and organisational roles had appeared too. A local printer had offered its services at cut price for posters and programmes. A small, loosely connected, group of men with an interest in carpentry had offered to take on set building, provided the materials were supplied. More importantly than all these there was an 'any other business' item due in front of the next council meeting to propose some funding, and Nick had received the tediously complicated application forms for grants from the County Council and from the Arts Council. He was spending some evenings ploughing through filling these in, aided by Adele.

These paperwork sessions usually happened at Adele's house, mainly because, somehow, by chance, the little cluster of houses on Greendale Road had become a nerve centre for the show. With nearly all the original team living on the street, and Duncan and Gemma's house being roughly the centre of them, it was Nick, living two streets away, who somehow seemed physically marginalised.

Nick hadn't been inside Adele's house before the show. It was comfortable and homely, in the way that only a house that has belonged to the same individual for fifty years can be. The narrow hall led to a snug back room and kitchen past a hall table that was old enough to incorporate an unbrella stand each side and hooks surrounding a bevel-edged mirror that was slightly foxed in a top corner.

Other furniture had been renewed during the decades, but piecemeal, with no grand 'designer' plan influencing it. A shrewd observer might have been able to deduce the colour and style of whatever piece had preceeded the current chair or settee, Adele having, like most of her generation would, replaced, due to wear, with as near a match for what she had been forced to part with as was possible. The rooms had been redecorated sometimes, but she had stuck rigidly to wallpaper, running from skirting board up to the old style picture rail, rather than bowing to the modern trends for white painted walls, or even the seventies gaudy colours.

Nick didn't see much of the back lounge, or the kitchen, being ushered into the front room on arrival on these occasional businesslike visits for the show. Adele's front room was not reserved by her for special formal occasions. Unlike many she did not keep it as 'best' for high feast days. In any case she had no immediate family to come calling at Christmas or Easter, and her few friends revolved around the museum, now her library days were over, Nick and the others she met in the pub. The front room seemed small, but this was because it had lost a foot or eighteen inches off every side due to rows of old bookcases that ringed the room entirely, interrupted only by the door and the front window. Some of the bookcases were low, some barely fitted below the ceiling, but all were crammed with volumes. These were not arranged by size, or colour, but, just like how she had spent her career working, arranged by subject. Nick wasn't immediately sure whether he could discern the Dewey system, but he would have been willing to place bets on it being in operation, just unlabelled on the shelf edges.

The immediate impression of small size was exaggerated by the main item of furniture aside from bookcases. In the centre of the room stood a huge, heavy kneehole desk whose leather top and inlaid wooden trim implied that it had once been in the office of a very senior manager of some company or other. It was a prized posession that she had bought at an auction almost immeditely after buying the house. A comfortable swivel chair was set at the desk.

Nick's visits involved dealing with the form filling for the show, and Adele had added a simple kitchen chair on the opposite side of the desk for him, so the two of them faced each other across the brown leather top. She had cleared her usual assortment of neat trays of paperwork off to a shelf so they had room to work. She had no computer, but a small copier lurked on a low side table.

On his first visit Nick sat on the hard kitchen chair, waiting as

Adele made them coffees, looking about at the room and studying the ornate gold embossed border to the leather top of the desk. The bookcases limited the wall space to a minimum, and there were only two pictures hanging on display. One was a small watercolour of a rural scene, the other a yellowing print of an engraving showing the town's main street sometime in the last century. He remembered the manager's office at the bank. There was a similar feel to this room. It was a room that told a visitor, 'I am permanent, established.' He envied Adele her comfortable security.

She brought the coffees, in mugs, but rather fine china mugs, not at all like the thick pottery ones he had at home. She set them down, carefully centering each on a cork coaster to protect the desktop, before seating herself in the swivel chair opposite him. He decided that the situation was rather as though he was being interviewed. He couldn't decide whether he liked this arrangement of their relative status. He was the director of the show after all.

"How have you got on with the bank," she asked. They had quickly discovered that they couldn't get far with grant applications unless a myriad of bits of officialdom were satisfied first.

"No problem. Well it is my field, so I had an idea what would be wanted. I had to drive twenty miles to find a branch now they've closed them all, but that's all right." He was still bitter about branch closures. "I've got the papers here. We need signatures from you, and I, and I've put Duncan on the forms as well. I invented the committee roles, I hope you don't mind."

"It depends what you've listed me as," she said, "I don't really want to be down as treasurer, it's not quite my thing."

"No. I had a long think about it, because what we put will affect who people like the press go pestering for comment when we get close to the performance, and who gets the cudos. I decided that

I'd better be the treasurer as I've got the banking experience..."

"I thought you'd have wanted to be the chairman."

"Not really. The chairman doesn't need to do anything. It's just a nominal position. So I put Duncan in as chair."

"Does he know?"

"Not yet. But it will be fine I'm sure. And you're listed as the secretary so we can refer everything to you. You're the most knowledgable about history and such. Very suitable for a quincentenary."

"I'm not that old!" she jested, "Anyway I see what you've done, you've sorted it so you don't have to deal with any enquiries at all, you just sign cheques when needed and fade into the background."

"Hardly. I'm directing it, remember. Anyway I think we'll all be mucking in together." He was quietly relishing the excuse for frequent meetings and discussions.

"Has Gemma agreed to your making Duncan the chairman?" Adele wanted to know.

Nick was unsure what to say. It hadn't crossed his mind to consider Gemma. He had been confident that Duncan could be foisted into his role as chairmen by promises that it was just a titular arrangement. The possibility of Gemma having an opinion, let alone an objection, had not occurred to him.

""Why? Do you think she might object?"

"I think she doesn't want him to spend yet more time on the show. I think she is secretly pleased, now he's delivered a script, that they can step back and let you do your thing without Duncan wracking his brains to come up with words."

"Well he's bound to find he's having to do some more writing for it as we get started. Things will need altering. Actually there's a bit near the start where..."

"Nick, I'm just suggesting you should probably have sounded them out before putting it down in black and white on official paperwork."

He turned the pages of the account application form back and forth rather sadly, holding the pen over it, wondering if he should make any alteration.

"Don't worry," Adele said, "I'm sure it will be all right. Where do I have to sign?"

He found the page. "Name, address, postcode, position in the society... we're calling it a society, it's easier to set up a club account than a business. Anyway a business would involve us in annual accounts and accountants and all sorts of costs, and it's only going to be for a year, well a year and a half." and he stopped, considering the timescale, acknowledging the way the calandar was ticking by. "Can you fill all that in there, please." He turned the papers round to face her and pushed them across the desk, handing her a pen.

Adele ran a finger down the edge of the sheet, speed reading the salient points with the skill of long practice, before filling in the details he wanted in the boxes, using block capitals where asked for and adding her neat signature in the inadequately small box printed at the bottom.

He took the papers back. "Is Duncan and and Gemma's postcode the same as yours?" he asked.

"I don't know. Postcodes never seem to make much sense to me. There might be a different code on the other side of the road."

"I'd better leave it then, and get Duncan to fill it in himself."

"Are you going over there now?"

"I might as well. It's still early and I could get this all back to the bank tomorrow if I did." He swallowed the last of his coffee. Adele looked a little disappointed, but he failed to notice. She rarely had a visitor in her house and his presence, even if only for business purposes, had enlivened her evening a bit. She debated whether to put her coat on and accompany him to the other side of the street, but it seemed foolish to make a big deal of getting a signature.

"Before I go," he said, and she brightened, "I wondered if you'd care to look at these council grant application forms. See if you think I've put the right sort of things on them."

Disappointedly she took the papers. The form asked for the name of the organisation, "I put Elveston Quincentenary Celebratory Show," he said.

"It's a bit of a mouthful."

"It's descriptive."

After details of any committee, which had been filled in, she saw, as he had decided before discussing it with anyone, the form asked for the 'objects'. He had written: 'To organise and arrange the staging of a historical retrospective performance celebrating the history of the town for its quincentenial year. The show will utilise local performers and trades to create a free admission event for the town.'

"I suspect you'll get a better reaction if you add some line about equal opportunities for all abilities and ethnic backgrounds," she told him.

"You think that would help sway them?"

"In this day and age, yes. You have to wave an equality flag to get anywhere. When we did up the library and the museum it was the main deciding factor at every stage. Access, equality.. no-one gave a damn about books or exhibits."

"You sound rather bitter."

"I don't care much for virtue signalling. Reams of paper being used to write down what everyone is doing anyway."

"OK. I'll put a bit in if you think it will give us a better chance.""

"Exactly. Nothing to do with what you want to produce. Just lip service to the current fad."

Nick scratched his head. How can you make something like this more, or less 'accessible'? I mean the audience is going to be on a flat grass patch, I guess we make sure that at least one of the portaloos is a disabled one, I'm going to cast it on the basis of who's best for the part..."

"And if someone turns up wanting to be Boudicea in a wheechair?"

"Oh for heavens sake.. I don't know. We disguise the thing as her chariot I suppose."

Adele wagged a joking finger at him, "Ah ha! You've got to learn to put the right things on official forms. There are some things that are no longer accepted, and making jokes about this sort of thing is a big no no. You'll get into real trouble. Keep your head down and tell them what they want to hear."

"It's gone beyond 'nanny state' and turned into 1984," he grumbled. But he added a few lines to the 'objects' paragraph before saying, "I made some estimates of costs for the finance bit. As we aren't charging admssion I didn't have to guess at income. What do you think of the expenditure?"

She frowned at the figures.

"Why so low for programmes?"

"Advertising space," he said shortly.

"And materials?"

"Edward and Tamsin are doing us a favour."

"Not that much they can't be. And I don't see lighting and sound, and performing rights for music, and contributions to whichever dance school you end up with, and print costs for copies of scripts and backstage refreshments and, wait a minute, how many portaloos do you think you're going to get for that!"

After another hour and half of drafting and re-drafting the guesstimated budget the financial situation looked dire by comparison to Nick's original up-beat version, and Nick was very depressed.

"Don't worry," Adele told him, "Grants will turn up, we'll find some sponsors from somewhere. Re-do it like that," she pointed to the revised figures, "and put it in and we'll see what happens."

Nick decided it was too late now to call in on Duncan and Gemma, and went home.

Chapter 20
Starting

It was lucky that he called at number 47 after Gemma had left for work. It was no real problem for Nick to persuade Duncan to be listed as chairman of the group. Duncan was willing to agree to almost anything to be rid of Nick quickly. For once he had a freelance commission to write a few paragraphs for a magazine, and he was eager to get on with the work. He supplied the postcode and signed in the box on the bank form without more than a glance, explaining that he was busy and never letting Nick get beyond the hallway.

It wasn't until Gemma came back from work that evening that he mentioned it, and she told him what a fool he was.

"The word I used originally was 'idiot', and you are! Just when you had got shot of the wretched thing apart from the danger of a few re-writes, you go and let yourself be pushed into being the figurehead of the event. I know, I know," she held up her hand to stop him speaking, "It probably is just that, a figurehead, but for the next year and a bit every enquiry is going to come here first, you're going to have to mediate on every petty argument between performers, you'll be the dogsbody of the society, and when it's a success, Nick will get the praise, and if it's a flop it will be your fault."

"I think I'll get the blame if it's a flop just because I wrote it," he said, "but Nick was very definite that I wouldn't have to do anything. He said chairmen never do anything."

"He's right, mostly they don't. But I bet you he'll have you running about dealing with all sorts of inconvenient problems."

Duncan slunk off, subdued. He'd been quite flattered when Nick had called and told him about the various nominal positions, pleased that he was still considered part of the team, because it would have been very easy for the others to have dropped him entirely as soon as the script was finalised. He liked the idea of being recognised for the work he had put in. He thought that Gemma was probably exaggerating the difficulties. And he spent the rest of the evening sulking. It didn't matter, because Gemma was giving him a silent time by avoiding speaking in her annoyance, a state of tension that continued through the whole evening and to bedtime.

The next day she said, out of the blue,

"The trouble is that Nick always gets what he wants. No-one seems to put their view across to him, especially you. Look at the script, he had you re-writing that endlessly, and you say there's still changes to be made. All the others are the same, agreeing with whatever he says, running around trying to please him."

Duncan was surprised by the outburst. It had come unexpectedly after a longish silence as they were getting up. Part of him knew she was right. He certainly hadn't seriously challenged Nick over any of his instructions. He didn't believe the others had either. The presumption, however much discussion took place, was that it was Nick's show, and his opinions held sway. He supposed directors always had their own way, though he had no experience of how staging a performance might work. Vaguely, in the back of his mind, he had an image, inspired by old black and white films he had seen, of a man with a megaphone sitting in a canvas chair telling people where to stand and what to do. He was conscious that the loud hailer was probably something exclusively reserved for the film industry, even that it might be old fashioned in this day and age, but the general principle seemed a likely scenario to him. Faint memories of school plays, which he had not become involved with in his childhood, had a teacher in the centre of the hall shouting at a cast on stage.

Time would reveal that Nick's direction was nothing like the image in Duncan's mind. Once rehearsals did start, several months later, all involved were to discover that Nick's style was hugely laid back.

In the first place he had an all consuming obsession with sightlines, which led to such concern about what did the show look like from extreme seats that he was seldom to be found in the centre of the seating area, being more likely to be wandering about in the areas close to or on one or other extreme edge of the stage area. Additionally he hardly ever raised his voice, so the large cast regularly strained to hear what he was saying.

For his part Nick had the theory that a soft spoken and gentle approach to directing would lead to a happier and more amenable company. In fact the gentle approach resulted in the cast themselves making most of the decisions, so the show slowly came together by a series of group agreements which favoured the more forceful and outspoken people. Outside organisations that had been dragged in, such as musicians and dancers, groups of school children and local societies, fought it out among themselves, sometimes through agreements, often though the muscle of a particular group leader.

Despite this the show was slowly coming together, and at least Nick produced a rehearsal schedule which meant that certain parts of the piece were rehearsed in turn. Since in many cases specific volunteer groups formed a whole scene on their own it was possible for them to rehearse at their own premises with the intention being that they would be fitted into the performance, in the order Duncan had written, as a series of tableaux.

In the vestry after morning service Rev. Luke Grainger began to explain to the choirmaster what they were being asked to do. The St. Georges choirmaster was intensely old fashioned. John Levante was earnest and serious. He was habitually insistant on the pronounciation of his surname implying that the final 'e' had an accent on it and was of some sort of continental origin, and he disliked any disruption of the routines that he had established for his small empire within the parish over the past forty years. Luke's explanation of the choir's requested participation in the coming event was going badly, his choirmaster resisting any suggestion of the singers 'performing', and certainly outside the confines of the church building.

"It's quite an honour to be asked," Luke was saying, "a major civic event, and surely, anything that attracts modern minds' attention to our church must be a good thing?"

John hesitated. He never really saw the choir, his choir, as having any particular connection to the church. It was the location they sang in, and by an unspoken agreement they mostly sang the hymns that the vicar chose each week. Sometimes they were allowed a bit of free licence and he let them perform some ecclesiastical piece that John had rehearsed as a display of their skills. But never did the choirmaster consider it anything other than a performance. However, performance or not he disliked the idea of being part of a show over which he had no real control. In church it was he who gave the nod to Mrs Henson, the organist, when he was ready to start, not influenced in the slightest by the vicar's blatant cue line at the end of a lesson or sermon. If he was honest, John was nervous about a situation in which he could foresee being made to comply with orders and cues from outsiders. Besides there remained the question of what the show would require them to sing. His choir was limited to ecclesiastical music, and he doubted that they would be able to adapt to other genres. He wouldn't want to anyway.

"Well within your field of expertise," said the vicar when he asked, "I understand they just want the second verse of 'Jerusalem'."

"Just the second verse?"

"So it would seem."

"It hardly seems worth turning up for just that. We'd have to get all the suplices and so on washed and ironed, arrange transport for some of the older members. You did know we have to fetch Miss

Turner and Mr Dunhill every Sunday don't you? And practices of course. And..."

"Apparently they only want you in cassocks, no ruffs and surplices, and it's just the one verse as you walk slowly across the stage space."

"It will be slowly with some of my choir," John promised him.

"Ask them if they'd like to do it, to be be part of the event." Luke told him, straightening a dusty pile of hymn books and hoping that the man might somehow be sold on the idea of participating in a big show in the town.

Catherine James and Simone had finished the day's dance classes and were in the corner café with cups of coffee looking at Duncan's script.

"I think it might be rather exciting," Simone said. She had been a pupil of the dance school since she was an infant, graduating through the endless exams and certificates until, having left school, and with no job, Catherine had taken her on as an assistant, mostly to supervise classes of toddlers and infants, allowing her, as the owner of the school, to spend more time with students who were going through exams.

"What? Appearing as armies on battle fields?" Catherine tried to put disapproval in her voice.

"We could choreograph them to march about very quickly, it wouldn't take up much time, and he can hardly refuse to let us do a couple of our existing dance routines if we play ball with him over being extras to make up his army numbers."

"You think our girls would want to be soldiers?"

"I can think of several who are ready made for it," Simone joked, she went off at a tangent, "Did you see Phoebe and Gillian on

Saturday morning? I thought Gillian would be bald if I didn't separate them."

"Yes, what was that all about, I forgot to ask."

"The excuse was something about Pheobe using Gillian's make-up, but actually they're at daggers drawn over some boy. It seems he dumped Phoebe last week, and had been seen out with Gillian."

Catherine shrugged and gave a short mirthless laugh, saying, "Oh god save us from teenage hormones. Anyway I don't see from this script that anyone actually fights, it all seems to be armies marching and setting up camps."

"I'm sure Phoebe would be pleased if there was some fighting."

"She'll have forgotten all about it long before, when is it? the end of April." She finished her coffee and started to get up, gathering a collection of cloth haversacks and a huge portable music player, the strap of which she heaved onto her green tracksuit clad shoulder. Simone rose too, helping to pick up the bags, which were half surrounding the little formica topped table they had been sitting at. "I'll tell Nick we'll do it then, if you're sure we've got time to teach them all to march. We'd better decide which dance routines we want to do too. It sounds as though it will be on grass, which isn't ideal, so possibly the Michael Jackson numbers are out. 'It's raining men' or one of the Bond themes might be OK though."

Chapter 21
First Rehearsal

Nick found that getting anyone to rehearse anything in the summer was quite impossible. Almost invariably one or more vital member of any scene was away on holiday, or about to be. He became frustrated by this. Adele found he was more and more frequently hanging around the museum, usually on a rather lame excuse about checking some historical detail for the show. It struck her that the director was spending more time looking into the town's history, despite having lived there for decades, than Duncan, who was a newcomer, had done when writing the script. She quickly realised that he was kicking his heels. She decided that he was killing time because he wanted to start the process of lifting the show from the page and turning it into a living, flesh and blood, performance. It didn't occur to her to wonder why he idled away his time in her museum instead of at home or in the pub.

It was late September before rehearsals properly started. Nick had his first intimation of how weather dependent the whole project was likely to be. He had called a rehearsal of those involved in the early scenes of the Romans and of Boudicea one Sunday. By pleading and wheedling he had succeeded in getting agreements from the Scouts and Catherine for the boys and the dancers to be brought for this initial 'blocking rehearsal'. He'd heard somewhere that the term was used to describe setting the moves for the actors, rather than going through lines, and felt that this was probably the most important thing at this early stage. He used the word 'blocking', now that he had discovered it, repeatedly. With great ambition he had also arranged for the volunteers who were going to build staging and scenery, and those who would be laying out the site, as well as the company that would be supplying lighting and sound, to all attend that day, ignoring the potential difficulty for him of trying to explain his vision to half a dozen different interested parties at once at the same time as instructing performers.

159

The day dawned dull, and grey with theatening clouds. It had been a wet week, and an optimist would have said that that morning was much better than the constant drizzle that had gone before. Duncan gave Adele a lift to Elveston Lodge. They arrived along the drive to find a number of vehicles already scattered untidily around the perimeter of the front lawn of the house. Tyre tracks across the lawn, pushed down into the wet, slightly too-long, grass showed the routes people had taken to where they had stopped. At one point on the far side a curved brown streak revealed the underlying soil where someone had turned too sharply on the slippery surface before coming to a halt to park. There were people wandering about. Adults, many with worried expressions, repeatedly calling to try to gather their charges together, and children of all ages, some huddled in groups, others wandering aimlessly around the space.

Duncan turned the car away from the house on the side where the driveway entered the lawn, feeling the wheels slip in the wet as he pulled up among some other parked vehicles. They got out. The house looked more drab and neglected than he remembered it from the original visit. Maybe it was the dull light of the day, but he felt that it had become more run down in the intervening months that had passed.

Basil emerged from the side of the house furthest from them, ducking below damp overhanging branches and giving an air of bemused berwilderment. He stopped in front of his house, at the foot of the steps that led to his door. They could see the confusion on his face. Adele made straight over to him. Duncan could see her taking his arm and talking to him solicitously. Basil shook his head a few times before her earnest words seemed to get through to him and he nodded. She led the old man back the way he had come.

Duncan went and joined Nick. The director was at the centre of a crowd of people, all wanting his attention. As Duncan arrived a man in a denim suit with a clipboard was saying, "We do need to know exactly where you want it.." at the same time as a young girl in a fluorescent yellow tracksuit was saying, "... and she says that the grass is too slippery for us to come down that slope..."

Duncan saw that Nick was overwhelmed by the sheer bulk of decisions that needed to be made, by his inexperience at this sort of thing, and by the poor weather. He felt an unusual urge to take control and beat some semblance of order into the mêlé. Nick had a loud-hailer dangling from a strap over his shoulder. It was as if he had dressed up as some sort of fancy dress idea of a film director, with his cord trousers and open necked shirt.

Boldly, and with his metaphorical fingers crossed, Duncan pushed his hand between two of the people crowding around, took the megaphone from Nick and lifted it to his mouth, pressing the trigger. "Thank you all for coming..." He was startled by the amplifed sound of his own voice and confused by the way what he said echoed off the front of Elveston Lodge and came back to him whole moments after he had said it. The delay in hearing what his brain thought he was saying confused him and he stopped.

Nick stretched fully upright and moved his head side to side to see through the throng surrouinding him, clearly wondering what Duncan intended to say.

Duncan tried again, concentrating to get the words out,

"...We know you all have lots of questions. Things will get clearer as we go along. Please be patient. We'd like to start with the Romans. Could the Scout leaders get their boys together and ready to enter over there.."

He pointed, though it was doubtful if anyone could see him, even if they knew where he was speaking from. In a way it didn't matter. The announcement had the desired effect of scattering the crowd back to their groups, leaving a very few hard core people to continue their demands on Nick.

Duncan handed the megaphone back to Nick, saying, "Get them under way now while they think something's about to start."

Nick grabbed the loud hailer gratefully and began issuing instructions, ignoring the persistant inqisition from the handful of adults around him. Away to the left of the house a group of uniformed scouts, led by a grown up, marched, rather smartly, into view from behind some bushes and came down a slope to the main lawn, where they halted and began assembling some small tents they were carrying.

More instructions came from Nick. Duncan watched, distracted after a few moments by someone coming very close behind him and whispering in his ear, "We'll make some more Roman looking tents for them for the show."

He spun round, startled, finding himself actually touching Jenny she was standing so closely as she had said this. He took a half pace back but somehow this was no better, for now he could hardly avoid looking at her. She had obviously been on the site for some time, because the thin cotton dress she ws wearing had become soaked from the drizzle and was clinging to her from its plungingly low neckline to its too short hem.

"Oh, sorry. I didn't see you there." Duncan blushed and floundered. He wondered again why the woman had this ability to make him feel embarassed just by being nearby.

Jenny took hold of his arm, saying, "Poor dear, I made you jump." but then didn't release her hold, starting to talk to him about things that were going to be made for the show. She described tents and banners and costumes and props, many of which he had never even considered as he had written the piece, but which she and Nick had clearly discussed and decided were needed.

Scout tents were up and a few, totally inaudible, lines of dialogue were being delivered by script-clutching characters as Nick could be heard getting Boudicea's army to enter from the same place.

A group of teenage girls, nearly all in tracksuit bottoms over leotards, appeared from the same bushes. They started down the slope. Many slipped and slithered, and Duncan saw that they were mostly wearing dance shoes. There was some chaos. A woman's voice could be heard shouting, "I told you this would happen," and the confusion was added to by several of the 'Roman army' starting to wolf whistle the girls.

Nick was saying "Stop, stop, stop.." down his megaphone. Duncan became aware that Jenny had still not released him. Adele joined them.

"I think Nick needs assistant directors to deal with large numbers like this," she said.

Jenny said, "Weren't there going to be horses for the ancient Britons?"

"Celts," corrected Adele absently, as she watched the small shambles on the other side of the lawn.

"All right, Celts then," said Jenny, "But weren't there?"

Duncan nodded, "I thought we'd approached the pony club."

"We did, and they agreed," Adele assured him, "We ought to remind Nick and see how that's going to work."

They crossed the lawn. Duncan was relieved that Jenny released him to do this, though he knew it was only because they were hurrying to join the discussion. Nick was fending off complaints about the wet grass surface from the girls and their tutor, not Catherine James, Duncan noticed, but one of her assistants. Someone was calling the scouts to order, but was having an uphill battle to restore order against the distraction of the arrival of the girls.

Adele asked Nick about the horses.

"Ah yes," he said, clearly having forgotten, then raising his voice said to the girls, "Have any of you done any horse riding?"

A few nodded and raised their hands. "We're trying to get the loan of some ponies for this scene, so if we do, when we do, we'll get those of you who can ride to enter on horseback."

Somewhere a voice said "Neat."

"At least something this morning has met with approval," Nick muttered to Duncan.

He made the scouts take the tents down and come back on again to re-erect them, but half way through this process the sky blackened immediately prior to a downpour which was accompanied by sudden and unexpected gusts of wind. Scouts fought with flapping wet canvas, and the Celts never did make their entrance again. By mutual agreement cast and crew abandoned rehearsal, rushing back to their cars to make an escape. Some cars became overloaded as people who had walked to the house cadged lifts with those who had driven. Duncan found himself with Jenny and two of the dancers in his back seat in addition to Adele in front alongside him.

He started the engine, waiting while the blower slowly cleared the condensation that had instantly formed on his winscreen as soon as they had all crowded damply aboard. He watched the headlights of other cars sweeping across the grass as they headed for the driveway and left. Eventually he followed a pair of red tail lights glinting in the refractions of the wet window and left too.

The dancers had to give him directions to their homes, because he still didn't really know the town. Back eventually in Greendale Road he pulled into the drive of number forty-seven, letting his neighbour passengers out to cross the road to their homes. Jenny leaned through the gap between the front seats and kissed his cheek, saying "Thank you for the lift," before getting out.

Adele gathered her belongings from the footwell as she got out. She stood outside the car holding one of her cake tins looking at Duncan almost coyly.

"I was going to share these round at the rehearsal, but the moment never came did it? Would you like them?" she asked.

Duncan had no real choice but to ask her in.

Chapter 22
A New Acquaintance

"Poor Nick," Adele said, as soon as she was installed on a chair at the kitchen table, watching Gemma boil the kettle, "it didn't really go very well did it? She looked to Duncan for his agreement.

Duncan shrugged, avoiding saying too much about what had clearly been a wet and demoralising shambles of a rehearsal by watching the rain dribbling down the window of the kitchen. Usually he would have been able to see out into the garden, where Gemma had made a serious start on planting and cultivating the beds. Today the view was one of bleary grey and little illumination came from there. Gemma had the kitchen light on, but this seemed only to emphasise the gloom outside. He was depressed by the morning's events.

"What went wrong, apart from the weather, obviously?" Gemma asked, looking back over her shoulder from where she was spooning instant coffee into the mugs.

"Too many people asking too many questions, so Nick didn't get any chance to tell them what to do. You tried with the loud-hailer didn't you, Duncan?" Adele told her.

"You did?" Gemma queried, "I thought you just went to watch."

"Well it did seem that Nick needed some help." Duncan knew what his wife was going to say. She would tell him to step back from it, to let Nick fight his own battles. Not to get further involved than his authorship had already made him.

Before he could begin to offer excuses Adele told Gemma,

"Duncan was very good, he called them to order and then handed straight over to Nick. We might have not got anything done otherwise, but a second voice was really helpful."

She smiled at Duncan. "Nick needs someone to help him with directing this," she added.

"Perhaps you could," Gemma cut in quickly.

"I thought Duncan might, after all he knows the show, he should do, he wrote it... thank you, do have some cakes," she broke off as Gemma handed her the coffee, and opened her cake tin. "And he did get them all to pay attention this morning." Adele held out the tin toward Gemma and then to Duncan, who each took a cake from the pile crammed in it.

They said 'thank you' and both told her how much they admired her cake making skills. After the slight interruption Gemma persisted, saying,

"I don't think Duncan has got the time, have you?"

"No, not really." he said, eager to let Gemma know he was agreeing with her. There was a second of excitement though, at the idea of being an assistant director and having some control over the way his script was performed. He wasn't wildly proud of the script, but he was very unimpressed by Nick's showing that morning, even if the circumstances, and the elements, had been against him.

He saw that Gemma was looking at him with a curious expression. Surely he had satisfied her determination that he should divorce himself from the show as much as possible by agreeing with her fiction that he was too busy? Adele too noticed Gemma's look.

With the confidence that only age could give she said, "I should wipe that lipstick off your cheek, Duncan. Gemma has spotted it."

Duncan's hand shot to his cheek where Jenny had kissed him, and rubbed. Adele said to Gemma, "We had to give Jenny a lift back when the rain came. You know what she's like when she says 'thank you'!"

"As long as it was only the lift she was thanking you for," Gemma muttered, adding, "These cakes are delicious. How do you always manage to produce such wonderful things?"

Duncan sank into one of his ruminative moods, drifting away from the inconsequential chat, thinking about his script, and the show, and, by association, and perhaps due to Adele's presence, the old Dragon Fair.

Gemma must have been thinking about it too because after a while, as the conversation flagged, she asked Adele, "Something's been puzzling me. Why did girls enter the raffle to be 'maidens'. What made you do it?"

"Apart from the cash prize you mean?"

"Yes, apart from the cash prize."

"Well there was always some peer pressure. Mostly groups of girls. You know the sort of thing, 'I will if you will'. And there was always an element of a dare about it too. But I suppose you have to remember the effect of teen hormones as well. It was a fairly frustrating period of time, lots of pop music about love, and precious little really happening in most girls' lives." she paused and thought for a moment, "Yes I think it was all of those things for most of us."

It was a quiet afternoon and evening following that. Gemma, some of her curiosity about the teenage Adele's motives satisfied, was now rather more concerned that Duncan would offer himself up to be Nick's assistant than about Jenny's recent behaviour. Logic told her that Jenny was an outrageous flirt, and that Duncan was perfectly safe with her. She worried more about Nick. Nick who seemed to have a facility for persuading people to do things he wanted or needed them to do. He'd wheedled Duncan into supplying the script, now the risk that he would press her husband into a longer lasting commitment to the event concerned her. She realised, with the sagacity bred of management roles in different firms, that Nick also seemed to be able to influence Adele. If both he and their neighbour were to work on Duncan she was sure he would cave in. She left for work on the Monday morning still worrying about this possibility. As she drove along the now familiar route to work, cursing the muddy spray from the vehicle in front, she seethed inwardly. The rain had stopped, leaving the roads wet and dirty, and the spray that hit her windsceen almost constantly dried in semi opaque smears if she used her wipers. She found herself hitting wash-wipe repeatedly, and wondering when she had last topped up the washer bottle.

Duncan stared at the contents of the kitchen cupboard. He had washed up and was wondering if he needed to make any advance preparations for his lunch. Gemma hadn't given him any instructions, presumably because of her continuing evident annoyance, and he'd been caught out like this before. Several times his self catering attempts had gone awry because he had forgotten, or not realised, that he needed to heat up the oven, or start something cooking long before he actually wanted his lunch. It wasn't that he minded cooking something for himself, but he wasn't keen on eating lunch at three o'clock in the afternoon.

He found nothing that was obviously intended for him or looked particularly perishable. Sure that he had avoided being told off for missing something that would have to be thrown out as a result he decided to eat out. A pub meal beckoned.

Backing his Fiat off the drive he made for the town centre and the old coaching inn. He could have gone to the local, the 'Dog and Dray', but something prompted him to try the old inn that was said to have been the centre of the Dragon Fair.

He turned under the archway and easily found a parking space on the gravel surface of the old coach yard. The building was quiet, an air of desperate desolation, the last image for a hostelry to project. Inside the furnishings were old and worn. He might have thought them welcoming if there had been people about, but the lack of customers gave the opposite impression. A woman in a black waitress dress appeared and asked if she could help him. Hearing his apologetic 'I was hoping to get something to eat' she directed him to a dining room. Several rows of tables, each with linen cloths and laid with cutlery and starched serviettes filled the room. Two customers sat about half way into the room, waiting to be served. They turned to watch him curiously. He recognised one of them just as the man's eyes lit with surprise at seeing him.

"Why, it's Duncan!" said the vicar. To his companion he said, "Duncan Newbon. You remember I was telling you, he's written the script for the quincentenary show."

The other man gave an 'Ah' of understanding, and said, "Come and join us."

Duncan didn't know what to do. He had no real wish to foist himself on their tête-a- tête, on the other hand sitting alone at a separate table in an empty room would be downright embarassing. The waitress hovered, waiting for his decision, one hand on a chair at another table, ready to pull it out for him.

"If you're sure I'm not intruding?" he said, getting predictable assurances from the two, and the waitress pulled out a seat at the table they were occupying, saw him seated, and immediately began relaying a place setting where he was. The layout as he sat down made it quite clear that only minutes before she had removed two unused settings when the vicar and his companion had been seated.

"This is Simon, Simon Dunbar," Luke told him as the waitress put a menu in front of him, "you'll be interested in his history, Duncan."

"Sorry, have you already ordered?"

"Yes, but only a moment ago. We're having the Steak and Ale

pie."

He looked up at the woman, hovering, notepad in hand, "I'll have the same, and a pint of lager please. Have you got a low alcohol one?" She nodded and went away.

"Sorry, you were saying?"

Luke became animated.

"Simon's agreed to tell me all about the details of the Dragon Fair. You see I've decided to write a book about it."

Duncan felt disappointment. The project he'd been nursing quietly in the back of his mind was suddenly blown out of the water. He'd assumed that the vicar had been trawling the church archives purely for his own interest. He'd even partly believed Gemma's guess that the man had been deriving some vicarious pleasure from the more raunchy details of the thing. If the vicar published an account, however small its circulation, however short on details, however badly written, anything that he produced about the fair would be seen as copying. He hated the idea that he might be thought to be plagurising the vicar's research, or trying to steal his thunder. He made suitable encouraging noises and wished his drink would hurry up so he could disguise his disappointment by sipping it.

"Simon was a dragon," Luke announced.

Duncan studied the man. He was probably in his mid seventies. Well built and quite smartly dressed for these days, when most of the population wore sweat shirts and jeans. Simon was in the sports jacket and pressed trousers club.

"Oh? Which year?" he asked.

"Nineteen sixty-one." Simon said, speaking confidently and with no sign of making any secret of it. Duncan found that rather refreshing. He had become used to anything dragon related being mentioned in mumbles and mutters by most of the town's population.

Duncan's drink arrived. He said 'thank you'.

"Was that the year Adele...?"

Luke shook his head, "No, she was the next year."

Simon said, "A pity really, she was a pretty 'maiden'."

Duncan's mind began trying to envisage Adele as a pretty maiden. He found it difficult to picture what the woman would have been like fifty odd years earlier, now his image of her was of an Agatha Christie character complete with coat and handbag. He was also slightly disturbed by Simon. He had been seated next to him, facing Luke, so he was unable, without obviously twisting around, to get a good look at the man's expression. The phrase about Adele being 'a pretty maiden' rang warning bells. Somehow the idea of this man of, what? seventy-something, commenting on the appearance of girls fifty years ago seemed odd. Could he have made a statement like that about someone he had only seen appear at an event that long ago? He doubted it. He would have needed to have at least been friendly with them.

Luke began saying, "Simon is able to tell me all about how the thing worked, what happened when and where.. things that the plain records don't tell you. So we thought that using his actual experience we could make quite an interesting book."

Duncan nodded. It was just what he would have wanted to dredge up if he'd been able to write the story. Sadly he had to acknowledge that the vicar had pipped him to that post. His only hope would be if Simon and Luke failed to publish, or if what they put in print was too bland or unreadable. Studying them and their eagerness he doubted either of these scenarios was likely.

172

"Mind you," Simon carried on, "my 'maiden' was very pretty too. Though she was a naughty little girl really," he added.

Duncan's ears pricked up at the phrase 'little girl'. He asked "Why, in what way?"

Simon gave a small sigh, as if this was something he had related already, and Duncan saw the vicar nodding thoughtfully, so he had obviously already heard.

"She and her friends only went in for the thing as a sort of dare. She kept it secret from her parents, particularly from her father, who happened to be the local Methodist Minister.. that caused some upset, as you can imagine."

Duncan noticed there was no reaction to this from Luke.

"When the weekend was over, and she had banked the cheque, she booked herself onto a round the world cruise. Remember, in those days that was almost unheard of. She came back eventually, but went to live somewhere in Essex, I think."

"She didn't patch things up with her parents?"

Luke shook his head and said, "I doubt there was any chance of that from what I've heard about her 'condition' when she finally got back to England. We don't know for sure, but that child may have been the last of the 'George and Dragon' offsprings. Equally we don't actually know who she may have met on board ship, or even ashore, on her round the world cruise."

"But it might have been your child?" Duncan asked Simon rather directly.

"You think I should have asked? It could equally well have been the bloke who played St. George that year, or anyone she'd met. You couldn't prove a thing in those days remember. At least not easily."

Chapter 23
Revelations

"Tell Duncan what you were telling me about the actual event," the vicar suggested, clearly trying to avoid the paternity subject that had arisen.

"It was supposed to be what you'd call today 'a family day out'. The kids didn't need to know about the overnight arrangements. But over the years, even from when I was a child and used to go to watch, somehow the crowd got rowdier. They drew the winner for 'Dragon' first. That was me. I'd entered for obvious reasons, along with dozens of others. So had 'St. George', he got drawn next. Most of the entrants were late teens or early twenties, but there weren't any rules about that.."

"Did you get older men entering then?"

"A few. Anyway my year we were both about twenty I guess. As soon as we'd been picked we were hustled off by some stewards to get changed. Well I had to. I don't think St. George needed to get into costume till the next day."

"Where did that happen?" Luke asked.

"One of the main street shops has a sort of store beside it. It was an ironmongers in those days, though it became Freeman, Hardy and Willis."

"I know it," said Luke, "The one that's now the British Heart Foundation shop."

"No. I think that's next door. The one we used is now the Pound shop. Anyway they put me in my Dragon costume. We could hear the crowd when the 'Maiden', Ella, was announced. Then there was quite a long gap while she was taken somewhere and dressed up, well undressed really, and they gave her a double brandy I think ."

He stopped as their meals arrived, and there was a brief period of ordering more drinks and asking for mustard. Once they were all eating Luke said, "And?"

"Oh, mmm," Simon was caught with his mouth full, "Well eventually I came out onto the Market Place in this dragon costume. Have you seen pictures?"

Duncan said he had, but still wanted to know what it was really like.

"Rather silly quite frankly." Simon said between bites, "It was very well made and robust, but it was just a sort of sleeveless jacket, with a long tail hanging off the back, all covered with cloth scales in different colours, and a dragon head that sat on your shoulders. It was strapped on and you looked out of the mouth. You could open and shut the mouth by a cord. Your arms were inside the jacket so no-one saw the cord. You couldn't see much if you shut the jaws, but you had to, once the maiden had been given to you, because they hung the end of her lead on one of your lower teeth and it would have fallen off if you didn't keep the jaw shut."

"The maiden was on a lead?"

"Not really a lead, she had one end of a ribbon attached to a collar round her neck, and the other got hooked onto the dragon's teeth." he noticed the shock on both their faces, "Oh it wasn't a proper lead, just a symbol. It was about three or four yards long. I, the Dragon, came out of the double doors of the store when it was time. They had a half a dozen stewards around me to keep the crowd at bay. I was pleased about that, they were pushing and shoving and shouting at me and I couldn't see properly, like I said."

"Did they have any sort of commentary or announcements?"

Duncan wanted to know.

"Yes, but I doubt anyone could hear. Especially when the maiden was bought out. I expect Ella must have been terrified. I mean she might have known what it was like, she must have known what was going to happen to her, but being on the receiving end of that mob... I mean she'd been picked out in the draw, taken to someone's house and undressed, put in that flimsy white gown. Then they led her out barefoot and hardly clothed into the square. Half the men were shouting obscene suggestions and half the women were calling her names like 'whore' and 'slut', and then she's confronted by a man dressed up as a dragon and she gets led the length of the street to here."

"To here?" queried Duncan.

Luke scraped the last of his pie around his plate to mop up the gravy and answered for Simon, who was glad to be able to attend to his meal for a while.

"Yes, here. This hotel, well 'Inn', they call it. It's always been the place where the maiden got deflowered and then used the next night by St. George." Luke said.

Simon said, "In the same room actually, the one at the end of that corridor," he gestured with his fork, "so far as we can make out that room every year since it all started."

Duncan leant sideways in a pointless attempt to see along the corridor outside the dining room door. The action caught the attention of an elderly couple who had arrived been sat at a table a little way away from the three men. They watched him curiously. They were old enough that they had long exhausted any conversation, and had been straining to hear what Simon was saying. Duncan was conscious, now, of their evesdropping, and said to the others more quietly, "And when you got here?"

"The stewards helped me out of the dragon suit and we were both locked into that room," again the fork pointed vaguely, and there we stayed till about lunchtime the next day."

"And you raped her?"

"Oh not you as well! Look the whole set-up might be old fashioned now, but it was accepted tradition then. The maidens agreed by entering, we men agreed too. The phrase 'consenting adults' applied."

"It might depend on the definition of 'adult' or even 'consent'," Duncan muttered, "What about food?"

"There was a very generous sort of buffet thing laid out in the room, and they brought breakfast in in the morning. Obviously there was drink too.."

"So as to keep the girl drunk?"

"The girl, Ella, was very willing once we got here. It was just the public that scared her in the street. I suppose she was lucky really, I mean I can remember one year, I suppose I was about thirteen or fourteen, when it rained so hard that the girl's gown got soaked and went all transparent. You could see everything through it. And a few generations back it is rumoured that the girls were paraded naked anyway."

Luke ignored that and said, "It's funny isn't it. This town's re-enactment of the George and the Dragon story lets the dragon win the girl at first and then be rescued later, and then hands her over to St. George, but usually accounts have her saved by him, and then he is offered her but goes all puritanical and refuses. I wonder why Elveston changed that plot line."

"I went to Heaton-Bassett the other day to look at stuff about their River Snake thing," Duncan told them, "The girl at the museum there said their girl was raffled just the same and given to whoever played the snake. They seem to think their event was based on a sort of ritual sacrifice, and she made the point that the snake was very phallic."

Luke nodded, "I looked into that too, but it finished so long ago now that it's hard to get beyond the few drawings and pictures."

"Surely there must be private photographs of the Dragon Fair in existence, even if the newspaper ones are all lost, I mean you were part of it in, what, nineteen sixty-one. There were plenty of cameras around then."

The waitress arrived to clear the table, and they chose desserts. When she had gone Simon checked with Luke. "Can I show him?"

"I think so," said Luke, "He might write things down that you've told him, but he can't copy pictures can he?"

Simon reached into his inside pocket and removed a paper wallet. It bore the advertising for 'Gratispool' and opened on the table to reveal half a dozen postcard sized colour prints in one half and some orange shaded negatives in the other. He slid the prints to his right so they were in front of Duncan. Duncan studied them. The first two were rather poor shots of a crowd in the market place. The people were hemmed in by the stalls of the Saturday market, not dissimilar to how he had seen the square on market days since he moved to Elveston, though with many more stalls and a lot more people. The next shot showed the Dragon emerging from the doorway of the store Simon had described. It was blurred from camera shake and a thumb had blocked the bottom right of the shot, but you could see the dragon, and some stewards having trouble holding back members of the crowd who were gesticulating violently. In the next picture a young, petite long-haired girl, apparently tied by the neck to the dragon's teeth was cringing away from the crowd, protected only by an inadequate number of crowd marshals. She was barefoot, and the sleeveless white gown which was cut to mid-thigh, left little doubt that she was otherwise nude.

Other pictures showed the back of the couple making their way out of the square and toward the inn, just visible in the distance. There was one final shot, of a man dressed in silver armour, clearly made of cardboard, with a St. George flag draped over him, slashing at the Dragon with a wooden sword as the Dragon rolled helplessly on the ground hemmed in by an excited throng. The girl was behind them, dressed as before except for an apparent stain on the front of her gown.

Duncan pointed at the stain. "What's that?"

"There was another gown for the second day," Simon explained, "It had fake blood on the front.. to show what had happened to her, in case anyone had any doubt."

"I think that may be the most disgusting detail of the whole thing," Duncan said.

"The most disgusting thing is how that year's George attacked me for real with that sword. I mean it might only be a wooden sword but in the dragon costume you haven't got any arms to protect yourself, you can see he's really properly hitting me. I don't remember any other year when that happened, but he was a nasty bloke, Angus, he was known for getting into fights."

Their desserts arrived, and Simon packed the snapshots away.

As they ate Duncan asked if there was any chance of seeing the room, and was told it would be no problem, as it was never booked out to the public and was kept as something of a shrine in memory of the fair. After the meal they went to reception and were given the key. The girl on the desk clearly recognised both Simon and Luke, because she smiled at Simon and said jokingly, "Revisiting the scene of the crime again?"

The long white walled passage led to a door right at the rear of the Inn. Simon unlocked it and stepped aside to let Duncan go in. The room showed its age. He saw at once why the Inn didn't let it out. The old flooring was uneven and canted slightly, so you tended to enter too fast, discovering, as Duncan did, that the space was fairly restricted. There was an old fashioned chest acting as a dressing table to the left, a double bed with a sort of canopy at the head. He remembered once being told this was called a 'half-testa', an old wooden chair, and the doorway to a bathroom and toilet. This had obviously been installed a long while ago, as the cast iron bath stood under an old fashioned geyser on its claw and ball feet, beside a crazed china toilet, with a cast iron cistern above, worked by a chain dangling from the arm weighted down by a white china handle. The door to this bathroom was missing, and splintered timber in the frame seemed to show that the hinges had been forcibly ripped away.

"What happened to the bathroom door?" Duncan asked.

"The year after me," Simon told him, "The maiden didn't like the dragon and tried to lock herself in there in the middle of the night. He broke the door down. They never replaced it."

"That would have been Adele then!"

Luke said, "Yes. Didn't you know she had a fight with her dragon?"

Duncan shook his head and turned to a pair of coat hooks by the door they had entered through. From each hung a hanger with a white gown inside a clear plastic bag on it. One gown had had a brownish red stain added low down on its front.

"The two gowns for the Maidens." Luke explained.

Duncan gently lifted the plastic cover up and felt the fabric of the unstained dress. It was thin cotton, almost translucently thin. He let go guiltily, somehow feeling he had intruded on someone's private affair.

On the way home he mulled over eveything Simon had told him.

He could hardly wait for Gemma to come back from work.

181

Chapter 24
More Rehearsals

She came into the house in a furious temper, flinging a bulging file of papers on the table, which he was mid-way through setting for tea.

"Good day at the office, dear?" he asked flippantly.

She snapped, "Does it look like it? I'm going to be hours trying to sort out this mess."

He curtailed his joking and asked what had happened.

"Damn fool driver! Got sent to Stamford Bridge with a load, and went to Yorkshire."

Duncan couldn't see the problem.

"Because he was supposed to go to Stamford Bridge in London, not the other one!" she explained.

"Ah. Oh well easily confused I suppose. Surely you just tell him to come back."

"I can't, he'd be over his driving hours before he did.

He crept quietly away, and while he got their tea ready he could hear her on the phone arranging for a relief driver to be taken as a passenger in another truck heading to Yorkshire. She came into the kitchen more calmly then.

"Sorry about that," she said, "but it gets me so angry. He had the post-code. All he had to do was put it in his sat-nav, but he just put the town in and it took him the wrong way. How was your day?"

As they ate he told her all he had discovered.

"I knew Adele didn't like her Dragon," she said, "more from what she didn't say about him than anything else. I wonder who it was. It sounds as though he was pretty violent to wreck a door."

Duncan was more interested in the risqué aspects of what he had been told.

"I never thought about how the crowd would have behaved," he told Gemma, "And I certainly didn't know the girl was dragged through the streets almost nude. I mean if that's what they did of course the crowd would be rowdy, heaven knows what it must have been like back in the days when they were actually naked."

"It's certainly got you interested hasn't it? Anyway you obviously can't write about it now. I wonder who Adele's Dragon was though."

"I don't know, but from what they said she certainly seems to have earned her prize money!"

At the end of the week Gemma accompanied him to the rehearsal at Elveston Lodge. It was a sunnier day than the last time he had attended. Once again the lawns were littered with parked cars, and this time with some horse boxes. There was also a significant smattering of vans, several of which bore the names of companies and what were to Duncan mysterious details of the owners' services. He vaguely understood lighting, and sound, but 'location services' and 'production company' bemused him. Gemma squeezed his hand. "It's getting a bit big," she whispered as they walked toward Nick, "Now remember not to get conned into becoming his assistant or anything, you've done your bit and you're going above and beyond by agreeing to do any re-writes he suddenly wants."

Duncan said, "Yes dear," but part of him hoped he would be directly asked to help.

Nick greeted them with smiles. They saw Adele was beside him also welcoming them. All around groups of people were moving about, forming into huddles to discuss things and dragging boxes and bundles of odd items to different parts of the grounds. They sat down on the grass, near enough to Nick's base of operations to look as though they were part of the production team, and far enough away to avoid constant conversation with him.

The loudhailer was in use. The cast were largely ignoring it, still talking among themselves, but the instructions were going out with the intention of making a start. A tall man with a commanding presence mounted a rostrum that had been placed roughly centrally in front of the house's steps. A small boy joined him. They began at the start of Duncan's script.

The child was softly spoken, Duncan knew what he was saying because he had written it. Possibly Nick knew too, he had the script on his knees. Most of the rest of the assembled people probably didn't even know that lines were being spoken, certainly they made no attempt to quieten down. Two men strode past wearing tee shirts that said 'Yes it does have to be this loud' on the back. One was saying to the other, "No they'll both have to have radios."

The child finished whatever it was he was saying and the man's voice cut across the background noise, "It was just over there," he pointed dramatically, "The Romans were setting up camp..."

"Where the hell are the Romans?" Nick said through the megaphone.

A distracted looking Scout leader peered out from behind the bushes, "We didn't know you'd started," he shouted.

"Do the cue line again Frank," Nick said using his loud-hailer.

Frank said, "The Romans were setting up camp," and pointed again. Scouts poured out from behind the bushes carrying canvas and poles which were assembled into a row of quite convincing Roman tents with commendable speed, before lining up, each holding a sword and a rectangular Roman style shield.

"...when the Iceni under Boudicea charged down the hill toward them..."

There was a slight pause and a handful of ponies emerged from where they had been concealed. Each was ridden by a teenage girl, incongruously wearing bright coloured dance leotards, but waving wooden spears. More dancers were to be seen, among the horses or following behind, all carrying spears and mostly with round shields. The Romans made a wall of their shields, touching the edges together, the attacking Iceni charged them, carefully aiming their cardboard ended wooden spears at the centre of the Roman shields. There was a ragged thudding and a single yelp of pain. The horses were in the way so Duncan and Gemma, and perhaps more importantly Nick and Adele, couldn't really see what had happened. One horse pranced sideways in defiance of any attempt of its rider to keep it still, and in the gap that opened they could see some dropped shields and a scout doubled up clutching his stomach as a Scout leader and two dancers bent solicitously to see what his trouble was.

The rehearsal ground to a halt.

The discovery that the attackers' spears could slide off the curve of the Roman shields and go through the gap between two of them led to long discussions, despite assurances that the boy wasn't really hurt. What little discipline had been achieved among the onlookers, both cast and crew, vanished as everyone expressed an opinion.

A full quarter of an hour passed before Nick was able to say, "From the top again," and the tents were dismantled.

The small boy delivered his inaudible lines again.

"It was just over there," said Frank and pointed dramatically, "The Romans were setting up camp..."

The tent assembly wasn't as slick this time. Some parts seemed to have to have been mislaid in the disassembly and there was considerable confusion before Frank could add, "...when the Iceni under Boudicea charged down the hill toward them..."

The Iceni were very slow appearing, and seemed short of numbers.

"Where's the rest of them? I thought we had five horses!" Nick said to Adele.

The girls attacked the Roman wall without incident this time, but also unconvincingly and gently, making the rout of the might of Rome rather unconvincing. Nick determind to press on regardless and for the next half hour Duncan's script was lamely delivered alongside clumsy action with frequent, often inexplicable, halts and delays.

Eventually Nick called a break and people produced packed lunches and thermos flasks.

Adele asked Gemma if they had brought anything, and being told 'no' immediately produced one of her tins and offered them cakes, sharing her flask of coffee too. Duncan asked what had happened to the missing horse and was told that it had become too frisky and its owner had put it in its horse box. Gemma asked if Nick was coping all right, and was told again that he needed an assistant. They were trying to ignore the implicit hint when they were saved by the sound of banging over to their left, near the site of the Roman camp. Jenny had a pile of Roman shields and was nailing strips of wooden beading around the edges.

"To stop spears sliding off and stabbing scouts," explained Adele.

"That's taken all the fun out of it," Nick muttered.

Duncan gave a short laugh, and saw Gemma frown at him. He decided she disapproved of jokes about possible injuries and deflected this by saying, "She works very hard at these props doesn't she?" realising instantly that he shouldn't have said anything that might be construed as praise for Jenny in Gemma's hearing. He scambled to his feet and walked off away from any repercussions and away from where Jenny was working.

His wander took him around the side of the house nearest to the driveway. The gable ended side wall was covered in ivy growing from a rather wild bed of weeds and neglected rose bushes. He hadn't explored there before, and was confronted by a large group of cast members who had set up what seemed to be a highly organised encampment hidden away toward the back of the building. There were tables and chairs, food and drink, even a tea urn, for which they had somehow acquired a mains lead to plug in to. He was greeted with some caution. Clearly they had little idea who he was, but he discovered that the assembly was made up of a selection of local clubs that had been roped in to provide crowds, whose numbers had been swelled by the addition of the amateur theatre group, who were supplying most of the principal, speaking, parts.

He fell into conversation with them. Having revealed that he was the writer he wished he hadn't. He was instantly bombarded with a succession of actors and actresses questioning and criticising specific bits of the script they had been given. At first he tried a sort of negotiation, 'what do you think would be better?' he asked time and again. This put him in an awkward position where he had to reject the suggestions more often than not. His rejections were often because he disliked the cast's version of his lines, but more usually because he had chosen the words for them because they referred to some piece of script or plot-line that had either just happened or was coming later. The cast, he quickly found, had never read any part of his script other than the piece they themselves were in.

He was pleased of the distraction offered by the arrival of Basil

Carnthorpe, wandering around his garden. He peered short-sightedly at the throng, and Duncan wondered again if the man had really expected this much of an occupation of his property. Duncan greeted him, more to escape the script debate than through a wish to talk to the house owner, and was surprised and flattered to find that the older man remembered him, and more than that remembered his role in the event.

"Difficult job, writing all those words," Basil told him.

Duncan agreed, "Sometimes you get stuck, sometimes it just flows for a while," he said, "I hope all these people aren't being too annoying to you, it's very kind of you to allow all this."

Basil swung his head from side to side exactly like a tortoise peering from its shell and surveying the world. His scrawny neck jutted from the collars of his shirt and jacket twisting as he studied 'all these people'.

"It can't last too much longer can it?" he suggested.
Duncan assured him, "It will all be over by the end of April next year," seeing what might have been shock at the timescale described on the old man's face.

Further talk was prevented by Nick, back on the magaphone, summoning everyone to return to the rehearsal. Duncan told Basil, "Sorry, got to go," and trudged back to Gemma who he was pleased to see had been chatting with Adele all through his absence. He tried to decern whether Gemma had forgiven and forgotten the fâux-pas of a few minutes ago, but she was deep in discussion with Adele and once the rehearsal resumed kept watching it intently, so he became sure she was ignoring him.

Chapter 25
A Council Meeting

Councillor Brian Andrews was restraining himself with difficulty. The meeting had been dragging on for even longer than usual. The local press reporter, from the paper fifteen miles away as Elveston's own publication had closed half a century earlier and the monthly advertising magazine never sent anyone to cover Council meetings, had been trying to find a suitable moment to escape for at least quarter of an hour. Andrews could see the young man playing with his propelling pencil, winding the lead in and out idly.

"Now we come to the application for a discretionary grant for the Quincentenary performance," the Town Clerk announced.

Several of the councillors shuffled papers. Andrews didn't need to. His copy of the application that Nick had filled in weeks earlier was at the top of the pile in front of him on the heavilly carved table, placed there ready so he could refer to it when he began to oppose the suggestion that the Council's funds should be used to subsidise this undesirable performance. He knew many of his fellow members of the assembly supported the idea of celebrating the Qunicentennary. His own view was that this should be done in a quiet and discreet way, possibly with a small reception for the councillors themselves here in the chamber, but not with a public event that was likely to raise the spectre of the Dragon Fair in the public consciousness again from its mainly dormant status at present. He was disappointed that the tweed wearing councillor who had spoken against the project a few months ago had sent her apologies to this meeting. She would have been at least one certain voice to add to his own.

"We have a submission from the organising committee, you should have copies, and you'll remember that at a previous meeting we gave our blessing to the general principle of this event. We're pleased that several local people have said that they will arrange to stage this..."

"So we don't have to bother," muttered the youngest, newest and most outspoken Councillor. He had only become a member of the body eight weeks earlier, as a result of an un-opposed by-election, and they had already come to realise that he treated the meetings with a ill disguised contempt. The Clerk frowned at him with the same disapproving expression as was painted on the faces of the portraits of former councillors looking down at them from the walls, but continued as if nothing had been said,

"... and you will remember too that we have stated that this will be the town's official event. This means that the public will see it as something we have done," he stopped and addressed the reporter directly, "Naturally that comment is off the record."

The propelling pencil stopped being twisted in and out in the man's fingers. The man from the Harville Herald had had no intention of quoting anything, so he found it easy to nod agreement. His game with his pencil now interrupted he settled to studying the wood panelling on the council chamber walls.

"Our staff will not have to be involved in any way, so we save any possible expenditure for overtime, while still appearing to have celebrated the landmark. The mayor and I are recommending that we agree to this application in full, as I'm sure you will agree it makes economic sense as well as being good public relations."

The Clerk paused momentarily, and, clearly expecting universal agreement, drew breath to thank the councillors with a view to rubber stamping the thing 'nem. con.'.

Brian Andrews coughed pointedly.

"You wanted to say something, Brian?" the Town Clerk asked rather informally.

"It seems to me that we are offering money to an event that we have no control over. An event that might, just might, cause the public to be grateful to the council very briefly, but which could, very likely, have much more long term adverse effects,"

He scanned the members to see how his words were going down. He found disinterest and even boredom, but pressed on,

"It seems likely that the 'show', which I understand is being written by a new-comer to the area, a man who has no knowledge of the background history of Elveston, and therefore no sense of the need for tact and restraint on 'certain matters', and who, I gather, has been meeting frequently with the Reverend Grainger, who you all know has an unhealthy interest in the old Dragon Fair. It seems inevitable that this means that the Dragon will feature stongly in this production we are being asked to finance."

"Subsidise, Councillor Andrews. A grant, not financing it." the Clerk cut in with pedantic accuracy.

"Subsidise then. The fact remains that we risk attracting all the wrong sort of publicity for the town. Publicity we have gone to great lengths to avoid in the past, because it is 'the past', on the off chance that a few extra bodies might visit one day and spend a pound or two in our local shops because there's an amateur local show on. I'd rather give the money we're talking about 'granting' directly to our local tradesmen. It would be safer. It would be more apt."

The reporter had stopped staring at the walls and started to pay attention. Would there be a heated argument? he wondered. He hoped so. It might give him a few lines of copy.

An elderly lady councillor spoke.

"Do you really think they might make a feature of the obsolete Fair?"

"I think it's a possibility, Miss Fraser. It's a possibility we should not risk."

The Clerk moved his notes about and said, "From what I can make out the project already involves so many organisations we might stir a hornet's nest if we scuppered it by refusing funding."

"What organisations?" someone wanted to know.

"I've been told," he consulted his papers, "the Scouts, the Guides, the church choir, four schools, Catherine James' School of Dance, the am drams... Well the list is quite long."

"A lot of people being involved doesn't make it right,"

"No, Councillor Andrews, it probably doesn't. But you only seem to be against the chance that they will mention the Dragon Fair."

"It would be disgraceful if they didn't," the new councillor put in, "It's part of the town's history and you shouldn't whitewash it."

"That's easy to say when you are young," the Clerk told him, "people who were involved might not agree."

"There can't be anyone still alive who was involved can there?"

Brian was about to disabuse the youth, when it dawned on him that pointing out the people who had been involved was exactly what he was trying to ensure didn't happen.

Instead he said, "We need to be sensitive to people's feelings."

""I'm sure they will be," said the Town Clerk, "Are you really going to force a vote on this?"

"Yes," Brian said shortly.

The Clerk sighed, sometimes chairing these meetings could be quite tiresome, and said, "Well unless anyone else has anything to say shall we just have a show of hands, those in favour of the grant?"

Hands rose, some promptly, some after their owners had looked about to see who else was voting, and some in idle boredom.

"Those against?"

Andrews put his hand up.

"Carried."

The 'Harville Herald' reporter waylaid Brian Andrews outside.

"Grant to Event Causes Dissent" Nick read.

Duncan waited. He'd already read the piece in the paper. Gemma had brought it home from work with her for him to see. Her workplace was close to Harville.

> *"There were angry scenes at last night's meeting of the Elveston Town Council when the application for a grant to stage an event for the town's Quincetenary next year was considered. Councillor Brian Andrews objected on the grounds that the proposed show intended to celebrate aspects of the town's history that included the notorious Dragon Fair. He told this reporter that the Dragon Fair, which finished in the mid 1960s, was a politically incorrect, sexist event, and that any mention of it at a Council funded event was unacceptable. Despite Councillor Andrews' objection the Council agreed the funding.*
> *The show, which is being directed by local man Nick Canforth, has been written by author and newcomer to the area, Duncan Newbon, and will be performed at Elveston Lodge by a huge cast, drawn from many local organisations, in April 2012."*

"Nice little mention for you there," Nick said, "I expect there'll be lots more before this is over."

He had called to ask Duncan to make a few minor changes to the script, an extra line here to give time for someone to get into position, a piece of explanation there to clarify the historical continuity.

They were in Duncan's house. Gemma was at work. Duncan wasn't sure whether she had intended him to share the article with

Nick. He had become more convinced than ever that she was anti-Nick, anti the show and anti his involvement in it. Mentally he was calculating how long there was to go. Nearly four months in next year, and things would presumably hot up during those, and a couple of months left of this year. Could he stave off her antagonism to the thing for another six months he wondered. It seemed such a long time, but he was also more than a bit worried that from what he had seen of rehearsals so far six months might not be anything like enough. He didn't want his play to be a badly performed shambles. In his imagination the thing was a spectacular, a tour-de-force. In reality what he had seen was a collection of less than competent performers stumbling over lines and unable to stand in any sensible positions accompanied by ill behaved horses and a variety of well meaning but unconvincing props. Gemma was right. He should never have agreed to be involved. He would become a laughing stock along with everyone else in high places in the production team. He resolved to ensure that no-one he knew from the world of writing and publishing should discover the thing was on. He would keep it a secret.

Nick was still enthusing.

"We ought to cultivate this bloke from the paper. If my guess is right the local reporters find it hard to come up with enough copy. If we were to feed him bits to put in we could get free publicity."

Duncan was unsure. He didn't imagine that reporters liked being given what was blatantly obviously advertising and being expected to find space for it.

"You could write press releases for us, couldn't you," Nick was continuing, "If you sent him something every other week.."

"I don't think I'd know what to write," Duncan tried to get out of this latest task.

"Don't worry, I'll tell you what's going on and you can just word it suitably."

He sighed in resignation. He decided to keep this new duty a secret from Gemma. Trying to turn the tables a bit he asked Nick how he thought the rehearsals were going. Nick was ebullient, full of praise for individual cast members and expressing delight at the few props and costumes that had emerged so far. He seemed oblivious to shortcomings that even Duncan's inexperienced eye had spotted.

"Anyway," he excused himself, "we won't do much good advertising this side of Christmas will we."

"Have you been invited to John and Jenny's Haloween party yet?" Nick asked.

Duncan shook his head. He felt some trepidation at the thought that they might find themselves dragged along to a party so close to their home that they could hardly find an excuse; would hardly have an excuse to leave early either. He could see the couple's house from the window. Idly he wondered if they would be forced to wear fancy dress. He found himself speculating what sort of costume Jenny might chose to flaunt herself in. He drifted off into one of his musings on that subject, losing all contact with the present until Nick said, "Did you hear me?" rather sharply.

"Sorry, what?"

"I asked if you and Gemma were coming to the next rehearsal."

"I think I'll leave it to you experts for a while," he excused himself.

Nick sensed that he was being brushed off. Rather indignantly he rose and headed for the door. He had become single minded about the project, and failed to understand anyone's reluctance to be one hundred per-cent devoted to it. Over his shoulder he said, "I should start a scrapbook of press cuttings if I were you. I'll let you know if I need any more re-writes," and was gone.

Duncan slumped in his chair.

Chapter 27
Halloween

They were getting ready, well Gemma was. Duncan had put on a dark suit, his funeral attending suit, with a black bow tie and Gemma had applied a few dabs of lipstick to the side of his mouth to look like a dribble of blood. He studied himself in the mirror. He thought he looked foolish. He hated fancy dress parties and had suggested to Gemma that they arrange to be away on the night of Jenny and John's Halloween function. He had been forced to conceed that there was nowhere they could legitimately claim to be going. Anyway, Gemma had pointed out, she was rather looking forward to mingling informally with their neighbours. Apart from Adele's occasional visits she had only really socialised with them when the planning for next year's show was happening. As she had done her best to divorce herself from that she often felt a bit isolated.

He watched the front of the opposite house surreptitiously from the living room window. People were arriving. He was pleased that, despite being the nearest neighbours they would not be the first there. Slipping in once the house was full of people gave a better chance, he thought, of slipping out before it became too late, and before he had reached that stage he knew so well, of having exhausted all small talk and longing to leave.

The arrivals opposite were clad in a wide variety of costumes, witches, vampires, and predictable Harry Potter style wizards mingled with some odd ball creations. As he watched an all green fairy was knocking at the door. Overhead he heard Gemma walking about. He guessed she was standing in front of the full length mirror and turning this way and that to make sure she was satisfied with her appearance. He wondered if there would be room for them in the house when they got there. There seemed to be a lot of guests.

He was still waiting for Gemma when he saw John and Jenny's

next door neighbours, Edward and Emily, come from their own house to join the party. He was rather surprised. The couple had not socialised at all since last Christmas and had been invisible since turning down the request for them to join in the preparations for the show.

Gemma joined him in their front room, and he ponted the older pair out to her as the door was opened to admit them.

"Well I suppose they think they might as well be at a party as just listening to it.. they do live next door. They'd be bound to hear it going on."

Duncan agreed with her. Already they could faintly discern the bass thump of some music playing on the other side of the road. When they reached the door to the party it was clear that it was going to be one of those evenings where no-one could actually hear anything anyone said because of the music,

Jenny let them in. Duncan handed over the bottle they had brought and she managed to use taking it from his hand as a means to pull him against her, looking straight into his eyes and licking her lips in a manner that he took to be suggestive. Afterwards Gemma told him the woman was just acting the vampiric part she had adopted, but at the time the very short, low cut black dress with a few scraps of black net as sleeves and the make up in the most extreme 'Goth' style he had ever seen combined with her double handed grip on the bottle and his wrist to send a chill which was not Halloween make believe through him.

Gemma followed him in. People shouted what might have been welcomes at them. Someone they didn't know came close to Gemma and began shouting in her ear. Duncan had no idea what was being said, but he saw her shake her head and point to him and the man drifted away. The kitchen was awash with spilt drink already, but they found some paper cups and helped themselves to cider, which seemed to be in plentiful supply.

Exploring rather tentatively, though feeling protected by each other and the drinks they were holding, they looked into the lounge. The furniture had been stripped out, huge cut out orange pumpkins had been hung from nails in the ceiling. A stereo system was blasting and had just reached Arthur Brown's 'Fire'. The dancing was restricted to rhythmic bobbing due to the crush. Gemma pulled on Duncan's hand. He shook his head 'no', but she dragged him into the mêlée and began to bob like the rest. He hated it. He found that, although it seemed crammed tight, there was a sort of natural circulation happening so he was slowly dragged away from the door and moved around the room as if in a slow moving whirlpool. This made him notice that Jenny had arranged coloured celophane over the various lamps on the walls, so that at some points Gemma was lit in a red glow, sometimes in green.

The music changed to some more modern number that neither of them knew and Duncan was able to lead Gemma out of the room and back into the hallway. Gemma had put her cup down somewhere and shouted, "Need to get another drink." at him. He carried on clutching his nearly empty one and they went back to the kitchen.

Like all parties the kitchen was becoming the centre for people who wanted to be away from the music and possibly to talk, though the music was still really too loud for that. In the kitchen you could loiter, prove you had attended, but escape the worst excesses of the active party-goers.

Nick was there.

Duncan heard Gemma mutter 'Oh no." though there was no way anyone else would have heard.

He had cornered a small group of three or four other guests and was clearly trying to persuade them to something. I didn't take much intuition for Duncan and Gemma to realise he was touting for volunteers for the show. Against the noise it was unclear if he was hoping for actors or leaflet distributors, but they had no doubt of his general topic of conversation. The guests included a wimpy looking young man, who seemed to have come as Frankenstein, despite his build working very much against this disguise, and a girl with fairy wings on her back. Nick saw Duncan and Gemma and interrupted his talk to wave. The fairy turned to see who he was waving to and Duncan realised that she was the green fairy he had seen knock at the door from his own window. Her short net dress was green, hardly covering any of her green fishnet clad legs. She had a green face and her bare green arms ended in green hands, in one of which she clutched a green wand, and in the other a glass of wine.

"Couldn't she find a green drink?" Duncan said in Gemma's ear.

Nick was beckoning them over. They waved and tried to replenish their paper cups while keeping the kitchen table between them and the director, but without success. With extraordinary skill Nick managed to work his way around the table to their side while still retaining a firm grip on his audience.

"Meet Duncan, our writer," he shouted. There were some brief handshakes during which Duncan failed to gather any of the names and the fairy, strangely, clutched his hand and stood on tiptoe to kiss his cheek. He noticed the green make-up had come off and was now all over the back of his hand. He wondered if he also had a green cheek.

He couldn't really hear what Nick or any of the others were saying and fought a long struggle to remain free of the group that Nick had formed. Gemma had taken a step along the table edge and was systematically lifting bottles and in some cases sampling the remaining contents. She eventually settled on one of the wines, Filled her paper cup to the brim, found there was some left in the bottle, swigged back most of the cup-full and poured again. Duncan saw her repeat this several times until the bottle was eventually empty. He tried to edge away from Nick on the excuse of finding a drink for himself but Nick's small tame gathering seemed to follow him.

Trapped eventually he was obliged to shout that he was very much looking forward to seeing what the cast made of his script, adding, as he saw Gemma leave the kitchen, "Must go, the good lady's on the move."

He followed her into the hallway. She had vanished. As he hesitated Jenny appeared from no-where, grabbing him by the arm and pressing herself against him so he was trapped against the hall wall. He had the mental image of a butterfly impaled on a pin in a collection as she pushed against him. She said, "Oh you naughty boy, you've been with that fairy!" rubbing his green stained hand between both of hers to clean off the smear of make-up before producing a remarkably clean handkerchief from no-where and rubbing his cheek where he had been kissed.

The cloth came away green.

"There," she said in his ear, and he squirmed with embarassment her nearness, "no more Mary the Fairy, all gone, nothing to give you away to Gemma."

"Nothing happened," he protested.

"But it could do," she said. The music made it impossible for her to whisper, even in his ear like this and she added quite loudly, "The bedroom's empty upstairs."

Some lull in the music, or maybe a change of tracks made this audible to the nearest party goers and heads turned. Duncan blushed. He blushed with embarassment because some people heard, and saw the hostess pressing herself against him. He blushed too because some hidden part of him was tempted by the blatant come on.

Instantly she laughed at him. "Poor dear," the music became

deafening again, "I won't make you.. I can wait for you to come to me," she said, and he could feel her lips moving against his ear.

She stepped a half pace away from him. He began looking this way and that for Gemma.

"She's in the lounge, dancing with John," she told him.

"Your John?"

"Of course. Otherwise it wouldn't have been safe for us to go upstairs." Again she laughed, but this time left him and vanished into the crowd.

He pushed his way to the door of the lounge. Jenny was right. There in the midst of the coloured lighting, surrounded by increasingly intoxicated witches and wizards, Gemma and John could be seen moving rather wildly in time to the music. They each seemed to have a wine bottle in one hand and occasionally swigged directly from them. He thought about just going home.

For almost an hour he perched on a small stool in the hall by the telephone table. The party grew wilder. At one point Edward and Emily, the neighbours, passed as they became the first to leave. They stopped and shouted to him. "..too old for all this.." was all he heard, but he nodded and agreed with them.

A very young witch, probably no more than a teenager, clearly drunk, reeled from the kitchen in a dishevelled state, tripped and slumped across his lap. Instinctively he caught her and found himself holding her. She wailed, ".... not fair!.." before putting her arms around his neck and burying her face in his shoulder to sob.

The embarassments were becoming too much for Duncan, "What's the matter?" he shouted.

The girl seemed to realise where she was through her drunken befuddlement and pushed away from him. She hadn't stood up when a woman appeared heading straight for them and saying, "Come on, Chloe, leave the man alone."

Duncan recognised Catherine James, the dance school owner. At the same moment she realised who he was.

"Oh, It's our 'playwright'. Hello Douglas."

"Duncan," he corrected.

"Sorry, Duncan, yes. Chloe's a bit upset."

"Why, what's happened?"

"She didn't get chosen as Boudicea for the battle sequence."

Chloe was standing between them now, swaying, and mumbling something that might have been 'not fair'. She made an unsuccessful attempt to put the strap of her dress back on her shoulder just as he saw that Gemma had emerged from the coloured lights of the lounge.

Duncan, who had been preparing himself to berate his wife for flagrantly dancing about with John had a dawning realisation that his standing with an evidently drunk teenage girl whose dress was half off wasn't quite the right image from which to start commenting on behaviour. He stayed silent. Gemma came to the trio and said, loudly and pointedly, "Introduce me then," before putting an arm round her husband's shoulder, either to steady herself or to assert ownership.

Duncan shouted the names, and a brief explanation as to who they were.

"Oh they would be something to do with this bloody show," she commented.

Duncan thought he should get her home and said so.

The cold air outside made Gemma stagger all the more, and he was grateful they only had to cross the road and make their way up the drive.

The sounds of the party carried on deep into the early hours.

Chapter 28
The Festive Season

Gemma and Duncan didn't talk much about the party the next morning. In fact they avoided the subject for several days. It was late in the following week when a chance comment about something one evening led Gemma to say, "What were you doing with that girl and her mother at the party anyway?"

Duncan was confused for a moment, then told her, "Not her mother, her dance teacher."

"Well whatever. It still looked very odd, you cuddling a teenager."

"I wasn't cuddling her. You make it sound like...oh I don't know, as if I was trying to seduce her."

"Well it certainly looked like it until she pulled away and stood up. No telling what it might have led to."

"She was hardly in a fit condition to stand up actually."

"You realise that only makes it worse. Now it looks like you were taking advantage of a girl who was drunk."

Duncan bridled at the false accusation. "She wasn't actually the only one who was drunk that night was she?"

"I went to a party and had a good time."

"With John."

"Oh god I think you are jealous. You are! You know damn well nothing happened, and you had green face paint all over you at one point. Green with envy were you? Or was it Mary?"

Duncan was sullen.

"It's stupid," she went on, "You let that floosie Jenny flirt with you all the time, but I can't have any fun."

"I didn't say you couldn't... shouldn't... just the girl wasn't my fault, she was upset because she didn't get the part she wanted."

"Part in the show or part of you?"

"Oh really!"

She burst out laughing.

"You are stupidly gullible. I know you wouldn't do anything."

Grudgingly he had to admit he knew she wouldn't either.

He was pleased, however, that one decision that the pair of them made in the wake of John and Jenny's party was that they wouldn't host a Christmas party at their house. Somehow there was an unspoken feeling among their acquaintances that now they were no longer really newcomers the Newbons might be expected to invite people round for a festive get together. Neither felt they wanted to.

Nick's requests to Duncan for new bits of script gradually dried up, and by the time they were seated at the table writing Christmas cards again he had stopped attending rehearsals completely.

The card writing was more frustrating than ever. The post brought greetings from people they had long lost contact with or hadn't spoken to or thought of for twelve months. Of these many had sent the card to their old address and they came to recognise the handwriting of the new occupant of their old home scrawled as a correction forwarding the card to Greendale Road.

Gemma sighed with annoyance as she picked another up from the mat. "What is the matter with people," she burst out, opening the re-addressed card and seeing who it was from, "I absolutely know that we sent your Aunt Hilda our new address."

"Did we?" Duncan wondered absently.

"I remember, because you queried why we hadn't got her post code, as if it was my fault, so obviously we must have sent her ours. Anyway she's sent us a card, to our old address."

He had a nagging doubt about this, but dutifully added the information to the greeting inside the card when he wrote this year's.

They had a quiet Christmas despite the occasional visits from their new friends in Elveston. Afterwards Duncan noticed it was now twelve months since he and Gemma had visited Heaton-Bassett, and was ashamed to be prompted by that thought to a realisation that he had neither looked any further into that town's 'Snake' nor, realisically, into Elveston's 'Dragon'. He promised himself to research both. Even if he was unable to write up the Elveston Dragon he would maybe get mileage out of a comparison of the two events.

He was twarted almost as soon as New Year was over by Nick starting serious and demanding rehearsals and arrangements for the show. The winter weather prevented him from using the actual site for his rehearsals with any guarantee of them not being rained off or of the cast not freezing in the open air, so he cajoled Duncan into booking time in the Community Centre for them.

He stood in the entrance lobby staring at the notice boards with their array of posters for aerobics and bingo. One board was enclosed in a glazed cabinet, preventing unauthorised additions or alterations to the information on display. This included the telephone number for who to contact to book the hall. Additionally, alongside a few legal notices about licensing and performing rights, a time-table of the weekly regular bookings showed that there were hardly any vacant slots for anyone to book, and that those that might possibly be squeezed in either fell in the mornings, or after certain evening classes had finished. Catherine James' dance classes were among these, and it looked as though Friday evening's class finished at eight. This was a bit later for a start of a rehearsal than he imagined Nick would want, but did have the advantage that some of the cast, the girls who were performing as Boudicea's army and others, might well already be on site due to classes. He rang the number.

The frail sounding and possibly harrassed lady who answered took his bookings, for eight till eleven every Friday from then until the performance week, and proceeded to lecture him for what seemed an eternity on do's and dont's chief among which seemed to be that, although the building would already be open, they were not to arrive before the end of Catherine's classes and must actually be off the premises at eleven for the caretaker to lock the doors behind them. He gave the woman Nick's details as Treasurer for her to send the bills, and assured her they would obey the rules.

He was quite proud of himself when he eventually hung up.

Nick was quite cross with him.

"I wasn't planning rehearsals on Fridays," he argued.

"There are no other evenings possible on the Centre's booking sheets, anyway it's good that Catherine and her lot will be there already."

Nick hurumphed, but conceded the point. A rehearsal schedule was produced and circulated, showing weekly sessions at the Community Centre, with provisional weekend dates at Elveston Lodge should the weather allow.

Nick and Adele met Duncan and Gemma in the pub one weekday evening a few weeks into the New Year. Gemma didn't really want to spend an evening discussing the show, but she was equally determined not to miss out on a few drinks and a social occasion. Her work was becoming all consuming. Duncan was getting dragged into more and more administrative aspects of the show. They were leading rather busy and isolating lives, and she welcomed time together, even in company.

Whether John and Jenny went to the pub every night, or had some sixth sense about the others being there, or had been tipped off, Duncan never knew. He suspected that Adele might have been responsible for them getting wind of the evening's drinks. He long had an idea that the retired librarian was a people watcher, and derived some amusement from his embarassment at Jenny's blatant flirting. However it happened he found himself once again sandwiched next to Jenny. Despite the winter cold she was, as usual, wearing a low cut outfit and short skirt. The group were talking, discussing the coming show, Nick was holding forth to her about some aspect of the event, and she was pressing her bare leg against Duncan's trousers again. He recalled she'd done this many times before, but it still bothered him. He looked at Gemma opposite him in mute appeal, half hoping she wouldn't notice, half hoping that she would and that she might berate Jenny, draw some limiting line in the sand that would stop the woman's blatant come-ons.

Gemma was talking to Adele. She seemed unaware of her husband's discomfort. Duncan was sure however that Adele had noticed what was happening and was supressing a slight smile as she nodded in agreement with Gemma's chat. He tried to concentrate on what Nick was saying, but eventually found he wasn't folowing it and buried his nose in his glass.

"That's right, isn't it Adele?" Nick cut across Gemma's conversation with the older woman.

Adele switched instantly to be attentive to Nick. Gemma surrendered and looked across at Duncan, who immediately tried slight nods of his head at Jenny to draw Gemma's attention to his discomfort. Gemma saw the gesture and with female intuition knew at once what he was trying to indicate, laughed, and said,

"You two getting along all right?"

He had thought Jenny might back away under the scrutiny, but she simply said, "Fine. He's a dear isn't he?"

Gemma put on a severe face and said, "If he is that's my training. He's quite a useless dreamer really."

"Oh thank you darling!" he said.

"... just remember he's my useless dreamer," she finished.

Jenny gave a hard press against Duncan's thigh with her leg before backing away an inch and giggling.

"Bless him," she told Jenny, "he's so up-tight."

"I'd better get another round in," he said, struggling out of the confines of the seat.

Chapter 29
Overworked

Friday evening rehearsals in the Community Centre were at least warm in those winter months. There were regular and frustrating delays to starting any session, partly due to members of Nick's cast arriving late, but mostly caused by the Centre's weird idea that one group could finish and another start a mere second later.

It was not that Catherine James' girls were slow about leaving, but several dozen teens and their bags take a finite amount of time to go out through a doorway, especially when a similar number of Nick's performers were trying to come in, accompanied by an array of mostly bulky props.

Nick was repeatedly frustrated by this situation and Adele used several techniques to distract him at the relevant time so he was less conscious of the clock. Mostly she brought up queries about the show that both needed his decision, and were complicated enough to require some thought. Duncan, for his part, adopted a policy of arriving a little late so as to miss the director's ill temper if the start was delayed.

He was ambivalent about the show. With all his writing up until then he had been unaware of his readers' reactions. He wrote, publishers printed, readers read; and there was no way that he, the author, could know what the readers thought. Now as he heard his lines spoken by the cast he was acutely conscious of lots of times when the actors and actresses said the line with the stress in the wrong place or pronounced the words incorectly. Some of the less able and more amateur players spoke in wooden tones as if they were infants, reading something with no understanding of what it was about. Often, when Nick did intervene to correct or modify the delivery of lines, Duncan didn't agree with Nick's interpretation. Actions that now began to appear and be repeated seemingly endlessly bore no resemblance to what Duncan had imagined when he was pounding his keyboard.

He began to dread some scenes. He itched to correct miss-placed stresses and erratic or downright dead speech. He didn't do so because he felt he shouldn't trespass on Nick's territory, and seethed gently.

At one point, after a particularly unimpressive attempt at a scene involving supposed villagers discussing a crop failure, he could stand it no longer and pulled Nick aside to whisper in his ear, telling him how appalled he was at the amateur delivery of his words. Nick regarded him with open surprise.

"You didn't think I was going to leave it like that did you? First we have to get them to say the lines and move about without falling over the furniture... then we try to make them act. Be patient. One thing at a time."

Duncan was unsatisfied by this response, but he noticed that Nick did seem to be starting to correct his cast's worst failings in that and subsequent rehearsals. Not that, to Duncan's mind, it seemed to make much difference. He still felt he was watching a very amateur performance. It seemed lack-luster. No-one appeared to be trying. His depressed contemplation of the rehearsal was interrupted by Frank, the narrator, wandering over to him and sitting on a neighbouring chair.

"Bloody awful, isn't it." the man said.

Duncan hesitated. Did the man mean his script? He couldn't remember if Frank had been introduced to him, and if so whether he had been annouced as the playwright. Frank carried on.

"Half of them can't deliver a line without sounding like a primary school reading lesson, and the other half, the ones who're in local theatre groups, can't seem to be bothered."

"I suppose it's still quite a long way off. Maybe once it gets nearer they'll be more enthusiastic."

"It's only another eleven or twelve weeks. Hardly a long time when you're only running one rehearsal a week. Most of this lot can't remember their lines from one week to the next. Nick needs to get them to put their books down or he'll never get any action rehearsed."

Duncan nodded. Perhaps Frank was right, perhaps Frank knew more about this than he, or more importantly Nick, did. Wasn't he supposed to be a leading member of one of the local theatre groups?

He was about to make some non-commital reply when Edward and Tamsin could be seen making a direct bee line for where they were, acoss the hall, weaving between the litter of stacking chairs and randomly dumped bags and coats that covered the varnished floor.

"Duncan," Tamsin said, rather ignoring his and Frank's conversation, "you must make some sort of decision. I keep trying to get Nick to make his mind up, but he always claims to be too busy or tells me to ask you."

Duncan felt a surge of concern. Nick hadn't previously passed decisions on to him, and he wondered if this was going to be a case of either-or, where whichever way he chose he would upset someone. He raised an eyebrow, saying nothing and waiting for the question.

"We've got to know about the costumes," Edward told him.

"Every show should have some," Frank said jokingly, "well most of them, unless we're suddenly staging 'Hair'."

"There were only some bits of 'Hair' that were nude," Tamsin said.

"Yes. It was the 'bits' that caused all the fuss," Frank said.

"What about the costumes?" Duncan asked, feeling uncomfortable at the flippant discussion of stage nudity.

"You know it's been decided that everyone will wear the same basic thing, and just add something on top to indicate who they are at moments when they are playing a character..?"

Duncan remembered some discussion like that. He said "Uhuh," rather vaguely.

"We must know what colour the basic costume is to be." Tamsin finished.

"I thought someone had said black, all black."

Frank said, "Oh no, surely not, we'll all just vanish on a dark night in the open air."

"That's what we think," Edward told him.

"What do you suggest then?" Duncan said diplomatically. A thought in the back of his mind was that Edward and Tamsin would probably want to costume the cast in a colour that they had a huge stock of material for in their shop, or could obtain very cheaply.

"Orange, like prisoners," said Frank with more than just a tinge of bitterness.

"We thought purple," Edward said, "It's dark enough to mostly vanish in a blackout, but will show up when the actor is lit."

Duncan nodded as if he understood.

"We can get purple tee shirts in bulk," Tamsin told him, "and if we buy in a bale of cloth we can run up sort of baggy trousers quickly like on a production line.. we just need to make a few different sizes."

"Won't that be a lot of work?"

Tamsin frowned. "Duncan, everything on this show is turning out to be a lot of work, or hadn't you noticed?."

Suddenly, it seemed, purple was everywhere. The first posters and flyers appeared, featuring purple, the girls from Catherine James' school were to be seen in the streets sporting purple tee shirts printed by a local shop with the slogan 'Back to the Past' on the back. It was, Adele pointed out, unclear if this was advertising the show or a statement from the teens that they had turned their backs on the past. Maybe the ambiguity appealed to the dancers, because these soon out-numbered the more usual ones advertising the Catherine James School of Dance.

"Perhaps we should call it that," Adele said at one point, "after all the girls are publicising it for us and we haven't given it an official title, and I rather like 'Back to the Past'.

"I prefer it to the rather formal things we've been calling it on paperwork," Duncan agreed.

So the show acquired a title.

Nick did not seem pleased.

"No-one asked me!" he said, "And why purple?"

Adele made soothing noises and told him, "You passed the buck for the basic colour to Duncan because you were busy with more important things, and the dancers put it on the back of tee shirts without asking anyone. It's a good title. We all like it. And the public has taken to it already so that's good. We couldn't delay any longer, you know. It will be time for tickets to go on sale very soon."

Nick shrugged, "I suppose we should have talked about this much sooner. Anyway what's done is done."

Duncan was surprised at the man's equanimity. He'd expected an outburst, a demand for some alternative title. Personally he quite liked 'Back to the Past' now. He rather regretted not having come up with it himself. It gave him a slim piece of news to release to the local press, 'Title announced for quincentenery show' and now they were within distant reach of the event he felt it needed every mention he could achieve for it even if he was still unsure what to expect in terms of the quality of the performance.

Gemma stood looking out of their front bedroom window late one night a week or two later. Duncan had already got into bed, and he wondered what had attracted her attention. She was evidently straining to see something on the other side of the road, but much further along.

"Have you noticed Edward and Tamsin's place lately?" she said over her shoulder.

"Not particularly. Why? What are they up to?"

"All their lights are on."

"So"

"It's a bit late at night for them."

Duncan rolled over and went to sleep.

At three o'clock Gemma announced, "They're still up. All the lights are still on." She got little response from Duncan. At four she put some shoes on and shrugged a coat over her nightie and crossed the road diagonally to the house, which was a blaze of light. As she got nearer she could hear bursts of vibration from inside. It sounded familiar, but she couldn't place the sound. She went up the path. Open curtains revealed Edward and Tamsin in a front room that was an explosion of purple cloth.

Satisfied that they were both all right she was backing away when

217

Edward caught sight of her in the spilt light from the house. He rose and came to the front door.

"I'm so sorry," Gemma told him, "I was checking you were all right."

"Thank you. We're fine, it's just that there's no way we can get all these costumes done in time unless we burn the midnight oil."

"Haven't you got to work in the morning?"

"Yes. But we'll manage somehow. We've been at this for days,, well I mean nights, now. At the rate we're going we'll hardly make the dress rehearsal."

"But that's weeks away."

"And we've got a hundred and ninety-seven costumes still to go."

"That's ridiculous. Are there really that many in the cast? Someone's got to help you!"

There was a big bale of purple material at the foot of the stairs when Duncan got up in the morning.

"Of course," Gemma told him, "we still need to find more volunteers. You have an ask around while I'm at work."

Adele said to him later, "I didn't realise they'd taken so much on. We'd better look up local organisations that might include people with sewing machines."

They extracted names and addresses from the library and began a campaign to whip up seamstresses. Adele pondered, "I wonder if John and Jenny need help too.. with the props and things. You ought to walk over and ask."

"Why me?" Duncan said, a vision of Jenny answering the door

and dragging him inside flashing through his mind.

"Because you're the chairman, and the assistant director, and you live right opposite them."

"And you're the secretary and live next door,"

"Oh go on, Duncan, you don't need to be afraid of Jenny."

Duncan felt that he did, and resented Adele's perception, but went anyway.

Gemma had been overwhelmed by the way the show dominated Edward and Tamsin's house, but Duncan found it occupying every inch of Jenny and John's. He'd expected an untidy scatter of bits and pieces under construction, but found instead row upon row of items, either completed or under construction, filling every part of the hall, both living rooms and the kitchen. He didn't enquire into the amount of props and things that might be in the bedrooms.

It was the armies that were taking up the space. If every Roman had a shield, sword and helmet, and every Iceni warrior the same, and the Roundheads and Cavaliers too, and two world wars were involving British Tommies' kit and rifles, and Medieval fairs needed pots and pans, and … He felt they might have bitten off more than they could chew. He wished he'd thought about the implications when he wrote the show. If only he had limited the numbers. He supposed it was superfluous for an army to march away to the 1914 trenches, for soldiers to return for VE day, for football supporters to be shown celebrating the 1966 World Cup, which someone had told him the population here did in the streets at the time, for schoolchildren to be seen with boxes for their gas masks, for half the cast to have shovels to clear the winter snow in the sixties...

And then there was St George's dragon. It lay across the front room table, the room where the dancing had been, great bundles of material with scales sewn on, a spike encrusted spine leading to a huge head which presently consisted of intricately curved and linked thin cane formers around the mechanics of a jaw. There would be no room here for a party now. The show has taken over the house, and clearly the lives of the occupants. From somewhere to the rear, through the kitchen, there is the sound of banging. John, who had answered the door, said, "Jenny's building something or other out there. I don't know what. Sometimes she just seems to have an unwritten list of things you need for this show."

"John, I'm really sorry," Duncan apologised, "We didn't realise how much stuff was involved. It was only when we found out how snowed under Edward and Tamsin were getting with the costumes that it occurred to us to check up on you two."

"Not a problem, come on, she's out here," said John and led the way through a small untidy kitchen into the cold dampness of a brick paved yard.

Jenny saw them. Duncan was grateful that she did not rush to him and embarrass him by her over demonstrative friendliness. It was only because her hands were full. She was gripping the two halves of what would evidently eventually be a cooking pot together. The thing was fully two foot in diameter, but somehow seemed moulded from rough rubber and she was sticking the sections together. A smell of fiberglass hung in the air.

"Won't be more than a couple of minutes now, sorry I can't come and cuddle you, I'm cuddling this," she said.

He tried not to show his relief. He saw now that the rubber was some sort of mould, and that it contained a fiberglass cooking pot. He assumed the rubber mould would peel away once the thing was assembled. He was surprised, once again, at the range of techniques the woman seemed to be master of.

"Duncan says that they hadn't realised how many props there

were. I think he wants to know if we need any help."

"Not easy to get other people involved, but we're going to need help at the performance making sure things are in the right place, and we're rather desperate for storage. You haven't got a spare barn or anything have you?"

She was still gripping the halves of the pot together, waiting for the glue to set, when he left, promising to find them storage and some assistant props workers for the shows.

Adele told him, "We need to put an advert in the press, we'll never get enough volunteers otherwise."

"I think what we need to do is get someone who's tech savvy to set us up some sort of website and get the appeal for help out on the internet. No-one reads the paper these days.. and anyway there isn't a local one any more, though I gather there used to be."

Doug was almost a characature technology geek. Duncan never knew where Adele found him. He was certain that the youth spent his life behind a screen in his bedroom, but find him she did, and there was a website and accounts on social media platforms within a couple of hours. Duncan doubted this would produce any immediate results, but was proven wrong. Quite swiftly a list of willing volunteers was created, and, even more valuably, Gemma's company, having seen the on-line pleas, offered some storage space. As Gemma said, "It proves it works, because I didn't ask them."

""Well done, Duncan," said Nick.

"It was Adele found the bloke to do it," Duncan told him.

Nick thanked Adele, and Duncan saw a brief flash of pleasure on her face.

They agreed that things were starting to get properly under way.

When he got home Duncan found Gemma already back from work and seated at her sewing machine, a piece of purple material hanging from it. She gave a brief, off-hand, 'hello' and immediately drowned out any further conversation by pressing on the footswitch, so the machine made its rapid thudding noise as it swallowed cloth, spewing it out away from Gemma sewn along a chalk line near the edge. She reached the end of the seam.

"Trousers," she told him, "fortunately no-one seems to think they need to be tailored, just done like overalls." she lifted the machine's foot and turned the cloth before lowering it again to grip the material and making the machine speed along another seam.

"And yes please, tea please," she said to him the next time the noise stopped.

He made for the kitchen.

"I left off a bit early. I thought I'd better make a start on these costumes," she shouted though to him as he filled the kettle and began putting teabags in mugs, "everyone at work seems to have seen all the stuff on-line about the show. It's a hot topic of conversation! It would be a shame if the cast had nothing to wear."

Duncan was surprised that Doug's various postings had been so effective.

"What were your colleagues looking at to see about the show?" he asked as he handed her the mug of tea.

"I think someone saw some social media thing first, then they shared it round the office and.. well you know. It just snowballed."

The sewing machine roared again for a second or two. She pulled the material out from under the foot, snipped the two cottons that attached it to the machine and held up a near complete pair of purple trousers.

"Just needs some elastic threading in the waist," she said rather proudly.

"How many did they give you to do?"

"I brought a dozen over, but they're ploughing through the other hundred and eighty. I do hope my firm isn't the only place that sees the appeal for help."

"I don't think it will be. This bloke, Doug, seems to know what he's doing with all this on-line stuff."

Gemma gave a sort of snort. "He's probably hacking everyone who clicks on his sites. I'm not sure I trust any of these teenage geeks."

"I think this one is probably genuine enough," he told her, "though I don't know how Adele found him. It's not exactly as if they advertise is it?"

"I bet she had some secret file in that library of hers, or at least the library had a file and she knew where to find it."

Chapter 30
An Oversight

Now that the word was being spread it seemed to Duncan that as the pace picked up the production became a whirlwind of activity. Volunteers appeared to help in all sorts of areas that he had given little or no thought to before. Even though the early months of the year were cold and damp Nick held some Sunday rehearsals at the venue. Duncan noticed that these were now often attended by strangers, who, like the various technical supply companies who had visited earlier on-site rehearsals, arrived in vans and trucks and spent a great deal of any rehearsal measuring and discussing mysterious things among themselves. He attempted to eavesdrop a few times, but found the discussions so jargon riddled as to be almost incomprehensible to him.

What he did bring away from these particular rehearsals, aside from frustration at having to make script alteration after script alteration to allow longer for people to get into positions, or make cuts where Nick felt the text dragged from being too wordy was a realisation that the business of staging a show involved a small army of vested interests. Sometimes too he wondered why he had sweated over the keyboard for this. He was compelled to make so many adjustments that often, when he saw his revised scenes the next week he often hardly recognised his own work. He felt that the piece was now so mauled about that any flow, any pace, any rhythm that it might have originally had was irrevocably lost.

He didn't know how to correct this. He wanted to confront Nick, to tell him of his concerns, but Nick seemed ever more harassed and busy. There was never a suitable time to have a quiet discussion. Even non-rehearsal times now saw Nick dashing about, visiting the homes of volunteers who were making things or even going off to the local radio station to say a few words about the show on some live chat show. Duncan doubted that was worth the effort. It was a truism that the local stations boasted no more than a handful of listeners, and that the majority of those were people who were, for one reason or another, effectively housebound.

Eventually he confided his concerns to Adele, hoping that she might be better able to bend Nick's ear. He found her reaction to what he said surprising.

"I think Nick knows what he's doing. He is making it look really good, isn't he? We are very lucky."

He grumbled to Gemma.

"Of course she's not going to like you criticising Nick," she told him, and carried on cooking their tea.

Duncan was puzzled by this comment. "Why not?"

"Duncan you are useless!" said Gemma. But he was none the wiser.

Posters began to appear, advertising the show. Duncan went from feeling that the long lead up to the performances would never end to a chilling awareness that the date was just around the corner. Now he could mentally count down; ten days, nine days. And eventually 'this time next week'!

Gemma saw that he was fearful and excited in equal measure, and despite her general antipathy toward the show she booked some holiday so she would be more available. She privately acknowledged to herself that she was arranging to be on hand chiefly in case it should be a resounding disaster and she needed to comfort him. Now it was so close she was glad to have finished the costume making she had volunteered herself into, because she could see that everyone involved with making things for the show seemed to be snowed under. She saw people she knew dark eyed from short sleep and grumpy from the pressures of the impending opening night. To add to the stresses the weather was very unfavourable. It rained more often than not. Those involved with the production peered hopefully, and hopelessly at the sky and devoured the guesswork of the weather forecasts.

Nick had been unable to rehearse on site for weeks now. He struggled in the confines of the Community Centre, working on individual parts of the show, without the benefit of linking them together in the open. Everyone involved eyed the grey skies with growing dismay, and many conversations revolved around how to squeeze the thing into the hall if they had to abandon Elveston Lodge.

Someone did some research, and relayed the depressing news that it was the wettest spring since 1910. Another Job's comforter arrived at rehearsal to announce that the papers had told him it was the coldest and dullest year since 1989. No-one was cheered by this news.

Duncan joined Nick at Elveston House on the Wednesday. They stood in the cold drizzle, joined by a small army of technicians from the lighting, sound and staging suppliers. There was only one topic of conversation. Strangely the various electrical contractors were not the least put off by the wet weather. Duncan had expected a great deal of explanation about how electricity and water did not mix. Or perhaps, he thought wryly, how they did. Instead there was a quiet confidence that weatherproof outside equipment was perfectly capable of surviving even heavy downpours. In the end it was clear that it was the audience's comfort that would decide the show's fate. Nick dismissed the cast's well being with a casual wave of his hand, as if they were of no consequence. Now that they were committed to the show he expected them to soldier on with a performance. He made it quite clear that he expected nothing to stop them.

He did concede that they needed some sort of contingency plan so Duncan was detailed to book the Community Centre for the performance times 'just in case'.

The lady who dealt with bookings was rendered even more

harrassed by his request than had been the case when he had spoken to her about rehearsal time. At first she flatly refused to consider the possibility of any of the regular bookings for that date being disrupted. When she did concede that it might be all right if the groups in question agreed she then refused to divulge their organisers' numbers to him so he could ask them, citing 'client confidentiality'. He begged her to ring them on the show's behalf and she flatly refused. The impasse would have continued, had he not remembered the notice board at the Community Centre.

Yes, she had to agree, the contact numbers were openly displayed there, and, caught out like this, she dictated them to him to save him having to go to the hall while someone was using it to get them.

He went through the explanations and begging three times to cover the organisations that might be affected, promising each that they would be told the moment a weather decision was taken, so they knew if their session was on or off. He became practiced in effusive thanks.

It was, he realised, an indication of how important the show had become in the public consciousness that all three organisations agreed to make way for it should it become necessary. This surprise awareness made him become even more nervous about the play, about what he had written and about the ways in which it had changed during the rehearsal. Nick had once referred to the time when it had seemed to Duncan that everything he wrote was getting butchered about as 'the gestation process', but a nagging doubt in Duncan's mind had punned this phrase to the 'digestion process', and he feared his original words had been taken in and converted somehow to little more than a rough basis for Nick's preferences.

He was trying to explain this feeling to the vicar as they sat over weak instant coffees in 'Mary's Tea Room' in the main street with the show only four days away. The plastic surfaces of the cafe seemed as damp as the street outside. The windows were steamed up, and, but for a calandar supplied to 'Mary' by the cash and carry depicting spring lambs gambolling in fields of daffodils which gave dates and days of the week for April 2012 you could have been forgiven for believing it to be mid February.

"Really bad luck," said Luke, stirring the coffee, "last month was as dry as anything, now look at it."

Duncan wondered why Luke had become such a regular caller. Neither he nor Gemma were church goers; in fact their attendance at the carol service nearly four months ago had been more out of duty than persuasion. Oddly it had happened the day after they had been to watch the local amateur dramatic society performing its panto in the Community Centre. He'd felt obliged to attend that too, as Frank, the show's compere, and several other members of what he thought of as 'his' cast were appearing in it. He'd never liked pantomimes as a child and the Elveston Amateur Theatrical Society's rendition of 'Puss in Boots' had done nothing to change his entrenched dislike. There were several amateur companies in the immediate area, with predictable overlaps in membership. 'EATS' seemed particularly 'amateur', pulling in a cast whose adult members were generally, what was the politest way of putting it?, vocally challenged, and children who had presumably been rejected by the area's two major dance schools. He grimmaced, now, at the recollection of an over-long period of discomfort on stacking chairs while stilted dialogue was, frequently inaudibly, presented by a cast clad in an assortment of old clothes and what appeared to be scraps of second hand curtains. The cat, he recalled being particularly distracted by. It had seemed lewdly clad, wearing thigh boots, a tight black leotard with a tail pinned on and a headband with ears. It was a costume that would not have been out of place in a strip joint, but on a late teenage girl in a village hall panto was somehow disturbing. The cast often delivered their lines in wooden tones, apart from the mute cat, who wriggled and put a fur-gloved hand up to an ear sometimes. They performed, standing in straight lines facing the audience in front of scenery that was not only wobbly but also

228

seemed to have been painted by the local primary school.

"I suppose it has some child appeal." Gemma had said.

But if it had the children in the audience still screamed and shouted and wriggled, not always in their seats, sometimes escaping into the gangways to run up and down paying no attention to the performance, un-fettered by any adults accompanying them. The stage was lit by a small selection of disco lights, on stands beside the seating, which generally seemed to colour the actors faces in an eerie mix of red and blue but became flashy during musical numbers. The band, a pianist, guitarist and drummer, ground out popular songs from time to time for members of the cast to attempt karaoke style renditions, with varying success. He worried for the coming event. He felt sorry for the author of the script, visualising him, or her, crouched over a keyboard churning out the words only to have them mutilated and mangled by this cast. He was pondering the fate of writers when Luke said, "What do you think?"

He had to admit to having been distracted.

"I was saying 'what will you do if it tips it down with rain on the night?'," he repeated.

"We're trying to hold the Community Centre in reserve as a contingency plan."

"Not my church? I could let you have it, as the show's on St George's Day it would be very apt, and it's Monday, so no clash with any services." Luke's disappointment was evident, as was his single mindedness about St George.

"Sorry, not big enough."

Luke sighed. "Big enough for all my congregations though." The cafe became darker suddenly as a large lorry crawled past, blocking the light. The word 'Andersons' slid across the window.

"Perhaps I need an advertising campaign like they run." Luke mused.

Duncan looked up, read the company name blankly as it vanished from view restoring what light the day had to offer, and blurted out, "Oh my God! Sorry, beg your pardon vicar."

"Something the matter, Duncan?"

"I've just remembered, I've got to do an article for a trade magazine for Andersons, and I think it's due in to the printers tomorrow!"

He grabbed his cup and gulped the coffee down, "I really must go, I'd forgotten all about it."

In his mind he could see his own calendar, black with notes about the show and rehearsals and eventually performance. He realised why the small note 'Anderson's copy' had been overlooked. It hadn't seemed either urgent or important when the order had come in. Now he would be burning the midnight oil to produce something in time.

Gemma came home from the shops to the clatter of his keyboard.

"Not another re-write?" she challenged.

"No. I forgot Anderson's piece."

"Oooops!" she said, laughing, "What reminded you?"

"I saw an Anderson lorry. I was having a coffee with Luke at that place in the main street."

"Mary's?" she said. He nodded. "Is he still banging the 'dragon' tub?" she queried.

"He does seem to be a bit obsessed," Duncan agreed.

He returned to typing, and Gemma, familiar with how he would now become absorbed until the task was done, went into the kitchen to unpack the shopping.

Chapter 31
Fatigue

Anderson's article took even longer than Duncan had expected, so it was dawn by the time he flopped down on the bed. Dawn on Friday, the day when all the equipment, scenic items, props, costumes, temporary dressing rooms, staging, seating, toilets, generators, ticket booths, catering outlets, in fact the whole show was due to move onto the grounds of Elveston Lodge.

It was cloudy, but for once there was no rain. The grass underfoot felt spongy, and before the morning was half over the wheels of dozens of vehicles that had carved tracks into the driveway and the lawn. Nick was trying to arrange for the council to deliver something to save the site from becoming a quagmire when Duncan finally arrived, tired and grey from a too-brief sleep.

Nick had a mobile phone to his ear and was turning this way and that in a somewhat vain attempt to improve the reception for his call to the Council. They had found Elveston Lodge to be a mobile signal black-spot some weeks ago during rehearsals. He was frustrated by this, a frustration exaggerated because he had bitten the bullet and upgraded his mobile only a fortnight earlier on the excuse that he would need it during their residency for the show. Duncan watched as the director struggled to communicate urgency to the Council office's switchboard operator and convince her that he needed to speak to someone who could help.

In the distance, near the house itself, a scrawny balding figure leant on a stick. Basil was watching as more and more vehicles arrived and disgorged their contents onto his lawn. He was not house proud, and he had long ago resigned himself to some inconvenience with hosting the show, the compensation for which would be the fee he had eventually agreed, but he was a layman where the requirements for a performance were concerned and had not envisaged so much equipment. From somewhere in his extensive gardens he could hear the metallic clang of a sledgehammer driving metal pegs into the ground. Nearer to the house an engine revved as a pick-up truck manovered to allow a row of portable toilets to be positioned out of sight of the audience, for the performers. The same company had already sited large trailer based units for the public behind what would be the 'auditorium'.

Basil turned away from the wholescale desecration of his garden to head for his back door, away from the noise and businesslike bustle, tripping as he did so on a thick cable that now crossed the path down the side of the building.

"Careful mate! Sorry about that, we'll have it covered up in a minute," and a strong hand gripped his arm and guided him away.

Duncan found a pile of folding chairs, extracted one, and set it up for himself facing the work. He slumped into it exhausted from his overnight session with a keyboard. Whether his presence had been unnoticed or the progress setting up the show had not required his input he never knew, but after only the briefest of moments, during which he watched the work, he found his eyes slowly closing.

The next thing he knew Jenny was dragging him toward the dragon, but the dragon was number 46, Jenny's house, and the front door was a mouth that was open and he was being pulled inside and.... it was Adele, trying to wake him.

For a few moments there was that confusion that can accompany waking. He felt detached, not physically refreshed at all, as his limbs had been too long in one slightly unsatisfactory position in this folding chair. The light was all wrong too, for the cloudy morning had given way to a brief gleam of ruddy sunset cutting across the lawn.

"Come on Duncan. Wakey wakey. They want to know about the closing speech," Adele said.

His mouth felt dry, he wondered if he had been sleeping with it open, whether he had been drooling and dribbling in this chair. He struggled to wakefulness and said, "Closing speech?"

"The bit where Frank's going to say 'So we turn our 'back to the past', and thank you for watching as Elveston looks forward to another five hundred years',"

"Yes? What's the problem with it?"

He was so used to any query resulting in a re-write over the past weeks and months that he automatically assumed this would be the case.

"No problem at all, but where do you think Frank should be?"

"Where does Nick want him?" he parried.

"Nick wants him somewhere out of the way, so the rest of the cast can all come on for the closing number.."

"OK,"

"Well the lighting people have pointed out that, as it will be properly dark by then they could put a spotlight on him and have everything else dark, so the cast wouldn't really be seen coming on for the end, and the audience would all look at Frank until they lit up the stage proper."

Duncan realised that there was a whole dimension to the show here that he had not even considered. He wondered if Nick had.

"I think that's a great idea," he told her, "Can we put him somewhere really striking, like up on the roof? Or maybe on a balcony?"

"The middle bedroom's got a sort of balcony sticking out from it," she said, slightly dubiously, "but we've done all this without

234

actually going into Mr Carnthorpe's house."

"Perhaps if it's just one person, for one line...."

"I'll ask him," she said, and was gone.

Duncan stretched and scrambled to his feet rather painfully. The garden had undergone a transformation while he had slept. The shambolic tangle had resolved itself into a businesslike array of equipment and facilities. Towers rose discreetly from behind outlying shrubs and bushes bearing lighting and sound equipment. Neat rows of huts and trailers lurked, mostly hidden, down the sides of the house with a large space on one side for the horse boxes still to come. Although it was expected that the audience would be entertained in an al-fresco style the rear half of the space that they all kept calling the 'auditorium' now boasted row after row of stacking chairs. Several rostrums had appeared in front of the house. He saw that there was a metal framed tent structure flanking the entrance driveway for the box office, and that at some point while he slept Nick's calls to the council seemed to have been successful because a lorryload of wood chippings had been spread from the rutted driveway across the grass to the edge of the stage area, providing a more stable base for arrivals than the mud that had been becoming evident that morning.

Someone had rigged over a dozen tall flag poles in a wide arc behind the seating, and these flew bedsheet sized flags, alternately the council's official one and a plain purple one for the show. They made a rear wall to the audience's space, but gave the place a look as though a joust was about to take place. Perhaps it was, thought Duncan, very conscious that another couple of days would see all their efforts held up for the public's critique.

Gemma was walking across the grass toward him carrying a shopping bag. She drew closer and said, "I bet you haven't had the wit to get yourself anything to eat,"

Guiltily he had to admit that he hadn't, but that this was mainly due to having fallen asleep.

"A good job I found your computer still turned on and clicked 'send' on the Andersons' copy then isn't it," she told him.

"Oh god, hadn't I hit 'send'?"

"Don't worry, I saw it. It got there for the deadline I reckon."

"Thank you." And the words were partly for sending the copy, and partly for the sandwich she was passing him from the bag.

"What's been happening here then, or did you sleep through it all? It's starting to look rather impressive."

Duncan explained that Adele was trying to get permission to use a balcony on the front of the house.

Gemma frowned. "Seems to me poor Mr Carnthorpe is putting up with quite enough as it is, without people trampling through his house as well."

"It's only one person, once," Duncan assured her.

"Until that Nick gets it into his head that he could have people upstairs in the house for all sorts of scenes."

"I've thought of that," Adele had come up to them unseen from one side. "I've told Nick that if he uses the same location at any other time in the show the whole impact of the ending will be lost."

"Clever lady," said Gemma.

"What did Basil say?" Duncan wanted to know.

"He agreed. In fact he said it was no problem. The room we want

236

to go through to get to the balcony isn't used. In fact it looks to me as though most of the house isn't used. It's almost derelict inside you know. He seems to be living in one bedroom and a couple of downstairs rooms, and the kitchen, but there's tons of rooms I don't think anyone's been into for years. It's rather sad really."

"The loneliness of single old age," Gemma said softly, and looked hard at Adele, who straightened up, opened her bag and extracted a tin, which turned out, not unexpectedly, to contain cakes, saying, "Help yourselves when you've finished your sandwiches, I must go and tell the lighting people which balcony to point their spotlight at," and she laid the tin on the grass and marched off to the lighting truck with a severe and determined air.

"I think I touched a nerve," Gemma said, looking after her ruefully.

Duncan looked puzzled.

"Don't worry about it dear," she told him, ""You wouldn't understand."

Chapter 32
The Last Weekend

It was a busy weekend. Saturday was cloudy, just like the rigging day had been. There were gangs of volunteers out in pick-up trucks on the nearby roads banging stakes into the verges to take the advertising and direction signs that had been printed. This was strictly speaking 'flyposting', but Nick had pointed out that as the council offices only worked a five day week no action would be taken against the bills and signage on a Saturday or Sunday, Monday would be taken up by deciding what to do about the signs and by paperwork and by Tuesday the show would be over, so who cared if the signs got taken down. It was a cynical bending of the rules, but even Adele had agreed that it was better than having to go through the hoops of applying for permission.

An unforseen result of these numerous announcements of the impending performance was to stir Brian Andrews into another flurry of antagonism toward the event. He had been out for his weekly shopping when he saw the first roadside poster. By the time he had prowled the aisles of the supermarket, mulling over possible courses of action, for he still had hopes of scuppering the entire show, and had loaded his groceries into the back of his Mini Clubman, his homeward journey had sprouted two more posters and a sign directing him toward 'Elveston Lodge'.

He pressed his foot harder on the accelerator pedal in some anger as he drove home. A randomly cruising police car saw him approaching at speed and the officers would probably have flagged him down, but before they were in a position to do so he swerved into one of the gateway to 'The Limes', spraying the driveway gravel as he shot up the curve to his front door. The police crawled past the end of the drive, looking up it, just in time to see him pounding up the front steps and vanishing through the front door. They exchanged glances, shrugged, and went on their way.

In the hallway Councillor Andrews was dialling the Town Clerk's number from memory. It rang for a long while before it was answered. Andrews didn't know it, but Nigel Warren had one of those phones that displayed the caller's number, and, if it was known, identity. Andrews was known. As he stood listening to ringing tone in the rather gloomy hall, and running his fingers impatiently around the carved swirl that formed the end of the bannisters Andrews was unaware that the Clerk was staring at the small display on his phone and wondering whether to answer. He had expanded the staff of office workers over the years, so he had a number of assistants in place who would be next in line if Andrews received no answer, but what was the point? The moment an underling had received the call from the councillor they would call him. He would not escape the irracible councillor's latest grumble, and he was sure that is what would be waiting at the other end of the phone line. Better to promote the image of being a helpful and available member of staff.

Eventually the Clerk's natural oily obsequiousness made him lift the handset and say, "Good morning," in an interogative tone of voice that concealed the fact that he knew full well who was ringing him.

He held the receiver few inches away from his ear as Andrews' voice issued from it in an impassioned tirade.

He was forced to admit that the fly-posting that was being described was not authorised by him, or the council in general, and that it was, as Councillor Andrews branded it, 'an illegal liberty that the public might see as being condoned by the council'. It did not seem to be the moment to point out that since the town had largely financed the event it was good that they get as much publicity for it as possible.

When Brian Andrews had exhausted his complaint about the billboards he turned to his long held opinion that the show would reflect badly on the town. Seizing a rare gap in Andrews' flow Warren smoothly interjected, "We didn't see anything to be concerned about in the script we were shown, but you are right, Brian, we should be very wary. I wonder if we could impose on you to visit the dress rehearsal tomorrow and watch, so you could report back to us?"

"But the show is on Monday. We'd have to work very fast to put a stop to it."

"I'm sure we can rely on your judgement as to whether drastic action like that is required, or to point out any small item that might need to be altered. I will let the other councillors know that you are going to vet the proceedings. I'm sure they will be most relieved to know that our interests are being guarded."

Andrews hung up. For a long time he stood in his hall. He was too savvy a politician not to know that the Clerk had swerved the issue. Yet the idea of attending the dress rehearsal was a sound one. In the first place his mere presence might ensure that any planned mentions of the Dragon Fair might be dropped, if Nick Canforth had thought he might get away with it. He decided he would make himself very visible at the rehearsal, and at the performance itself. They wouldn't dare adapt the performance if they knew he was observing them.

At Elveston Lodge the time for the technical rehearsal gradually drew nearer. Nick, Duncan and Adele had little concept of what a 'technical' might consist of. They had been told that they had to have one, and had dutifully put it into the diary. Nick, who had been under the impression that it was another opportunity for him to rehearse cast movements, was quickly diasbused by the various lighting and sound technicians, and Jenny, all of whom told him quite firmly that this was nothing to do with him, this was to deal with the things that had never yet been tried out.

"You've been rehearsing the cast for months," Jenny told him, "If they aren't sorted out now it's too late. The 'tech' is for us, for the invisible backstage people."

Duncan, listening, thought he had never considered her to be an 'invisible' person. As usual there was far too much of Jenny 'visible'. In a true traditional theatrical manner she had started wearing all black clothing. Somehow it accentuated the pale flesh it wasn't covering, as the contrast between the black clad and bare parts of her was startlingly conspicuous. Gemma, who was now beside him through the long days, and evenings, saw where he was staring and muttered, "You can't complain it's her fault if you gawp at her like that all the time."

"I thought stage crew wore black clothes to cover themselves up and be inconspicuous."

"Now when have you ever known Jenny be inconspicuous?" his wife asked him.

They were interrupted by a burst of music from the PA system that had been installed. The music was nothing to do with the show, merely a snatch of an old pop hit. It was faded out almost immediately, leaving both Duncan and Gemma mentally continuing the well known lyric.

'Still waiting all night for yo⌣ou..' they finally mouthed quietly together.

It was unlikely that the sound engineer had intended being ironic with his choice of a test track. Had Duncan and Gemma known it the random snatch had simply been what was available on the man's phone at that moment. None the less the number stuck in their minds and through the long grey day, and even longer seeming evening, came back to them repeatedly as mysterious hold-ups kept them 'waiting all night for yo⌣ou..' and they would whistle or hum the melody to each other before dissolving into almost childish giggles at the aptness of the line whenever a delay dragged for them.

Duncan saw Nick scowl at them for this sometimes, and even Adele gave an inquisitive stare, but he felt beyond caring now.

The show was almost upon them. Barring some major catastrophe with timings his work was done. He was feeling an unusual excitement, relief almost, that he never normally had from any piece of his writing making its way to press. This was different, though he couldn't define why. He wondered if there was a real and intrinsic difference between having people read his work, and seeing people act it out while an audience watched. Could he, he wondered, ever normally expect this sort of thrill at seeing words on a printed page as opposed to, what was the phrase? Seeing 'A' impersonate 'B' while 'C' looks on. Yes, that was it. The simple formulaic definition of 'theatre'. And now he, a complete outsider to the world of entertainment, had created something that 'C' would 'look on' to. Even as he watched this progression of mechanical arrangements he anticipated Monday, when there would be an audience. An audience, if the advance bookings were anything to go by, that would fill this open space to its utmost capacity.

"One, two... Try that, Frank."

The sound engineers were adjusting levels, playing around with radio mics. Frank, with a tie-clip microphone attached to his lapel, bent his head toward the fluffy windshield that covered it and said, "Testing."

It was loud, and somehow distorted.

"Don't bend into it, just ignore it and be natural. Do a little bit of a speech please."

"It is 1940, and the first evacuees have arrived in Elveston," Frank recited.

Knobs were twiddled, the sound became more natural and comfortable. There was general satisfaction. And the whole process was repeated over and over again for each memebr of the cast.

Gemma yawned, and reclined in her seat.

"Wake me up when they get to something interesting," she told him.

They worked their way through the show, cutting great chunks so they only saw entrances and exits and moments when scenes were changed or music needed to start.

By the time they reached the church being dedicated to St George half the company were bored and had taken to lying about on the damp grass reading, eating or playing games. People were no longer ready when they were needed and the pace slowed. A background buzz of chatter had slowly risen and Nick's attempts to 'shush' people were becoming less and less effective. And then the dragon came on.

Frank was explaining the legend of St. George to the evacuee who was the show's device for the whole history being enacted. The boy was very young, but perversely probably the only person there who was utterly concentrated on the task in hand.

The dragon emerged from the side of the house. No-one had really seen it before, except as a bundle of parts. Now it was being operated by two men and moving like a live thing. It was dark enough for the lighting to be taking effect and there was an audible 'oooh' as the cast and crew saw it enter. The reaction was delayed by people not paying attention, but this merely meant that instead of one momentary gasp the noise lasted, spreading across the space slowly. The chatter died as the gasp took hold and Duncan thought he had never seen a group of people gripped in such a way before. He nudged Gemma.

Jenny's dragon was lithe and sinuous. It wound its threatening way across the front of Elveston Lodge. The lights made it seem more real somehow. Frank was continuing to recite Duncan's descriptive lines about the legend, but no-one was listening to them. Jenny's construction was revealed as the star of the show.

A few feet from Duncan and Gemma there was a movement, a slight gasp, and Adele got up and turned her back on the scene and walked away to the back of the auditorium space. Nick jumped to his feet and went after her. Gemma craned her neck to see them, torn between watching the dragon and her curiousity about Adele's unexpected reaction.

It was hard to see what went on between Nick and Adele. The evening had slowly darkened, so away from the lit space of the performance things were obscured, but Gemma was almost sure that Nick put an arm around Adele before the two of them came back. It was all very brief. Nick was back in his place before an armour clad St. George dispatched the dragon and the church choir was processing over the lawns.

Under cover of a ripple of applause and the singing Gemma whispered, "That upset her. I always thought she had her feelings about the dragon very much under control."

Chapter 33
The Dress Rehearsal

Brian Andrews drove to Elveston Lodge, his annoyance rising as the road led him past the posters advertising the show. He deliberately ignored the signs directing him to an adjacent farmer's field that had been reserved for car parking and went through the gateway, past the square pillars and the white barred gate. The gate had been pulled more to one side and straightened up now so that, although it clearly wouldn't open and shut easily, it didn't look quite as neglected as it had when Duncan and Nick had first visited.

Brian's Mini ventured onto the curving driveway, betraying its small wheels and poor ground clearance immediately as it wallowed into the deep ruts that the commercial vehicles combined with the wet weather had created. Andrews grunted with annoyance and steered to one side of the roadway so that at least two of his tyres were running on the higher and firmer part of the track. He was concentrating on this so much that he almost failed to noticed the house as he emerged into the huge lawned area. Now, unchallenged and mostly ignored, he drove across the space and parked at what would eventually be the back of the audience. He saw that a succession of white painted right angle lines marked the corners of catering concession pitches. Cryptic abbreviated names were written in the middle of each rectangle. He parked exactly over the top of one saying 'Bennie/Ices' and turned off the car.

There were lots of people milling around, many seemingly busy and actively readying the site for the show, but some, he noticed, simply lounging about. He took his chair and a bag from the rear of the car and went a few yards toward the house, which he guessed would be the focal point of the show. Picking a random spot centrally between two pre-positioned banks of seats he unpacked his folding canvas chair, sat down and waited.

People drifted onto the site. Parents and siblings of performers, wives or husbands of singers and musicians all scattered themselves and their rugs and blankets across the space and settled to watch the dress rehearsal. A few stole a glance at the councillor in his folding chair in the middle of a gangway, sitting with his arms folded across his chest and a sour expression on his face.

Nearer to the front of the audience space, closer to the action and to the house, a trestle table and some chairs stood with opened files and paperwork flapping in the gentle evening breeze. Now the rain had stopped it was possible to hope for a dry evening. Andrews saw Nick and Adele walk over to the table and sit with their backs to him facing the 'stage'. He assumed they hadn't seen him. Somewhat to one side, and perched on folding chairs Duncan and Gemma were waiting for the show, his show, to start.

Adele said to Nick, "Did you invite him?"

"No, and I wish he wasn't here, for your sake."

"I'm all right."

"If I thought we'd get away with it I'd get someone to tell him to leave."

"Nick, he's spying to see if he can find anything to stir up trouble with. If we chuck him out he'll pull rank and point out that the Council is paying for this. Just pretend he isn't there. I'm going to."

Under cover of the table Nick squeezed her hand.

The dress rehearsal began. There had been real doubt earlier in the day. Noon had brought another of this month's downpours and Nick, peering from the windows of Adele's house, had been certain he would need to move the show to the Community Centre. He mentally applied a sort of sympathetic magic. 'If I accept that I have got to move indoors then the rain will stop to spite me.' Slowly and reluctantly the deluge had decreased and stopped.

Andrews saw that stage lighting was on, though it was still daylight and half an hour or so to go before sunset. Even on this cloudy evening he couldn't see the lighting was having any effect. He made a mental note about this wastage. Lines were delivered, locations and historic periods portrayed. He couldn't find anything contentious in the show. He sank ever deeper into his canvas chair, an air of sullen gloom evident on his face.

Relatives and friends watching clapped at the obvious places. There was some clearly partisan cheering at times, usually for Catherine James' Dance School girls, who appeared in different roles, mostly whenever a crowd scene was called for.

Slowly and imperceptibly the daylight faded, so the stage lighting took hold, lending the scenes magical artificiality. By the interval it was almost like watching a show in a proper theatre.

The interval produced a stream of visitors to Nick's table. Questions and complaints in equal measure were fired at him, but he was pleased that his company's mood was generally up-beat and tolerant.

"I think it's going to work," he told Adele, after fielding tricky queries about whether the horses should be allowed to leave the site in their horse-boxes during the interval. She nodded.

"Of course it is," she assured him, pouring him coffee from a flask dragged from the seemingly inexhaustible bag she had beside her. "You haven't eaten either," she pointed out, and pressed him to some cake.

Gemma was producing sandwiches for Duncan at the same time. Her words of encouragement were interrupted by the arrival of Luke, who walked straight across the stage area and joined them.

"How's it going?" he asked.

"Haven't you been watching?" Gemma wanted to know.

"Just arrived with the choir," he told her, "Why's Councillor Andrews here?"

"We think he's come to see if he can find anything to object to," Duncan told the vicar, "I think Nick probably thought it better to ignore him than to try to throw him out. Anyway directors always say they like to have some audience for a dress rehearsal so there's some reaction."

Luke surveyed the field. "You aren't short of audience are you? If you got this many tomorrow you'd be reasonably pleased."

Duncan realised that his friend's attendance ambitions were way below his own, and certainly a very long way short of Nick and Adele's. They, he was sure, would be mortified if the attendance tomorrow was at this sort of level. Presumably the vicar was judging it against his own best congregation sizes.

"I think we're hoping for a lot more than this, that's why your church wouldn't have been big enough."

Nick's raised voice, encouraging his cast back into position to start the second half curtailled much more chat.

As the interval music began to fade Luke said, "Anyway Councillor Andrews doesn't want to be making too much fuss. His own family background might come out."

Duncan wanted to query this, to ask what he meant, but the show had re-started. He made a mental note to try to get Luke to explain his cryptic comment.

The dew came down as the second half began and people sitting on the grass were made conscious of the damp chill of the spring evening. Gemma thought it was probably proof that the show shouldn't have been staged on this date. An English April was not reliable enough to even consider staging outdoor events, she decided. She reached down beside her seat and idly plucked a daisy from the grass. The evening midges began to circle, rising from the Lodge's lake away to her left.

Brian Andrews felt the damp. It aggravated him. He was already silently annoyed at how uncontentious the content of the show was. He was desperate to find some firm and uncontestable salacious content that he could present to the Town Clerk. Without it his attempt to scotch the presentation would lack ammunition. Warren had made his position fairly clear in their phone call. He would do nothing to upset the planned event, now that the Council had funded it and was seen by the public to be the driving force behind it, unless there was a very good reason. It was, Andrews told himself, exactly the kind of impasse you got into when you funded something with the intention of allowing outsiders to do the work so you could take the glory.

There must be something to be found in the second half. Andrews was sure that the piece had been written with some intention of following categorical order. That meant they must be getting nearer to the present day. That would put the show on shaky ground he was sure. The nearer to the present they came the more chance that they would have included something to upset the living, to cast the town in a bad light by modern standards.

He remained disappointed for the next three quarters of an hour. It was not until Frank was speaking of the parish church's dedication to St. George that he began to pay serious attention again. He was relating the saint's legend. Little to do with the Dragon Fair that Andrews dreaded being featured, but dramatic and startling as in what was now proper darkness the spotlight picked out Jenny's dragon costume. It wasn't the bundle of cloth with scales applied that Duncan had seen in Jenny's lounge. Even the technical rehearsal had failed to do it justice. The operators had managed to get the hang of the thing now, and it writhed threateningly in the light, its spinal spikes glinting and the mechanical jaw snapping as it went toward the dancer playing the maiden.

The girl was demurely clad in a long white gown and standing by a post that had been placed on stage. Brian had not noticed its arrival. The impression was that she was tied to this stake, although there were no ropes. Despite himself, and his determination to dislike the scene, Andrews had to admire the theatrical artifice that was being employed. It was nothing like the dragon costume he had worn. It was two men rather than one, and it had a more menacing appearance. For the first time in fifty years he wondered if Adele had felt genuine fear when he had first approached her in his costume as part of the fair.

The dragon reached the girl and the front operator made the jaws open wide close to her as if to bite. Catherine James' dancer turned her head away from the puppet melodramaticaly. Andrews heard Catherine shout over to the dancer in a stage whisper, "The other way, downstage, otherwise they can't see your face!"

The girl obediently turned away from the dragon the other way and showed a transparently fake look of fear to the audience. It didn't matter. The dragon was stealing the show. In any case St. George entered in full silver painted cardboard armour, waving a wooden sword and challenging the monster.

The staged fight was brief and ended with the saint driving the dragon away rather than 'slaying' it. Music started up. Andrews recognised the strains of 'For all the saints'. The church choir emerged from the side of the house. Their slow processional singing was visually spoilt by John Levante trying to walk backwards in front of them, waving his arms to conduct. Frank launched into a narrative piece about the church and its history over the top of the unamplified singing and the tune segued into 'Jerusalem' as the choir made its way across the stage area.

The lights faded out as they departed, and a single spot stabbed at an upper balcony. There was a brief pause. A hiatus as the flow was interrupted. Then Frank appeared in the spotlight and gave the final line. The lights changed to reveal the whole company coming onto the stage singing an up-beat number that Andrews did not recognise.

And then it was over. He had to admit, grudgingly, that it was better done than he had anticipated, but his antagonism was undiminished. Sullenly he admitted to himself that he had nothing to take back to Nigel Warren that would justify a cancellation.

Chapter 34
A Revelation

The Councillor returned to his car and started the engine. His headlights sliced across the lawns, which were still occupied by groups who had been watching the dress rehearsal. In most cases at least some of the members of any group were standing, stretching, or starting to repack bags they had brought with them. With no hestation Andrews drove straight across the grass to the point where the driveway could be seen and left.

Many of the families scowled after his tail lights, disapproving of his driving through the middle of an audience. They didn't know who he was and their angry looks were wasted. Nick, Duncan and the rest also watched him go, unsure if they were more pleased he had gone without passing comment or nervous from not knowing what his next action might be.

The tail lights jiggled noticeably as the Mini lurched over the rutted drive, its brake lights flashing on every so often until the red glows were lost behind the early undergrowth.

Nick accepted a microphone from the sound engineer and coughed down it noisily.

"Can we all gather round for notes please!"

There was a considerable reluctance among his cast and crew. The dress rehearsal had gone well they felt; better than most had expected. They were buoyed up and full of anticipation. They were tired and ready to go home. They had no wish to spend a potentially tedious hour having each and every detail picked over.

Nick began. He thanked them all. He made the usual encouraging noises. Many of the cast, still gathering around after changing out of costumes or returning props, missed much of this.

"I have got a few notes," There were audible groans. "I'll be as quick as I can." he squinted at the note pad he had used, realised he couldn't read it in the dark, used his phone as a torch and decided he couldn't really decipher his own writing, and would have to work from memory.

"In no particular order:" he failed to observe the gradual drifting away behind him as scouts and guides, dancers and singers, schoolchildren and amateurs met with their parents on the dark grass and wandered home. "where's Mr Levant?"

"Levanté," the man corrected.

"..and your choir?" Nick ignored the quibble.

"They've been taken home."

Nick took a deep breath and said, "Anyway, we can't have you walking in front, especially backwards, can they not sing without a conductor?"

This was clearly considered to be sacrilige and a few minutes were lost while oil had to be poured on troubled waters before Nick could suggest that Mr Lavante..

"Lavanté!"

...might perhaps find a distant corner where his choir could see him but he was out of sight for the audience.

Luke leant nearer to Duncan and whispered, "He's lucky John didn't walk out. He's very defensive about the choir."

Duncan muttered, "You were going to tell us about Councillor Andrews."

Nick turned that way and said, "Quiet please! We've got a lot to get through."

Duncan had a feeling that he had not experienced since he was a schoolboy, of a slight conscience at having been caught and a resentment at being told off.

From somewhere out of sight around the side of the house came sounds of things being packed away and of the doors of vehicles getting slammed.

Nick ploughed on. He queried Frank's late arrival on the balcony, being told it was purely because the route was both unfamiliar and in the dark. He praised some parts, queried others, all the while aware of a slow but steady drift away. By the time he gave up and repeated his thanks and reminded everyone of the arrival time for tomorrow's performance he was noticably short of listeners.

He shrugged and looked helplessly at Adele, who still sat beside him.

She said, "They're all tired and it's late. We can't do any more tonight."

Luke said to Duncan, "I'll drop round tomorrow and tell you about Andrews."

Duncan said, "I think I shall be here most of tomorrow."

Gemma looked at her watch. "If we are really quick we might make last orders."

They sat in the 'Dog and Dray' staring into their drinks. Duncan felt it should have been a boisterous celebratory occasion, but somehow everyone just drooped. It was the same crowd. Himself and Gemma, John and Jenny, Nick, Adele beside him.

Nick was grumbling quietly, saying, "They didn't listen to my notes. I'm going to have to go round them all individually before the performance tomorrow."

The group had acquired Luke too, and, somehow, the vicar's friend Simon who was, Duncan remembered with some jealousy, supposed to be doing a book on the Dragon Fair.

Duncan was about to ask how the book was coming along when Luke bluted out, "I suppose I've got to tell you about Councillor Andrews. It's safe enough now.. too late for you to add anything to the script!"

Gemma made a slight attempt to hush him, telling him that there might be people who would rather not talk about Andrews, but he said perceptively, "I don't think I could tell you anything much that Adele doesn't already know."

"She doesn't have to be reminded though,"

Adele could be seen to be shrugging.

Luke launched into his tale. "You see what Simon and I have found is that the whole Dragon Fair thing was prone to rigging all through its history. We can't prove it, but we think that Brian Andrews fixed the 1962 lottery so he could be the dragon. He was connected with it of course because of his family background."

"Family background?"

"I thought you all knew. He is the illegitimate offspring of a previous 'maiden' from either the Dragon or the George of that year. So his money was inherited originally from the prize his mother won in 1938."

He paused, aware like all of them that the whole bar had fallen silent and was listening intently. It was a Sunday, so not a crowded evening, but there were groups and couples scattered around, all now turned and straining to follow what he was saying. In the gap the barman rang the bell, but instead of chivvying them all out he walked purposefully to the outer door and locked it, returning to a vacant stool near their table to listen.

"A lock in?" someone queried.

"I figure if you're the people putting on this show you deserve something. Anyway everyone here wants to know about our revered councillor." he managed to put a sneer on the word 'revered'.

There was a quiet flurry of agreements.

"Do I gather that Andrews is a bastard?" someone asked.

"We all knew that."

There was more laughter and agreement.

Almost imperceptibly the vicar's experience with addressing an audience made his voice carry to the eavesdroppers as he continued.

"Simon thinks that there's some evidence from gossip at the time that the draw drum was tampered with, in fact that it had been, shall we say 'influenced' for a couple of years previously too. Obviously you can't make all the names in the drum yours, but you can make it a big percentage of them, so you stand a better chance of winning. There's a risk your name might get drawn twice, once for the dragon and then again for George, but you can always suggest that your ticket got put back in again by mistake.

"We think that the reason Simon was attacked so violently the previous year, 1961, in what had always traditionally been a very light and fake George versus the Dragon fight was that the attempt at fixing obviously failed. Simon won. And we think that Angus, who got to be the knight, was probably either in the pay of, or a close friend of our Councillor Andrews."

"So the violence was just a sort of punishment for winning?"

"Probably, but it might also have been supposed to be seen. A visible threat in order to discourage entrants next year."

"Would it? Did it?" Gemma wanted to know.

Luke said, "Well numbers were down the next year...""

Simon told them, "One night of fun is a nice prize for red blooded males, but not if its followed by being beaten up."

"Maybe they should have been beaten up," said one of the locals who was listening in, "the whole thing was disgraceful. It's a good job it doesn't happen now."

Clearly there was some agreement with this sentiment. Duncan could tell that there was a good proportion of those around who didn't entirely agree however. Trying to check who held which opinions he noticed a man some distance away across the room, alone at one of the small round tables. He had a notepad in his hand and he was scribbling furiously with a propelling pencil. Sensing Duncan's eyes on him the man said, "Marcus Wainsthorpe. I'm a reporter with the Harvile Herald. I'm coming to do a review of the show tomorrow."

Duncan mumbled, "Thank you. Be kind," and there were a few laughs.

Someone was asking why anyone would want to fix the draw so they could be the dragon.

"Why do you think," Simon said, "You wouldn't expect young men to turn down a chance of a night with a girl would you?"

"Is that why you..."

"Candidly? Yes."

Chapter 35
Performance

Nigel Warren waited all morning at his desk in the council offices for the expected phone call from Brian Andrews, hardly paying attention to the small mound of papers in front of him, sometimes looking out of his window at the cloudy sky, sometimes worrying what possible authority he could utilise to pull the plug on an event that the full Council had both sanctioned and financed. He was convinced that Andrews would come to him this morning with a string of complaints and would bamboozle him into becoming seen as the judge and executioner.

He had no real opinion either way. There was advantage in being part of the Council and claiming cudos for arranging an event for the quincentenary which had involved next to nothing in terms of effort or imagination. A successful show tonight would allow the council to continue to mislead a confused public into believing that it had arranged an entertainment for them. Having to cancel would undoubtedly cast them, and worse him, as the kill-joy villains of the piece, but if Andrews produced incontravertable evidence of content that would be suspect or dubious there was no avoiding it. He studied the sky and hoped for a return to the rain of the past weeks. It would provide a much needed excuse. The phone resolutely refused to ring. He fiddled with the button on his plastic flip-over calendar on his desk, until he inadvertently clicked it on another day, to Tuesday 24th April. Cursing he set about getting it back to todays date.

St Georges' Day. The 23rd. The day of the proposed show. Still nothing from Andrews. Just before midday he could bear it no longer and rang the councillor's home.

Brian Andrews had been pacing his house. He had run through every excuse or grumble he could think of to come up with a reason to force the Clerk to cancel this show, but he could think of nothing. He couldn't bring himself to dial the number and tell

Warren that he thought the show should go ahead.

The phone rang in the hall. He knew who it would be, He had vaccillated too long, now Warren was chasing him.

The exchange between the two men was embarrassing. The one unwilling to admit he had failed to find enough, or any, amunition to close down the show, the other trying to pretend that he was sorry that was the case, while secretly being delighted that he would no longer be facing the disapproval of nearly all the councillors and half the population. The population didn't matter; they could be fobbed off with pseudo corporate speak using phrases about public safety or ethnic minority equality, but the councillors...

Anyway he no longer needed to worry. There was no fudging to be done, no attempt to hide the total expenditure on an event that was called off, The show would go on. If the weather stayed dry.

Duncan and Gemma went to the Lodge in the late afternoon, expecting to be among the first to arrive. They were surprised to find the lawns a teeming mass of people. It seemed that most of the performers had already arrived and big groups of school children, scouts, dancers, local thespians, musicians and extras wandered the site, forming queues at the catering vans that now ringed the rear of the audience space, chattering excitedly and giggling in anticpation.

When the public itself began to arrive, long before the scheduled start time of the show, Duncan saw that the townsfolk had decided to make a gala occasion of the show. Despite the gloomy clouds and the still not quite dry grass the public had come in smart clothes, posh party frocks and suits. Picnic rugs bore food hampers and bottles in ice buckets, rather than the crumpled carrier bags and fast food wrappers that had been in evidence at rehearsals. Elveston Lodge took on the look of Glynebourne.

He and Gemma pitched themselves on chairs well back from the marked performance space, behind the rug sitters, but at the front of the rows of seats. They could see Nick slowly and methodically visiting each backstage gathering of cast members.

"I bet he's giving them notes again," Gemma said.

Duncan agreed, thinking how frustrating it must be to have a picture in your mind of how a scene of a show should look, only to have performers ignore your instructions and move about however they wished. He recalled how through most of the rehearsals he had cringed and been infuriated by actors slaughtering his carefully crafted lines by incorrect stresses and mispronunciations. How he had tried to modify these errors and been amazed how often once a line had been wrongly learnt it would never change to its original scripted form no matter how often he mentioned it. There would be several, he knew, that would crop up this evening. He could tell you what they would be, and who the perpetrators would be, for some of the cast were more prone to mangle words than others, and he knew with dull certainty the bits of script that would become meaningless through corruption.

"Penny for them," said Gemma.

"Just thinking about which lines will get tortured into incoherence by the cast tonight."

"Too late now, unless you want to go tramping round the backstage area seeking out your favourite script modifiers to threaten them."

"I think I'll pass. They're probably getting enough 'notes' from Nick."

Gemma was studying the growing crowd. "Look, there's the reporter bloke from the pub last night."

"And Luke and Simon," he told her, as the vicar and his friend trudged over to take seats near them.

"I'm glad someone seems to have thought to take care of Basil," she said, watching as the house owner was ushered into a seat by a couple of the front of house staff.

The box office hut and gateway was rapidly vanishing under the press of arriving bodies. The catering traders were inundated, and long winding queues tangled together near mobile units. Everywhere there was a steady hum of conversation and the occasional sound of laughter or of glasses clinking. The sound system began playing soft background music. He could see that some of the lighting was on, though it was ineffective yet against the daylight. He wondered where Adele had chosen to sit.

The gloomy clouds made for a darker feel to the Lodge's grounds than they had experienced at this time of the evening before. He hoped it would not dampen the crowd's mood.

The available space was almost entirely filled now. No spare seats seemed available and places on the grass were few and far between. At least the crush at the entrance seemed to be thinning. His watch told him there was just five minutes to go. Five minutes to the start of his first show. A lump formed in his throat. What if...

Gemma seemed to sense his nervousness, for she reached over and took his hand, giving it a reassuring squeeze. As she did so a haze machine started to pump out a mist on the downwind side of the performance space. Slowly and reluctantly the thin artificial fog spread across the front of Elveston Lodge and over the grass spaces reserved for the action. The background music changed to an instrumental version of the song that had been written especially for the show.

The sound of a world war two air raid siren cut through the music and drowned it out. Moving searchlights, just visible in the machine generated fog in front of the house swept back and forth.

Afterwards the older generation discussing the show said that the moment had made the hairs on the back of their neck stand up. Either way it rivetted the audience's attention. Frank walked to the centre of the space, paused and began.

"In 1940 Elveston, just like many country areas, received evacuees from the East End of London...."

The school children, dressed in drab forties style coats, with cardboard labels and gas-mask boxes, trudged across the stage from one side to the other, passing Frank, till, when they were gone a single small boy was left staring up at him. Frank dropped to one knee to conduct a conversation with the child.

In a few lines he promised to tell the boy all about Elveston, the town that he had been evacuated to.

"Let me," he said, "take you 'back to the past', to the time of the Roman occupation."

Off to the side, where the chldren had come from, a gang of boy scouts dressed as Roman soldiers emerged and proceded to set up tents and establish a Roman camp before forming up into a military parade just as some of Catherine James' dancers, a chariot and several of the pony club's horses arrived to attack, defeat and rout the Romans.

Jenny's shields and swords and Edward and Tamsin's costumes with some clever fight choregraphy combined to hold the audience.

Duncan had a brief recollection of a girl, Chloe, that was her name, crying because she wanted to be Boudicea in the chariot. It seemed so silly now, it was such a small part in this great sweeping sprawl of history which had become almost a pageant.

Gemma whispered reassuringly to him, "It's going to be all right, you had nothing to worry about."

And she was right. The show continued, using the conceit of Frank telling the town's history to the evacuee, through the decades, through the centuries, to the destruction of the town by Cromwell's roundheads, portrayed with much screaming and running and projected flames, the dancers crossing and recrossing the space with long red and yellow ribbons on sticks, as well as some carefully carried real blazing torches.

Incongruous though they were the dance school's numbers helped to break up and enliven the somewhat sombre and serious nature of the historical content. Some musical interludes helped too, and the time sped by unexpectedly quickly.

A small army of 'Tommies' marched away to the First World War before flower girls scattered poppies.

The evacuee's question about the church being dedicated to St. George and claiming not to know the legend was transparently artificial, but the appearance of Jenny's dragon costume and its defeat by the cardboard armour clad St. George were a theatrical moment that captivated the public. The church choir processed, slowly, at a rate to accommodate Miss Turner and Mr Dunhill, as they sang. Frank appeared, spotlit on the house balcony to say, "So we turn our 'back to the past', and thank you for watching as Elveston looks forward to the future and to another five hundred years," before the whole company joined to sing the show's special number as a finale.

It was over.

The applause was long and loud. Duncan gulped and found he was crying, felt foolish and was glad of the anonymity of the dark. Gemma kissed him and said, "Well done."

Chapter 36
Afterwards

Duncan was never sure why their house became the venue for the post show get together a few days later. It was crowded, and noisy in a self congratulatory way. People had brought bottles and food and were spread through the whole of the ground floor. There had been much back slapping, and kissing from Jenny, much to his embarassment, though Gemma seemed to take it all in her stride.

The evening had wound down and they were all lounging about, mostly having had too much wine. The empty glasses cluttered the mantlepiece, jostling the solitary 'Thank you' card he had received, from Nick. Tongues were loosened. The team that had staged Elveston's 'Back to the Past' relaxed.

At one point someone had asked whether they should do it again next year, and had been roundly shouted down. Now a smug tired and relaxed mood had settled over them. The copy of the newspaper had been passed from hand to hand.

Spectacular open air show for Elveston Qunicentennary.

The review gushed in congratulatory style. It went on to try to mention as many names and organisations in connection with the performance as possible in the available column inches.

> *'Back to the Past', staged last night in the grounds of Elveston Lodge to a packed audience....*

Each reader at the party had scanned the lines of praise hoping to see their own name in print. Duncan had been unsurprised to find himself reduced to *'a script by Duncan Newbon..'* but found that in the end he didn't care. He nursed his personal pride quietly.

More shocking and creating more comment than any of the review was the final paragraph:

The production, which received financial support from the Town Council, was put on against strong opposition from Councillor Brian Andrews. Councillor Andrews, who has been recently revealed to be the son of one of the Elveston Dragon Fair 'Maidens', has long campaigned to eradicate all mention of the infamous historic event, which was discontinued in 1963. His objection that "Back to the Past' would 'glorify' the old annual tradition proved unfounded last night.
Councillor Andrews was unavailable for comment.
However this newspaper has been told that there is a book about the Dragon Fair planned. The collaboration between the vicar of Elveston's St. George's Church, the Rev. Luke Grainger, and Simon Dunbar, a former 'Dragon' is due to be published later this year and promises to reveal the previously hidden secrets of the Fair.'

Luke and Simon had perched on the arms of adjacent chairs and remained uninformative about the 'hidden secrets' under repeated questioning.

Nick had excused himself and gone off upstairs to the bathroom. Duncan asked Adele a question that had bothered him for a long time now, "Who was your St. George then?"

Adele regarded him carefully, seemingly considering her answer, maybe still unwilling to discuss the events of almost fifty years earlier. Before she could reply Gemma said,

"Nick, of course. You are so stupid sometimes, Duncan."

The older woman nodded, asking, "When did you know?"

"Oh, right from the start," Gemma told her, "You were both very coy about the history, but there's obviously something between you two. Why aren't you together?"

Adele gave an 'I don't know' shrug.

"Talk to him now it's all out in the open. Especially if there's a book coming out. I think you'll find that he feels the same. What have you got to lose?" Gemma told her.

"Maybe you're right. I think I will."

Also by Cliff Dix
'Theatre Wagon'
'In Which Case'
'And Burnt The Topless Towers'
'All Invited To A Murder'
and
'Up The Fire Escape And Through The Kitchens'